Olivia Varrus and her Uncle Archer own a profitable bookstore on Henrietta Street in the heart of London. As such, Olivia, has practically everything a young Victorian lady could want to live a pleasant life … except for a stalker!

But Olivia wasn't especially frightened because of her quirky ability to "just know things." She sensed that the man who lurked in the shadows wasn't malevolent even though his presence was a little unsettling.

Then a troubling situation arose. The proprietor of West End Brokers directed his attention to the shops on Henrietta Street when he discovered he could make a tidy profit if he acquired the entire block of businesses. If his offers to purchase were refused, the man had methods to encourage reluctant people to change their mind.

It didn't take long for matters to escalate. The once pleasant street soon became a war zone with windows shattered, goods destroyed and store owners attacked!

How could a twenty-six-year-old spinster combat thugs hired to make the shopkeepers sell their homes and businesses for next to nothing? Perhaps the secretive Mr. Brandyce could help. Olivia had quickly realized there was a great deal more to the gentleman other than a handsome face, piercing blue eyes, and a wild infatuation. She would have to think on it.

More Than You Know

JENINNE TAYLOR

MORE THAN YOU KNOW is also available as a Kindle edition from Amazon.com

10 9 8 7 6 5 4 3 2 1

ISBN 978-1-57550-094-2

Printed in the United States of America
Cover Art by Johanna M. Bolton

I would like to dedicate this book
to family and friends who
supported me over the last year,
with love and appreciation
for the caregivers
who took time off work
and traveled thousands of miles
to be with me.

Chapter One

I stood outside the bookshop near the front door, and looked up and down the busy walkway, then directed my gaze across the street.

A slight shiver and a tingling sensation traveled up the back of my neck, a familiar awareness, yet, difficult to describe.

One might consider these impressions a gift or curse. For as long as I could remember I could sense what people were thinking. Not exactly a "mind-reader", more what a person was feeling . . . anger, sadness, pain, good will, falsity or deceptiveness.

I knew someone was watching and had been doing so for quite some time. The feelings directed toward me were

1

fiery, emotional and intense, but not dangerous, at least not to me.

Sooner or later whoever it was would make himself known, there was little doubt this "watcher" was a man.

I took a deep breath and a last look around before stepping inside.

My uncle, Archer Varrus, owns the Ink on Paper Book Gallery . . . Uncle Arch.

We live over the shop in a pleasant but cozy space. One reason our place is especially comfortable is the recently installed plumbing that provides bathing and lavatory facilities.

Such luxuries are no longer only for the wealthy; many of us so called, socially vertical groups, can afford a few extravagances now and again.

Our book gallery is located around Cavendish Square in the West End of London, not far away from the fashionable Oxford and Regent Street shopping area.

The three-story building was built in the mid-seventeen hundreds.

A commercial space on the bottom and two-story living accommodations on the upper floors. Out front was a small iron-columned loggia running the length of the building.

Perhaps a little old fashioned, but charming. The front door was of sturdy oak; on either side were bay windows that projected outward a few feet. The interior space was ideal to showcase a variety of tomes that might entice customers to investigate the magical world of books.

Within, one could find works by popular authors, Dickens, Thackeray, Bronte Sisters, Haworth, as well as a variety of used and rare publications.

Along the walls were shelves over pullout drawers, down the center, rows of bookcases that stood about seven feet tall. Sections were arranged according to subject . . . medieval literature and history, folklore, politics, biographies, poetry, and children's publications.

In the back was a labyrinth of interconnected rooms accessed through archways; the space featured mismatched antique bookcases full of used books. Customers could settle on sofas in alcoves to hide away and read.

Under lock and key upstairs, we kept a selection of rare volumes and manuscripts that Uncle Arch had collected. He allowed a few customers access, and perhaps purchase, if a price could be negotiated.

Some of the treasures were plays by the Roman author Plautus, edited by Saraceni and Valla in 1511, the manuscripts were fully illustrated and featured a full-page woodcut of a theater.

The 1496 edition of Terentius comedies edited by Gruninger, found in a library collection in Scotland, would probably be sold to one of our frequent patrons.

There were manuscripts on political economy, moral philosophy and mathematics. A 15th century illuminated Dutch songbook and a beautifully illustrated Bible from Germany dated 1483.

Centuries old, complete manuscripts, or sometimes only a single page, called leaves, were fragile, extremely rare and expensive.

Henrietta Street was full of interesting businesses, enamel and glass shops, tailors and dressmakers, bakery, leather and dry goods. Further down the street buildings were being bought up, pulled down, and replaced with offices or expansion of the ever-encroaching emporiums on Oxford Street.

1885 London had become a financial and trading capital of Europe, possibly the world, but all the glitter didn't make up for the poverty, dirt, and disease that existed in many areas of the overcrowded city.

My parents died in one of the recurrent cholera epidemics that claimed thousands of lives.

Thankfully my uncle had the financial ability and the inclination to take on the responsibility of raising a five-year-old girl.

Archer Varrus, a confirmed bachelor, did his best to nurture my intellectual curiosity and accept that I was quite different from most people.

I guess he really wasn't aware that girls shouldn't be educated, or thought of as frivolous, flighty and feather-brained.

So . . . I . . . Olivia Varrus, spinster at age twenty-six, was manager and partner in this thriving world of books.

Uncle Arch devoted much of his time to the scholarly pursuits, and I was mostly responsible for the everyday activities of the home and business. I had help in both the house and shop.

Jennie Marsh handled the cleaning and cooking upstairs, and Nyles Patton assisted in the store.

It was time to change the display in the windows, a new selection of books had arrived and Nyles was separating them into categories.

I looked through something called *Last Days of Marie Antoinette.* Might be worth while, hopefully not too graphic, I wasn't interested in ghoulish descriptions of how the poor woman's head had been separated from her body.

"Nyles please rearrange the toys in the window and make room for these two titles. *Little Adventurer, and Grannie's Rhymes of Olden Times.*"

"Yes ma'am, do you want the one about mental arithmetic included?"

I chuckled. "Don't think a child could be enticed to spend leisure time perusing arithmetic concepts. I know from experience it would make my blood run cold,

put it with the other educational items in the children's section."

Nyles was a sweet young man, not yet twenty. One

could say he was rather homely with ears that protruded from his head like small wings, light brown hair and large, brown eyes. He was tall, thin and somewhat awkward but Uncle Arch and I appreciated his keen mind and love of books.

"I'm sure Mrs. Collingswood will be stopping by, she knows the shop receives new

inventory at the first of the month," Nyles stated.

"Indeed, you should put the *Selected Poems, by Edmund Gosse,* aside for her, I think she enjoyed another offering by Gosse."

Nyles paused for a moment. "Yes, she purchased *English Odes* several months ago."

"You never cease to amaze with the ability to recall such things," and handed him the book of poems.

I placed the *OPEN* sign into the front window, then pushed the large door ajar to let the fresh morning breeze waft into the shop. Inside could get a little stuffy after being closed for the night.

I was arranging books on the center table when a man entered. He studied the room carefully.

"Good morning, may I help you find something?"

The fellow removed his hat. "I'm just looking, I understand you have quite a selection of used books."

Not entirely the truth, he wasn't much interested in reading material. "Indeed, browse all you like."

He nodded his head and wandered toward the archway and became lost in the stacks. I'd send Nyles to turn up the lights and see what the gentleman was really doing.

I could hear Jennie descending the stairs on her way to do some marketing, rather her than me, shopping wasn't a pleasurable activity for my keen awareness of emotions in others.

Too many people milling around made it difficult to block out their moods, human drama and conditions, be they good or bad.

"Just need a few things for dinner, carrots, potatoes and onions," Jennie announced.

"Thrilled you didn't mention peas, can't abide the slimy green things."

"Fresh, young peas that haven't been overcooked are quite tasty, Miss Olivia."

I shuddered and made a face. "So you keep saying, but will never convince me."

Jennie chuckled and continued on her way with the large basket dangling off her arm.

I guess the term "girl of all work" was the best way to describe Jennie Marsh. She had been with us since the age of fifteen, ran away from the workhouse, after her mother died. The girl came into the shop to get out of the rain and cold and never left.

Jennie had a certain quality, a quiet dignity in one so young. She learned to keep house and cook from Mrs. Akins, our former housekeeper, who planned to retire and go home to family in Yorkshire.

Uncle Arch provided a nice bonus when the woman left six months later.

Jennie had dark hair and eyes, not especially pretty until she smiled. The delightful grin and contagious laugh changed her whole face. One could only take pleasure in such expressions.

She was happy with her situation for the time being, but I had little doubt some fellow would be attracted to this bright and capable young lady.

Nyles returned and leaned close. "I don't think the man has a passion for books, he seems absorbed in the physical attributes of the building. I could see him writing in a small notebook and studying the walls and ceiling."

"Interesting, but nothing wrong in looking about the place it's quite pleasant."

"Nevertheless, I'll continue to observe, he could be a sneak thief."

I resumed placing new books on the table as Nyles made his way to the back.

It wasn't long before the man wandered in my direction, took one more look around and approached.

"I'd like to have a word with Mr. Varrus."

"My uncle isn't available right now, perhaps I may be of help?"

He reached inside his coat pocket and produced a card and handed it to me. "This is a business matter of some importance."

I took the card and regarded it carefully. "George Clegg . . . Agent. What or whom do you represent Mr. Clegg?"

The gentlemen inhaled and brushed something off his coat sleeve. "As I mentioned, an important business matter."

"I'm not sure when Mr. Varrus will return, but will give him your card."

The fellow nodded and left, I watched as he examined the front of the shop and made a few more notes in his little book.

Curious, but not unexpected, I had heard rumors of offers being made to several small business owners further down the block. So far no one had been persuaded to sell.

When Uncle Arch returned from Bristol we could discuss what was going on in the neighborhood. Right now I had work to do and would think on it later.

❧

Saturday was always busy; quite a few mothers with their children in tow browsed through the shelves and usually purchased something.

Fashionable young ladies sought out the latest romances

and one woman asked for a recommendation on "something chilling and ghostly".

One could never go wrong with *The Old Nurse's Story* by Elizabeth Gaskell . . . spooky old haunted house. Charlotte Riddell's *The Open Door,* another haunted house with a mysterious door that wouldn't stay closed.

The Body Snatcher, by Robert Lewis Stevenson could keep one awake and unnerved at sounds in the night.

I had become interested in detective novels; I quite liked the solving of crime riddles and following clues. It had all started when I read *The Moonstone* by Wilkie Collins.

I enjoy Edgar Allan Poe's Dupin tales, the American, Anna Katherine Green; author of New York based detective stories, the Lecoq novels by Gaborian, and Forrester's female detective who works undercover for the police.

I admire the intelligent skill that eventually solves the crime, satisfied that the criminal will be caught, human relationships restored, evil, violence, and crime alleviated.

I suppose a reason my favorite books are called fiction, a narrative of imaginary events and people, a fabrication, as opposed to fact. One could get lost in the adventure.

Unfortunately, reality has a way of popping up no matter what, I guess it's how one deals with the actual events of life that make us who we are.

❧

Sales had been steady throughout the morning, but were slowing down since it was past noon, I sent Nyles upstairs to have lunch with Jennie.

Two Metropolitan Police Constables strolled inside, looked around, and waited until I finished with a customer.

They wore the traditional uniform of navy-blue trousers and tunic with raised leather collar, helmet, whistle, and truncheon attached to a wide belt.

"Good afternoon, is there something I can help you find?"

One of the officers moved a little closer to the door, he seemed a bit edgy, the other, a heavy-set constable, came forward and stood in front of the counter. He had a faint smile on his face and his hand caressed the wooden baton.

"We're collecting for the Crime Prevention Fund. For only a few shillings a week, your charming shop will be protected from acts of vandalism. Saved from broken windows, defacement of property with vile words, even harm to yourself and them's that work here."

Was this a subtle threat, extortion, from those who were supposed to safeguard the public? He tapped his fat fingers on the club.

I hoped my voice didn't sound too quivery. "I believe that is the reason I pay taxes."

He leaned closer, his manner intimidating. "Me and my mate would hate for something bad to happen, if a break-in was to come about, them books could be damaged beyond repair."

I noticed the repulsive copper had an eye that looked a little milky. Probably found it difficult to see much of anything.

I took a deep breath and concentrated on the distasteful looking eye. "It would be terrible if something happened to your other eye, might be a disadvantage in your profession."

The extortionist jerked away then began to rub his good eye. "What did you say?"

"I said it would be a shame if you had no vision." I concentrated all my thought processes on that eye.

He fumbled for the truncheon and knocked it off the counter, then screamed, and covered his face with both hands.

The other fellow rushed to his partner. "What's wrong Frank, you sick or something!"

"Help me . . . can't see!"

The frightened, smaller rozzer, had no idea what to do for the frantic fellow who lurched about and held his head.

"Take your friend and leave, if either of you ever return, the blindness will be permanent and the headaches you suffer will be severe enough to cause bleeding from your ears. Now get out!"

I had no idea if any of things I had mentioned would actually happen, rather doubtful, but the power of suggestion on weak minds could prove hazardous.

Chapter Two

The two odious policemen stumbled from the shop. The heavyset creature clutched his head with one hand and grasped his partners sleeve with the other. I doubted they would trouble me again.

I gathered the heavy truncheon from the floor and placed it under the counter. It was brightly painted with a black and red snake encircling a gold crown. Rather apropos, its former owner was as loathsome as a snake.

Not that all snakes were abhorrent, I'm sure there were some perfectly delightful serpents somewhere . . . far away from me.

Some minds were malleable, especially when one might feel inadequate, guilty, frightened, essentially lacking in some way.

The paunchy copper was afraid he would suffer the loss of his sight, and was also engaged in a criminal act; his smaller friend was terrified of the consequences of being caught. They were both vulnerable to suggestion.

The channeling of emotions is draining; I didn't resort to such things often. The first time I realized I could mentally be assertive was at The Somerville Academy.

Uncle Arch wanted to make sure I acquired all the social graces of a practical education. Good manners, precise needlework, music, singing, flower arranging, and a bit of poetry.

So three days a week were spent under the watchful eye of Mrs. Somerville and her sister Miss Hopkins. The other two days and late afternoons I was tutored in areas such as languages, literature, history and mathematics. My education equaled or surpassed most university-enlightened males.

The rotund Miss Hopkins had her "pets" of which I was not. She was partial to Josephine Parker and two other nasty creatures that made life miserable for the rest of us.

I was furious that one of the smallest and shyest girls had been severely disciplined, which included a hard slap to the face, then ridiculed by Miss Hopkins.

Josephine had invented something about Emma that deserved punishment in the eyes of the teacher.

I glared at Josephine as she looked at each of us and simpered. She pushed the curls away from her face, stood and loudly announced that Miss Hopkins looked like a fat pig and smelled like one too.

At the time I was thinking of how much the forbidding and disapproving instructor resembled a great sow, and wouldn't it be lovely if Josephine said as much.

Everyone gasped; Miss Hopkins went pale, then turned an interesting shade of puce. The enraged teacher dragged the shocked girl out of the room and we never had the pleasure of seeing Josephine Parker again at Somerville Academy.

Another time was at the Bodleian Library in Oxford. Uncle Arch and I were examining The Anglo-Saxon Chronicle, the Mercian Register segment. The manuscript was written in the late 9th century in Old English, and considered the most important source of British history between the departure of the Romans up to the Norman Conquest.

This part of the library was a closed section and only people with special permission were allowed access to the fragile and rare documents.

My uncle was a friend of the Head Liberian of the Bodleian, Edward Nicholson, thus our means of entry.

I was having difficulty concentrating on what Uncle Arch was saying about the Battle of Holme because of the emotional turmoil coming from the man in the corner. After a few minutes I murmured my suspicions to my uncle, who also began to watch the fellow, then motioned one of the security officials to our table.

As two guards walked toward the man, he abruptly stood and began to babble about "needing the money, he could get out of debt . . . it was only a small picture".

The pathetic man was removed and turned over to the police for trying to steal a one of a kind fragment from the Caedmon Manuscript, called The Fall of Lucifer; the drawing was by the 7th century poet Caedmon. A "small picture" . . . indeed.

Never did find out who the fellow was working for, but someone must have wanted the illustration very badly to have gone to such lengths.

Nyles interrupted my thoughts to say that Jennie had prepared a savory chicken and rice soup, fresh rolls, and a pound cake just out of the oven. One couldn't pass up such a meal, so hurried up to indulge my healthy appetite.

Thomas Brandyce watched through the window of his second-floor office across the street from the Ink on Paper Gallery. He was concerned that two policemen stumbled out of the door and hurried away. Something was wrong, he could feel it, the thought of Olivia in difficulty was unbearable.

It was time to come out of the shadows, stop lurking about and meet the woman face to face. He knew the skulking and spying, yes; this furtive observation was spying, had to stop.

How in the hell could he explain this overwhelming affection and desire to protect a woman he had actually never met, a certain madness perhaps?

In all other aspects of his life he was relatively sane, if one could call his business sane.

He owned an agency called Privatus, as the name implies, private matters, mostly assisting those who had nowhere else to turn. The advertisement in the newspaper was short and to the point.

INSURMOUNTABLE PROBLEM?
ODDS AGAINST YOU?
CONTACT PRIVATUS
PORTLAND STREET POST OFFICE
BOX 37 LONDON

It was time to present himself, couldn't put it off any longer, especially if Olivia was in trouble. That was what he did . . . protect people, solve their problems.

Thomas squared his shoulders, took a deep breath and walked out of the office.

Nyles greeted the tall, formidable looking gentleman. "Good afternoon, may I help you find something?"

Thomas carefully looked around. "I would like to speak with Olivia Varrus please."

"Miss Varrus is unavailable at the moment, I will be happy to assist you."

Brandyce knew the lady had not left the store. " Thank you, but I'll browse for right now."

The young clerk nodded, smiled and went back to placing books on shelves.

Thomas wandered toward the back and tried not to be impatient. He selected a book, returned it to the shelf, moved on to another section, removed another book and sat on the nearby sofa.

After about twenty minutes he heard voices and ventured toward the front of the building.

She was standing a few feet away. He contemplated her abundant auburn hair, fair skin, and striking amber gold eyes that grew wide when he approached.

I knew instantly who he was, not his name, just that this was the man who had been watching, observing me for a month, possibly longer.

"Nyles, there is a box of books in the back that requires unpacking, I'll tend to the gentleman."

My assistant scurried away, and I let my eyes roam over the fellow who stood much too close. "I was wondering when you would make an appearance."

"My name is Thomas Brandyce. You don't seem surprised or unnerved, I'm greatly relieved you are not frightened; I would be devastated if that happened."

"Dismayed rather than frightened Mr. Brandyce, perhaps an explanation is in order.

The man brushed a hand through his hair, then took a deep breath. "Difficult . . . beyond comprehension, perplexing at best. I realize this is out of the ordinary, but will you walk with me to Cavendish Square where we can talk."

I studied Thomas Brandyce; his piercing blue eyes were exceptional. He was tall, his dark blond hair thick and a bit unruly, I had little doubt he could take care of himself if provoked.

I imagined that his size could be intimidating, but quickly realized he was a right-minded man, but full of shadows and secrets; nonetheless I'd be safe with him.

I nodded slightly. "I shall let Nyles know where we are going."

The small park is an oasis of calm tucked away from busy Oxford Street; there are benches, grass and big shady trees, a tranquil bit of green in the heart of London.

We sat on a bench in the shade of a large tree, the leaves rustled in the slight breeze.

Mr. Brandyce looked up at a branch overhead. "Do you know the word Obsessus?"

I frowned in thought. "It's Latin, the meaning is something like "to watch closely" possibly even "to haunt"".

He inhaled deeply. "Correct . . . I don't claim to understand or even know why I have this overwhelming desire to possess and protect you . . . and realize I sound completely mad."

People strolled near our bench, I could hear snatches of conversation, the breeze continued to make the leaves shiver softly. "I don't know what to think of your disclosure, it's both disturbing and flattering at the same time. What do you intend to do about this . . . obsession?"

"I intend to marry you."

I could only stare at his interesting face in disbelief. "You can't be serious?"

"Very serious . . . so will you accept my offer of marriage?"

"No."

"Why?"

"The reason should be obvious and I'm perfectly happy

as I am. Besides this obsession of yours will probably vanish just as quickly as it started."

"No, it won't, but now that everything is out in the open it will be easier."

"Easier in what way?"

He smiled confidently. "To convince you to become my wife."

I closed my eyes and pressed three fingers against my temple. "Mr. Brandyce, whatever your affliction, you must realize this whole situation is absurd."

"I'm sure my mother thought the same thing about my father when he announced his intentions."

I folded my hands together tightly. "Are you saying your father pursued your mother in the same manner?"

He nodded. "Seems it runs in the family, this "fine madness". The whole story will take some time and tolerance on your part."

"At this moment, I have little time and limited tolerance. Nyles will be wondering what has happened to me."

We walked the short distance to the shop, our conversation centered on Gilbert and Sullivan's comic opera The Mikado that recently opened at the Savoy. I refused his invitation to attend, which didn't seem to discourage him at all.

As we arrived at our destination, he removed his hat, bowed slightly, announced he would see me the next day and walked away.

That was probably the most provocative and thought-provoking experience I had ever encountered. There was little doubt he was serious, which was unsettling, yet intriguing on an emotional level.

I had decided long ago that matrimony was out of the question for me. It would be far too difficult to constantly deal with someone's state of mind, their moods and perceptions of the world.

Right now there were customers to take care of, I would think about Mr. Brandyce and his obsession later.

It was almost six o'clock, closing time. My feet hurt and I wanted to remove shoes, put on slippers and unwind before dinner.

Uncle Arch should be home in about an hour; the train from Bristol would be arriving soon. Finding transportation could be time consuming and traveling from point A to point B frustrating depending upon the congestion of people and vehicles on the streets.

Archer Varrus placed the well-worn case on the floor beside his favorite chair, removed his hat and coat and lowered himself onto the leather cushion. He sighed with satisfaction as he rested his head against the back of the comfortable chair.

"You have a look of contentment, must have come home with something interesting,"

"Biblical Achieves, four original leaves from the Geneva New Testament,

Translation of Matthew, published by Conrad Badlus, and written in English."

I had to do some thinking about the new acquisition. "If I remember correctly the Geneva Bible was before The King James Bible."

Uncle Arch smiled. "Very good . . .the Geneva Reformation Bible was published in 1557 and translated by William Whittingham, and the first to use verse numbers. The King James Bible didn't appear until 1611."

"I'm sure the three-hundred-year-old pages will survive until you have something to eat." I gestured toward the dining room and waited for him to accompany me to the table.

My uncle rarely suffered from lack of appetite, he enjoyed his food perhaps a little too much. He was mostly round, from his face to his mid section, which included the shape of his spectacles that he frequently pushed on top of his head and often forgot where they were.

He was mostly bald, but had a fringe of white hair that encircled his head. Dark, intelligent eyes gazed under thick brows, his broad, large nose added character to a cheerful face. No one would ever say Archer Varrus was dapper.

Nothing on the outside mattered, I loved him because he was kind, intelligent and supported me in everyway possible, which was unusual for most men. Times being what they were held little consideration for women, tradition placed limitations on females.

Women seeking something other than the role of wife and mother were considered arrogant, presumptuous and lacking in the knowledge of their place in society.

"Did you encounter any problems, other people interested in the same artifacts as you?"

Uncle Arch shook his head and dipped a piece of bread in gravy that had accumulated on his plate. "Since this sale wasn't publicized as anything unique in regards to rare manuscripts and books, none of the usual dealers made an appearance. Caught a gimps of David Lang, but didn't stop to talk, he was in a hurry."

I helped myself to some more potatoes. "So how come Mr. Lang missed the fragments of the Geneva New Testament?"

"Probably the same reason other people did. The leaves had been inserted inside an old, but not especially valuable, tome on garden design. The book was in a box of similar material, which I purchased after telling the rather self-important person in charge that he might want to examine the four leaves.

I was informed that an expert had been through everything and if I wanted the book please make my way to the clerk and pay the price marked on the tag. So that is what I did, I might add that the cost of the volume on English gardens was rather inflated."

After dinner we sipped the sweet berry flavored port and munched on roasted nuts. The large glass doors to the balcony in the sitting room were opened to let in the cool evening air. I wondered if Mr. Brandyce was watching from across the way.

"Oh, a rather peculiar man stopped by, he wasn't interested in books, more in the composition and structure of the building. I put his card on your desk, I believe his name was Clegg."

Uncle Arch frowned. "Don't recognize the name, but there has been talk from other business owners about an estate agent making a nuisance of himself."

"I would imagine the envoy represents someone interested in buying this block of properties for whatever reason."

I could envision new office buildings, modern apartments, retail establishments offering a wide range of consumer goods, gobbling up buildings to expand into Arcades. Shopping for pleasure rather than necessity was becoming popular.

Places that once consisted of a single shop grew to encompass as many as ten or more neighboring stores. The idea of different departments was in vogue, goods were more accessible. A person could shop for furs, silks, lace, gloves, jewelry, clocks, dresses and home goods in one place.

Somewhat unsettling, a hoard of people milling about was not my idea of lighthearted pleasure.

Chapter Three

The morning was overcast; it would probably rain a little later. I had planned to wander Oxford Street and observe the latest construction; the place seemed to be in a constant state of development.

Not wanting to be wet and uncomfortable settled for a brisk walk to the newsagent at the end of the block. I could purchase several papers and look for estate sales scheduled for the coming week. One could find nice bargains in regards to the printed word.

Most people had no idea about books and their value. Usually relatives of recently deceased family members wanted to dispose of superfluous items as quickly as possible. Small libraries seemed to fall into that category, a collection of great "Uncle George's" old books were sold away posthaste.

Three papers should be enough to see what sales were taking place this week. One could usually tell by the address if it was worthwhile to have a look at whatever was being offered. Family members would have had time to select what was near and dear to their hearts, the left overs were put on the market

I wondered if Mr. Brandyce was slinking about, if so, he was keeping out of sight, but then again, since our discussion there was no need for him to lurk. It didn't really matter much to me, his obsession was likely to dwindle away. I also knew from our brief encounter he was being honest about his feelings, which was flattering in an odd way.

It had been slow all morning, the intermittent showers made it difficult for browsing shop windows. Nyles was having lunch with Jennie and I was writing information on two estate sales that might prove interesting.

Mr. Brandyce swept into the shop, removed his hat and tried to smooth his disheveled hair into place. He studied the room, then walked to where I sat taking notes.

"Good afternoon Miss Varrus, it's a pleasure to see you today."

"Mr. Brandyce . . . have you given up observing from a distance?"

He nodded; his eyes regarded the newspapers stacked neatly on the table. "After our conversation, there is no need to conceal oneself. I hope you have thought about what we discussed."

I returned the pen to its holder and took a deep breath. "Naturally I reflected on your surprising request and the answer is still . . . No."

"Understandable, but your response shall not deter me from my purpose."

I sighed. "Do you actually know anything about me Mr. Brandyce?"

The serious face offered a slight smile. "I know enough to realize we belong together as you will become aware soon enough."

'You seem sure of yourself."

He leaned over the table. "Very sure."

I watched him through the window as he walked across the street after our brief chat. One had to admit the fellow was persistent, almost single-minded when it came to me. The man was starting to unsettle my predictable life and I didn't know how I really felt about his regard. I would have to think on it.

After the fourth day in a row of polite but determined refusal of marriage I agreed to meet Mr. Brandyce at one of the estate sales. It was within walking distance of the shop and public. If I found something worthwhile he could carry whatever . . . might as well make use of his tenacity. Books proved to be rather cumbersome after a few blocks.

I glanced at the folded paper once again to make sure the address was correct. There wasn't any indication of a sale from the street. It wasn't until I reached the front door that I saw the small sign posted by the brass doorknocker.

I entered the house, stood quietly for a moment to look around the spacious entry. All the doors were open to the various chambers; at the back was a wide staircase. I would imagine the more public rooms were in this area and the private family space on the second level.

Since I was interested in the library, assumed it was located in one of the rooms off the hall.

There were voices coming from somewhere in the house. I peeked around the door and found what might be considered a sitting room. It was partially furnished; the better quality furniture had probably been removed.

A quantity of gimcracks and figurines were displayed on a long table, a young woman stood by the window. She looked nervous, not especially happy about being here.

"Everything in the room is for sale, prices are written on the small tags," she said softly.

"I'm looking for the library, the advertisement mentions a selection of books."

"Ah, yes, the library, its down the hall, last door on the right," her eyes darted around as if looking for something.

I could feel her apprehension, but the cause could be anything, and none of my business.

"Thank you, this is a lovely old house, a little gloomy, perhaps due to the dark wood."

She clasped and unclasped her fingers together and offered a tentative smile. "It is somewhat dreary even with the drapes open.

Hopefully there will be great interest and the contents

will be gone soon," she stated.

"Yes, one can look forward to that expectation."

I made my way out of the sitting area and headed for the library. A movement on the stairs drew my attention it was Mr. Brandyce making his way toward me.

He hurried down the last few steps.

"Miss Varrus, how delightful."

"I wasn't certain you would be here, most gentlemen are not interested in things of this nature."

"I must admit I've never engaged in such activities before but couldn't pass up an opportunity to be in your company."

His words were sincere enough, but sure he would prefer to be elsewhere. "Find anything interesting up there?"

"A rather nice pair of Georgian Wingback chairs in desperate need of new upholstery, and what was once an arched stone doorway with strange designs carved into the masonry."

"An entryway?"

"It was in pieces on the floor, a notice said something about Northumbria."

"A curiosity to be investigated after perusing the library," I murmured.

Another dark room awaited us, even with the heavy curtains open; the space was probably a combination study and library. There were significant gaps on the shelves where books had been removed; no doubt family members had found volumes worthy of their attention.

Mr. Brandyce moved to a table to examine items that

had once graced a desktop, the desk was nowhere in sight.

Many of the remaining books were religious or philo-sophical in nature, some written in Latin. *Essays on Religion* by John Stuart Mill, an edited version of *Chronicles of Bede*, *Consolation of Philosophy* from Boethius, the last two were recent publications of Anglo-Saxon writers of the seventh century.

The bookshop already had several copies of the works of Caedmon, Bede, Cynewulf and Boethius, no need to pur-chase more.

On the last row of shelves in a dark corner were two volumes tied together, a neatly written tag stated a price of eight shillings. I pulled the books from the shelf to get a bet-ter look at the title. *Travels into Several Remote Nations of the World in Four Parts.*

I untied the coarse string and opened the well-worn calf binding to the title page. Benjamin Motte had published it in 1726, no mention of the author's name. One could discern this was also a *First Printing*, a book that supersedes all oth-er editions chronologically.

I could feel my heart begin to beat rapidly as I carefully turned the pages of this trivial travelogue.

Part one, chapter one, began with Lemuel Gulliver re-counting the story of his life. I was holding a first edition of *Gulliver's Travels* by Jonathan Swift, a prize to be sure and the cost was in shillings not pounds.

Mr. Brandyce was engaged in conversation with the at-tendant regarding an ornate ink blotter made of brass.

I waited a little impatiently clutching the books in one

hand and eight shillings in the other.

My companion paid his five pence for the blotter and stuffed it in a pocket. I showed the tag to the attendant and counted out eight shillings. Mr. Brandyce took the books, and glanced at the title.

"A travelogue to somewhere exotic?"

I nodded and smiled. "Could prove absorbing reading, fascinating people with strange customs on a remote island might be entertaining.

Shall we see what interesting items await upstairs, you mentioned something about stones."

The large drawing room contained more trinkets displayed on tables. A few pieces of dark, heavy furniture that looked worn and over priced were against the wall.

In one bedroom the tattered Wingback chairs Mr. Brandyce had mentioned were positioned next to a headboard that might be nice if refinished.

The last room we visited was empty except for the stones arranged on the floor in the shape of an arched entryway. Odd symbols were carved in each segment of masonry.

Brandyce bent down to inspect the tablets. "As I said, rather nonsensical, don't know many people who keep something like this in their house."

There wasn't much light and the room smelled musty. I leaned closer in order to see the etchings. "Undoubtedly the owner had a reason, the marks are Anglo-Frisian used from the 5th century onward. This kind of runic writing in England became associated with the Anglo-Saxon Christianization and Latin scriptoria in the 7th century."

My friend chuckled softly. "I'm not sure I fully comprehend what you said, but not surprised you can decipher these scratches."

I took a deep breath and smiled sweetly. "A person interested in vintage books and venerable manuscripts would recognize an early form of Old English. Given a little time I could translate what is recorded here, might be fun," I pointed to one of the stones. "I think this one mentions something about St. Paul."

"St. Paul the man or the church?"

"Anglo-Frisian from the 7th century could refer to the abbey of St. Paul at Jarrow. The tid-bit of information on the placard refers to Northumbria, which is where the monastery of Jarrow was located in the late six hundreds."

"Looks like scratch marks to me. Still can't understand why anyone would want a bunch of stones."

"My uncle might be interested, especially since the price is two pounds."

Mr. Brandyce touched one of stones and grunted. "Two pounds and the cost of hiring someone to haul this . . . whatever it is away."

"One should remember the old adage of "One person's trash another person's treasure.""

"If you want these slabs of rock then you shall have them, I'll find someone to help with the transaction."

I placed my hand on his arm to stop him from leaving. "I can't accept your generous offer, please don't trouble yourself."

He brushed his hand over mine; his fingers lingered

against my skin. It took a moment to realize that I was holding my breath.

His intense blue eyes took in my face. "Don't deny this small courtesy, it's important."

I knew his statement was true; it was essential for him to do me this service.

"Very well, but my uncle will insist on repayment."

"We shall discuss the matter later, excuse me for a moment."

I probably shouldn't have allowed Mr. Brandyce to purchase the stones. It would only encourage his behavior. But for some reason I knew it was the correct thing to do. I guess one might say the fellow was growing on me; he wasn't the least bit discouraged by my refusal of his outlandish marriage proposals.

We should have another discussion soon, there were so many questions to be asked and answered.

I was burning with curiosity to know where this man came from. He was well spoken, had manners, his clothes were of good quality, and probably attended some university somewhere in England.

At the moment didn't know what to think about his determination to fulfill any desire I might have. A reminder to keep impulses to myself, no telling what the man might do if he decided I was in need.

Another thought . . . what was I going to do with the stones once they were delivered home? I guess room could be made in the back storage area, Uncle Arch would enjoy translating whatever message was inscribed, after that . . .

something to discuss and figure out.

I had not mentioned Thomas Brandyce to anyone. Nyles had seen him several times when he came into the shop but didn't presume to ask questions. I would inform Uncle Arch of the existence of my gentleman friend since the stones would probably be delivered later this afternoon.

Right now I would enjoy a cream tea in the café Mr. Brandyce suggested only two blocks away from the sale.

We sat in the small-enclosed garden located in the back of the café.

"This is lovely, do you come here often?"

"Not really, but it was close to my old place of business."

"A place of business indicates you are employed?"

"I have a profession of sorts, rather difficult to explain."

I smiled and said lightly. "So you're not a beneficiary of family assets and receive a significant income."

Mr. Brandyce stirred his tea. "Let's just say I have been fortunate in having access to substantial benefits when necessary."

"How deliberately ambiguous, what exactly is your occupation?"

"I help people in crisis. I have certain connections, resources . . . skills if you like."

I raised my eyebrows and studied his face. "Wonderful, so I could hire you if necessary?"

"No need for that, I would never let anything happen to you."

This person sitting across from me was genuine in his

feelings rather like a defender. I could envision a hero from the court of Charlemagne or King Arthur . . . a paladin.

I mustn't let my thoughts run wild. "You mentioned your parents when we first met, that whatever this obsession might be has happened before."

"No harm in telling you some of the family history. My father met my mother at the home of neighbor, she was a governess, he fell madly in love and eventually persuaded her to go away with him. They lived happily together in London, had twins a year later a boy and a girl. My sister Thea is married and lives in America, I have two nephews and one niece."

I waited for him to continue but after a moment realized he was finished with his narrative. "I know there is more to the story, but will settle for the abbreviated version for the moment."

He chuckled. "Come, I will escort you home. I must contact haulers and have the tablets transported.

"I have some explaining to do before the delivery, Uncle Arch will not be expecting anything so dramatic. The first edition of *Gulliver's Travels* will help."

Mr. Brandyce looked at the books placed on the table. "You mean to say that these two sad looking things are by Jonathan Swift?"

"Indeed, Mr. Swift wrote a satire on human nature, published it anonymously because it was also anti- government."

"So these two volumes are scarce?"

I nodded and traced my fingers over the creased leather. "Scarce and valuable."

"How valuable?"

"Some collectors might pay as much as twenty-five pounds, maybe more."

He whistled softly. "That is quite a return on your investment. I believe you paid eight shillings."

"Money well spent, Mr. Brandyce."

Chapter Four

Uncle Arch examined the first volume of *Gulliver's Travels*. "It's in decent condition, I know just the person to contact about this delightful acquisition. You did exceedingly well my dear."

"Thank you, Uncle, I must also apprise you about another object, or rather objects, I obtained. I expect delivery late this afternoon."

Uncle Arch peered over his glasses. "Delivery, what kind of delivery?"

I took a deep breath. "Stones that once surrounded a doorway a few hundred years ago."

He looked a little puzzled. "I'm not sure I understand."

I really should start from the beginning, which included Mr. Brandyce, and try not to sound barmy. Uncle Arch listened quietly and after I finished he steepled his fingers, then tapped them together in thought.

"Are you certain this fellow isn't dangerous? He could be mad, have you reflected upon what he might do if you continue to refuse his offer of marriage?"

I slowly exhaled and leaned back in the chair. "Thomas Brandyce would be extremely dangerous toward someone wishing to harm me, that is a certainty. As for his obsession, something for me to work out."

Uncle Arch pursed his lips. "As long as you aren't frightened of this man, which you don't seem to be, I'll try to keep an open mind about his unorthodox behavior. You say he will accompany the engraved stones?"

"Yes . . . I will enlist Nyles and Jennie to help make room in the back for our unusual purchase."

He pushed away from the table. "I should look for the Anglo-Saxon

Futhorc alphabet, it's been quite a while since I've translated Old English. I must say I'm looking forward to the challenge."

Nyles, Jennie and I moved and stacked items, placed battered and rickety bookshelves against walls and cleared space for the stones to be assembled on the floor. We would need more light than just the single gas fixture that flickered; the carvings were worn in many places and difficult to see.

There were several lanterns packed away that would help, we could also keep the door to the alley open for a while.

Uncle Arch eventually found his Anglo-Frisian alphabet along with glyphs and notations of sounds that would translate into words.

Hours later Mr. Brandyce entered the shop. I was bundling several books in brown paper for a customer. He lingered near and observed.

"Nyles, please fetch my uncle, I believe he is upstairs."

The young assistant came forward, stared at Mr. Brandyce, then hurried away. I said good-bye to the shopper and turned my attention to the tall, quiet man who waited patiently.

"I hope you haven't been inconvenienced too much, I'm sure you would have preferred to spend your time elsewhere. Thank you for such consideration."

"I admit this has been an irregular activity, but a pleasure to be in your company. I'm a few minutes ahead of the haulers, where do you want the consignment delivered?"

I began to walk toward the back. "The storage area has been rearranged, there should be room to place the stones on the floor."

The door leading to the storage area was open; I turned up the light, which cast a dim glow over the contents.

Uncle Arch hustled inside the room and made his way to my side. He peered over his glasses at my companion; I took a deep breath and began the introductions.

"Uncle Arch, I would like to introduce Thomas Brandyce, Mr. Brandyce, my uncle, Archer Varrus. I have told him of our unusual acquaintance."

Uncle Arch continued to observe the tall, reserved man, then extended his hand. "Mr. Brandyce, you have a remarkable way of presenting yourself."

The two men shook hands. "I agree Mr. Varrus, but intend no disrespect to your niece, only my deepest admiration and consideration for her welfare."

At least they were being civil, which was a relief. Nyles interrupted to announce the arrival of the haulers.

My uncle was enthralled with the stones and spent the next few hours making detailed drawings and notes. He didn't even notice when we left him alone with his latest endeavor.

Mr. Brandyce had business elsewhere and departed after he asked his usual question and received my usual answer. He also refused to accept payment for the artifacts or the cost of hauling.

One couldn't help being beyond curious and drawn to this mysterious man. To be honest I looked forward to his daily visit.

Uncle Arch was still working when I went to my room later that evening. I tried to convince him to stop, but knew when he was in pursuit of something he was relentless.

I prepared for bed and listened to the rain; it had slowed to a soft steady beat on the sidewalk below. Thoughts of Thomas Brandyce intruded, what to do and how to manage this situation left one perplexed.

I should be annoyed but wasn't . . . the only logical thing to do was wait and stay calm, most things worked themselves out. I almost convinced myself he would grow tired of this game and one day soon, stop coming around.

Thomas balanced carefully on the wet ledge three stories off the ground. This little exercise should have been a
cakewalk if the rain had held off. Danny would think it terribly funny, as he remained dry under the shelter of the garden
loggia.

The prowler worked the glasscutter, made four swipes
in the shape of a square and softly tapped out the pane and
maneuvered it into his hand. Twisted the latch, opened the
window, and was inside the study.

He stood quietly in the dark room to let his eyes adjust.
His client had given him detailed information about the
house, the contents of the study, and the disreputable individual that lived here.

The letters were in the mahogany safe cabinet near the
desk, at least that is where Miss Pronsonby, in her tearful
account, thought they should be.

The, not so respectable, fellow was blackmailing the
young woman, with threats of informing her father and fiancé of their relationship if she didn't pay a considerable sum
for his silence.

Brandyce couldn't help but wonder why the girl would
be so foolish as to put anything in writing. Not his place to
judge, his job was to find the letters and return them to his
employer.

Slowly he made his way across the room and stood in
front of the desk, then contemplated the tall cabinet close by.
Gas pilot lights flickered at several places around the room
producing enough of a glow to be able to move about with-

out running into the appointments.

The mahogany cabinet was designed to look like an ordinary piece of furniture; in reality it was a diversion safe. One must locate the "secret" keyhole that opened the cabinet door, then hopefully pick the lock to the safe inside.

There were several brass embellishments at the top of the cabinet. Such emblems or decretive plates were used to conceal a keyhole. Thomas had seen many such devices, family crests, shields, faces; this one was an oak leaf.

He started at the left and gently manipulated each one; the second to the last swiveled to reveal the aperture.

He removed the strap from across his chest that secured the leather bag and set the kit on the floor, then carefully extracted a ring of keys. This particular barrier was a standard warded lock. A well-designed skeleton or master key can easily bypass the wards. With that small task out of the way, he opened the cabinet door to examine the safe.

Not especially difficult, the iron safe had a pin tumbler lock that shouldn't take more than a few seconds to open using a pick set.

The interior was lined in red velvet and contained two small drawers above a large space for bulker items and important papers.

After looking through the pack of letters to make sure they were from Miss Pronsonby, emptied the entire contents into his bag.

A few moments later he was out the window, across the roof, and down the sturdy, rambling, wisteria vine that covered the loggia. Danny St. Jules, his friend, as well as employee-companion was waiting in the shadows.

"I was about to come looking, what took so long?" Danny whispered.

"In case you haven't noticed its raining, the bricks are slippery, and the ledge not especially wide."

Danny peeked around the thick foliage and pulled the wool cap down over his ears. "Best get out of here while the rain provides cover."

Back at the house in the fashionable district of Mayfair, Brandyce and St. Jules entered through the door that led into the basement kitchen. Climbed the back stairs to the second floor and into the library.

"Shall we see what the scoundrel wanted to keep away from prying eyes?"

Danny lolled in a comfortable leather chair and watched his friend empty the bag.

Thomas put the letters to one side and read through the other small stack of papers.

"Seems Mr. Webster doesn't own the house we just burgled and is behind on his rent. He's part owner of a race-horse called Smartly Run, costing him quite a bit.

This is interesting; the gent is being sued over some real estate deal that went awry.

Looks like the fellow isn't doing very well, perhaps someone should contact this lawyer who wrote the scathing letter and inform him of Mr. Webster's whereabouts."

Thomas counted the cash, a little over twenty-five pounds. Removed a nice gold and pearl bracelet, silver cuf-flinks and a gold ring from a small purse.

41

He held up the bracelet. "This little bauble will be re-turned to Miss Pronsonby, part of the blackmail payment. Rob can take the rest of the jewelry to Clifford's in the morning, should get a few pounds."

Danny stifled a yawn. "Which charitable institution do you want to endow this time? Schools, widows, and orphans . . ."

"I'm sure the Burlington Charity School will make good use of Mr. Webster's funds. You staying here the rest of the night?"

"Might as well, it's still raining."

The dining table was covered with papers; Uncle Arch was having coffee. As I entered, he looked at me and smiled.

"I think I know most of what was written on the stones, the essential part anyway."

I hugged the tired looking man and sat across from him. "Hopefully you didn't stay up all night."

"Not all night, did sleep a few hours."

Jennie came in with a carafe of fresh coffee. "Would you like breakfast now Mister Archer?"

"Yes please, I'm famished."

"Miss Olivia, breakfast or just coffee?"

"I think an egg and toast will be fine Jennie." I picked up one of the sheets of paper and tried to make sense of the scribbles. "So what have you found?"

He smiled and carefully gathered the papers. "Let me put these in order. Do you know who lived in the house where the stones came from?"

I added milk to my coffee. "I don't have the slightest idea . . . why?"

"Just wondering how such historical items came to be in London."

"How historical are we talking about?"

"I have an idea the stones once framed an archway at either Jarrow or Wearmouth, the twin monasteries in Northumbria."

"So the inscription dates from the late 600's?"

Uncle tapped the stack of notes. "It would seem so."

I set my cup carefully back on the saucer. "How interesting . . . what does it say?"

"As you know the monasteries were the center of scholarship and book production for around two hundred years, until the Vikings came along and wreaked havoc."

I had to smile. "Ah, yes, the Northmen, they caused the Anglo-Saxons a spot of bother. But I guess turn about is fair play, the Saxons did their own ravaging and pillaging of the Britons after the Romans left."

He humphed a bit at my comment. "That is neither here nor there, do you want to know what the good monks had to say?"

"Of course, something profound I'm sure," I teased.

Uncle Arch shuffled through the piles of paper, selected several and arranged them in a row on the table and began to read.

Almighty God bless the works of thy servants.
Guide our hands to spread the glory of thy word.

"The last two inscription seem to be a list of places where books were sent."

*Four pandect gifts to St. Peters, St Paul,
Hartlepool and the Pontifex Maxamus.*

I was a little confused. "Pandect, as a code of laws?"

Uncle Arch tapped the papers. "I believe it means "pandect" as in a name given to the Latin Vulgate Bible. It has long been thought there were three large single volume Latin Bibles produced at the monasteries. One went to Wearmouth or St. Peters, a copy to Jarrow or St. Paul's and the third delivered to Pope Gregory II in Rome."

I studied my uncle who looked rather excited. "The inscription mentioned four gifts, so where or what is Hartlepool, other than a small town up north."

"I don't have the slightest idea, but intend to find out."

"Now that is intriguing, so there might be a forth Latin Vulgate Bible around somewhere? Have you ever seen one of these twelve hundred year old books?"

"Not a complete one, just fragments, the Bibles at Jarrow and Wearmouth disappeared or were destroyed by your Viking friends. The one presented to the Pope resides in Italy, Florence, I believe. It's said to be the oldest and only surviving Vulgate Bible in the world."

I narrowed my eyes. "Are you speculating, or do you know this for a fact?"

My uncle smiled and reached over to pat my hand. "You wouldn't ask such a question if you had read the works of the Venerable Bede with more care."

I offered a slight grimace. "The Venerable Bede, the father of English History, was rather long winded."

"Long winded or not, he mentioned the Vulgate Bibles and where they were distributed, but nothing about Hartlepool."

"The man was a prolific writer, he wrote poetry, letters to everyone important, history, scientific tracts, and endless commentaries on the scriptures. But quite a few of his works have gone missing or exist as fragments, could be a reference to Hartlepool has been lost over the last twelve hundred years."

Jennie carried in a tray from the kitchen and placed dishes containing eggs and bacon, toast, jam, cheese and slices of caramelized apples. The delightful aroma of cinnamon was irresistible.

It didn't take much prodding to include savory apple slices with my egg and toast.

"Now that you have an idea about the inscriptions, I'm sure you plan to investigate."

"Indeed, I shall see what information there might be on Hartlepool. I have an idea it's a monastic place, in Northumbria, curious to know what would make it special."

I spread strawberry jam on the toast. "So you're off to the archives?"

"The archives and the British Library, see what I can find."

"I should go back to the estate sale, perhaps I can learn who the owner was. You were curious about how the stones

45

traveled all the way from Northumberland."

He nodded, then sipped more coffee. "Most people don't have Saxon etchings laying about the house, did you notice any other object d'art on display?"

"I didn't go into all the rooms, but most of the items I did see weren't especially collectable, some ceramics, glassware, a few brass whatnots."

Uncle Arch folded his napkin. "If there were anything of great value, the relatives would have removed it, but it couldn't hurt to find out the name of the individual who resided there."

"Archer Varrus, you don't really believe there is another "one of a kind Vulgate Bible" do you?"

He shrugged and smiled. "Well . . . I might have given it a thought or two."

"If such a rare tome existed, don't you think someone would have let the world know?"

Uncle Arch chuckled. "Not if it had been hidden away like the *Stonyhurst Gospel of St. John.* It was written in the six hundreds and not found until the eleven hundreds.

We seem to have a mystery worth investigating."

Chapter Five

A face peered through the shop window. It wasn't quite time to open, but resigned myself to unlocking the door for Mr. Clegg, the estate agent who had wandered through the shop a short while ago.

My uncle might as well talk to the man; the library and archives could wait for a few minutes. It wouldn't take long to convince the fellow we had no desire to sell the property.

Our neighbors, Mr. Sullender and the Portman brothers had spoken with Uncle Arch about this Clegg person being rather persistent. They were not interested in selling either.

The fellow entered the shop, removed his hat, looked around and addressed me in a rather curt manner. "I need to speak to Mr. Varrus, I have tried to do so on numerous occasions and found him unavailable."

I studied the impatient man. He wasn't especially memorable, pale skin, mouse brown hair and gray eyes. Even though he appeared assertive, it was a pretense, a show of confidence.

"My uncle has been away. I'll see if he can spare a few moments to meet with you."

Mr. Clegg puffed out his chest and looked irritated. "I'm sure he will find what I have to say worth while."

"Please make yourself comfortable," I gestured to a workspace with a table and chair in the corner.

"I'd rather not, I'll wait here."

I nodded my head slightly. "Nyles please advise my uncle he has a visitor who is most anxious to speak with him."

My assistant headed for the stairs and I placed the open sign in the window. I glanced through the glass pane, no rain, people would be strolling about soon and I hoped the new display would catch their eye.

I had positioned a bottle of poison with skull and crossbones, a wanted poster and a replica of a tombstone on copies of books about mystery and crime. Chosen titles were *The Woman in White, Things as They Are, Scenes in the Life of a Bow Street Runner, Bleak House, The Moonstone, The Female Detective and The Notting Hill Mystery.*

Mr. Clegg paced nearby, occasionally drawing his watch from his pocket to check the time. The stairs made their usual creaking sound as Uncle Arch slowly made his way down. He carried his old leather case in one hand, a hat in the other.

He only managed to travel a few steps before being set upon by Mr. Clegg, who began to rattle about "opportunities and progress" and presented his card.

Uncle Arch examined the card, listened politely as he edged toward the door. "Mr. Clegg, I do not wish to sell and don't care about missed opportunities. Tell whomever you represent to look elsewhere for expansion possibilities. Now I must have a few words with my niece, excuse me."

Mr. Clegg didn't look pleased; perhaps indecisive would be a better description.

Uncle Arch hastened to my side and spoke softly. "Hopefully this will be the end of any more attempts to purchase the shop. I have things to do this morning, many questions to try and find answers . . . be home for dinner," and walked quickly out the door.

I should be courteous to the unhappy looking Mr. Clegg. "Is there something I can help you find, we have many of the latest publications."

The irritated man surveyed the room, took out a small notebook and pencil and scribbled something, then came to where I was standing. "It would be in your best interest to convince your uncle to sell, my employer rarely takes "no" for an answer."

I smiled sweetly. "Please tell your employer that Archer Varrus has no intention of selling and not to trouble us any further."

He took a deep breath, placed his hat carefully on his head and strode out of the shop. Nyles approached the counter. "Not a happy man, his last words seemed almost menacing."

"I didn't feel threatened by him, he is a messenger boy, have no idea about the person he works for . . . we can only hope this is the end of it."

Thomas left the small public gardens located west of the Chelsea Old Church. He and Miss Pronsonby had met at an out of the way corner where he returned the letters and bracelet.

He assured her the sordid individual wouldn't bother her again, since his creditors, a solicitor and the police had been notified of his whereabouts.

The tears flowed in excessive amounts. Eventually the young lady gained control of her emotions and stated she would heed his advice about expressing feelings of a personal nature in writing. Hopefully she would pay attention to the recommendation.

He had an appointment with another possible client in an hour. The summons was rather mysterious, but the address was in one of the most fashionable areas of London. The short note expressed the need for confidentiality and the date and time for this audience.

Thomas made his way toward the Victoria Embankment, hurried along the walkway by the river and thought it would be nice to wander about the place with Olivia. After his meeting he would stop by the bookstore, see if he could persuade the young lady to accompany him on a leisurely stroll.

The opulent and too warm room was cluttered with furniture and ornaments, burgundy and gold wallpaper attacked the senses. The place was filled with fresh flowers in crystal vases, and the mantel of the marble fireplace displayed pictures and ceramic figurines of various sizes and shapes.

Thomas could feel the sweat trickle down his back and the urge to open a window was almost overpowering. He moved away from the brightly burning fireplace in hopes of getting a breath of cool air.

The double doors opened a small woman stood in the entry and stared at him. She was elderly, lines of age embedded on her face, the almost white hair artfully arranged with small combs that sparkled when she moved.

The cane she leaned upon was of a dark gnarled wood and had a silver handle. The lady walked slowly into the room and sat down on one of the two sofas near the fire.

"I can only assume you are from the organization called Privatus. The name implies whatever is discussed will be held as a private matter."

Thomas studied the woman, then approached. "All business is considered confidential."

She looked at the object partially concealed in her hand. "The card has no name, I surmise you have one."

He nodded. "Thomas Brandyce."

Dark eyes peered at him for a long moment. "Please sit down Mr. Brandyce, through the years I have acquired several designations, Cecily Lydstrom will do for the time being."

Thomas recognized the name. Her husband was the late

Robert Lydstrom, 2nd Baron Newmark. Interesting. "How may I be of service Mrs. Lydstrom?"

The woman didn't speak for several moments, then smoothed the material of her black dress and leaned the cane against the gold cushion of the sofa.

"I have been approached by a solicitor who represents a young woman claiming to be my granddaughter. I would like this assertion investigated."

"Did the solicitor present any proof of this alleged relationship?"

"I was shown some documentation; a license that shows one Julia Margaret Lydstrom married Liam Moore. Also a letter from a vicar in Keswick stating there is a baptismal record in the Parish Register for a child born to a Julia and Liam Moore."

"I gather that you and your daughter are estranged?"

Mrs. Lydstrom ran her hand over the silver handle of the cane. "Many years ago my daughter was sent to school in France. It was my husband's idea; he wanted her away from a young man. Robert felt it was the best way to put an end to Julia's infatuation for this painter.

A few months later we were notified she had run away. That was more than twenty years ago, tried to find her with limited success, we know she left France and returned to England, but after that nothing.

As you might imagine, Julia's disappearance created quite the scandal in the eyes of the social elite, I would prefer the past not repeat itself."

"So the news of her marriage and subsequent birth of a

child is the first information you have had in over twenty years?"

"Yes, I recognized the name, Liam Moore, the young man Julia was determined to marry."

"The first thing I would recommend is to find out if the solicitor is reputable. Did he present a card?"

Mrs. Lydstrom furrowed her brow. "I was thinking about sending someone to Keswick as soon as possible."

"I suggest that mission take place later, I would be curious to know if the solicitor is perpetrating some kind of fraudulent scheme. As you mentioned your daughter's disappearance was gossiped about even if the family sought to keep it private. Some enterprising individual might wish to capitalize on the unfortunate incident."

A slight smile appeared on the woman's face. "It seems what little I could find out about you and your agency is true, you do have a certain ability with delicate situations.

"I have a small reputation to maintain," Thomas admitted.

"Very well, I'll have the solicitors card and important information regarding my daughter provided before you leave."

Mrs. Lydstrom used the cane to help rise from the sofa. "Please try to settle this matter, I would like to know about Julia, if her decision resulted in a happy life or became a tragedy."

Archer Varrus searched the history of Hartlepool, a flourishing seaport on the North Sea. The town started as a

Saxon settlement in the Kingdom of Northumbria in the 600's, around an Abbey, a double monastery for both monks and nuns . . . unusual.

For unknown reasons the religious house declined in importance in the 700's and finally destroyed by the Vikings around the year 800.

The book dealer had an idea there must have been some kind of monastic establishment if the name Hartlepool had been inscribed on the stones.

He doubted if anything was left of the Abbey, the Vikings usually did a wonderful job of obliterating such places.

Now that he knew there had been a monastery, why was it important enough to carve the name? That would require more digging, which he enjoyed; one could never tell what exciting developments were waiting to be found in the old dusty archives.

Archer smiled at the thought of the existence of another Latin Vulgate Bible, it would be an incredible find. Imagine stumbling upon this uniquely English Codex.

The only other copy was in Italy and would never be returned to England. The few fragments that survived of the Bibles from Jarrow and Wermouth are preserved in the British Museum.

He had seen and knew the history of the eleven leaves, called The Ceolfrid Bible, found in the 1600's. The pages were being used as covers for a chartulary, a collection of documents, title deeds and so forth in volume form, belonging to an aristocratic family.

The Willoughby family included the Baron's of Middleton. Where and how the remnants got to the Willoughby estate at Wollaton Hall, in Nottingham was anyone's guess.

There had to be more information on Hartlepool Abbey. Might take some time to trace the history . . . who founded the place, who were the abbots, was there anyone historically important with ties to the area.

One of the first tasks Thomas considered would be to investigate the solicitor. He looked at the name on the card, Norton Engle, didn't set off any feelings one way or another.

A visit to The Law Institute to find if Mr. Engle was a member in good standing was a place to start. This group represents and governs solicitors, gives support and training to it members and holds them accountable for their actions.

It might be possible to learn what court cases the advocate participated, was there a particular type or specialty.

Does this person solicit business from hapless victims of crimes; involve himself in frivolous litigation and groundless judicial proceedings?

All good things to know before spending time running around the countryside and paying a visit to Keswick in the Lake District.

Thomas hailed a cab to transport him to the bookshop, he was eager to see Olivia; it always made him feel better when he was around her.

She had a calming effect and it was important for him to know she was well and not experiencing any difficulty.

He knew his feelings were irrational; nonetheless he had to make sure.

❧

I felt the presence of Mr. Brandyce; aware he had entered the shop even though I was hidden away in the stacks, the man never missed a day. I found myself waiting for his arrival, becoming restive by the late afternoon if he hadn't made an appearance.

Nyles must have directed him toward the back where I was dusting. He appeared in one of the archways and watched as I placed several books back on the shelf.

"Miss Varrus, unfailingly busy as usual."

"There is always something that requires my attention, this particular activity is one of my least favorite."

"Then it shouldn't be difficult to convince you to take a walk, come away from this tedious chore, stroll along the river before it rains again."

"The invitation is tempting, almost beyond my ability to refuse."

"Don't decline, we have many things to discuss."

I chuckled. "Our discussions, as interesting as they might be, eventually turn to the subject of matrimony."

"Then we should get the topic out of the way first. Olivia Varrus please accept my offer of marriage; our life together will never be dull. There will be adventure, excitement, and most of all my undying devotion."

I approached my admirer who was lounging in the archway. "You might not find me as delightful as you think."

He took the feather duster and placed it on the small sofa close by. "Why, have you a dark secret you wish to con-

56

ceal?"

"Most of us have something to hide, things one wish to remain hidden for whatever reason . . . especially you Mr. Brandyce, a man of mystery."

"I prefer to call myself reserved, no mystery about what I do. I help people who have been victimized, have no resources, or require some assistance in finding a solution to their problems."

The sound of voices carried from the front of the store. Nyles was chatting with a customer.

"You feel I might be a problem in need of a solution."

"The solution is obvious, agree to be by wife, not difficult at all."

I had no doubt he was being honest, his regard for me was significant. "Let me

get my shawl and bag from upstairs, I'll join you at the front of the shop."

❧

George Clegg adjusted his coat, tugged at his sleeves and slicked back his hair before pushing through the double glass doors. Mr. Hodge's secretary made him nervous, his employer, Ruben Hodge terrified him.

Standing in front of the assistant's desk was always an exercise in tolerance. Wilfred Fiske was a little man, painfully thin with thick, dark brown sideburns. As usual he pretended not to notice Clegg for several moments.

Eventually he looked up, adjusted his spectacles and huffed several times to make sure the visitor knew the interruption wasn't appreciated.

"Mr. Hodge is expecting me, "Clegg stated in a firm voice.

The secretary smirked. "He has been most anxious to see you, I will let him know you have arrived . . . finally."

Chapter Six

Ruben Hodge stood with his back to the office door. He looked out the window and studied the buildings across the street. "I expected you earlier Mr. Clegg."

George Clegg nervously shifted his weight from one foot to the other and fiddled with the watch in his pocket.

"I had appointments with several business owners around Cavendish Square."

Mr. Hodge slowly turned toward the tense estate agent. "The outcome of these meetings was positive?"

"Not especially," Clegg said softly.

"Speak up! I didn't hear what you said."

"I haven't had much success in convincing the property owners to sell. There are three rented places with absentee landlords that might be interested if a better price can be negotiated."

Mr. Hodge moved to his chair behind the large desk and sat down. "Three buildings in the entire block doesn't lend itself to much of anything, don't you agree Mr. Clegg."

"I think I can persuade a few owners of the smaller shops, two of them said they might consider selling, but not at the amount offered."

"It seems these shopkeepers are under the impression their properties are far more valuable than expected. Perhaps they require some convincing to see the error in judgment."

George Clegg knew his employer would bring in the thugs and riffraff, to wreak havoc upon the shops, employees, and owners to scare them into selling. It was a tactic Ruben Hodge seemed to enjoy as much as making money.

Quite often he wished he had never become involved with the man. But needed the job, a family to support, and could almost convince himself that he had nothing to do with the more sordid side of West End Brokers.

The initials of the company name . . . WEB . . . was exactly that, a web of deceit, duplicity and fraud.

As long as Hodge provided what the large and powerful corporations wanted, no one cared. Expansion was the objective, the bigger the better, growth and development were a top priority regardless of those hurt in the process.

"I'll visit everyone again tomorrow Mr. Hodge, try to convince them it will be in their best interest to sell."

"Do that Mr. Clegg, persuade these shop owners to come to terms before something unfortunate occurs."

The emissary took a deep breath and hurried toward the door.

"On your way out ask Mr. Fiske to come in."

The secretary scrambled for his notebook and pencils, knocked softly, then entered the office and made his way to the desk. "Yes sir."

Hodge looked up from the newspaper. "Send a note to Ellicott and Rush, their services will be required relatively soon. Advise them to bathe before coming to the office, I can't abide the stench."

"Yes sir, right away sir."

"Oh, and prepare a list of shops and store owners around Cavendish Square, don't forget the landlords of rental property."

Ruben Hodge watched the diminutive man scurry out. He pushed away from the desk and rested his head on the back of the soft leather chair. His thoughts were about his wife, Roanne, the beautiful and self absorbed Roanne. The woman he bought and paid for.

Another lavish dinner tonight, something she reveled in partly to enjoy her friends, more typically to display a new gift of jewelry. He took the key from his pocket, unlocked the drawer, and removed the oblong box.

The lid snapped open to reveal a necklace of verdant green emeralds set in gold. Reuben brushed his fingers over the stones and smiled. Roanne had hinted that her new gown was a deep green silk; this bauble would match her eyes and make her wildly happy.

Keeping Roanne happy was something of a chore, but a commitment he accepted. He closed his eyes and envisioned her long dark hair and milk-white skin, eyes that would flash with pleasure when he presented the necklace.

He had first seen her riding in the park with her brother, Charles Bartlett, and was besotted with her beauty. The family moved in the best circles despite drowning in debt from years of poor management of their considerable assets.

The Bartlett's had acquired a loan from the bank Reuben was involved, so made it his business to find everything he could about the family. Hodge assumed the loan, became acquainted with Charles and Roanne and eventually a member of the family.

One might say Ruben Hodge bought a wife, a reverse dowry; he forgave the loan and in return gained a bride. Roanne, reluctant at first, eventually accepted the arrangement and made sure she had everything a woman could want in the way of material comforts.

I really should visit the house where the sale was taking place. Hopefully it hadn't ended. Uncle Arch wanted to find the name of the owner; it wouldn't take too long if those in charge knew the answer.

When I arrived the front door was open. I entered the foyer and went into the first room. Most everything was gone; the young woman who seemed so nervous when I was there a few days ago was packing curios into a box.

"Sorry to interrupt, hopefully you can answer my question."

The girl startled at the sound of my voice. "My goodness, you surprised me."

"I am sorry, won't take much of your time, could you tell me the name of the former occupant of the house?"

The girl placed one more item into the box. "The gentleman was quite elderly, his name was Edward Selby. I understand the residence now belongs to a nephew, but can't remember his name."

I looked around the dark room, the heavy drapes were open but didn't provide much light. "Thank you for the information, I'm sure you're happy this event is over."

She sighed. "The few things that remain will be donated to several different churches. Hopefully the next sale will be in a less depressing place."

After saying goodbye I made my way back to the shop, dawdled in front of a few windows along the way.

I guess Uncle Arch would devote some time looking into Edward Selby, and try to find a connection to the old monasteries, a task he enjoyed.

Henrietta Street was relatively busy, nothing like around the corner on Regent Street, but the shops did quite well most of the time.

A few doors down I saw that Clegg person go into the leather goods store. He was a persistent fellow; the Portman brothers were not interested in selling.

I should get back to the shop; it wouldn't be long before the agent came asking to speak to Uncle Arch. He would have to be satisfied with me, which in the past seemed to make the man unhappy. After all, women didn't have the brains to discuss business; only men had the acumen for that.

Mrs. Sullender waved from inside the bakery as I passed. It was tempting to stop and purchase a few lightly glazed custard filled pastries, a favorite of Uncle Arch. But my chubby relative didn't need any such sweets; I had enough trouble making sure he only had one slice of pie or cake at mealtime.

Nyles had the newspaper spread open on the counter. "Another body was pulled from the river yesterday, the police identified the victim as Siggy Fawcett, a well known villain in the East End."

I made room on the counter for a basket to display a few small books of poetry. "I guess the chap received some kind of final justice for whatever he was involved in, not many people are saved from the Thames."

Nyles grunted. "Don't go to the East End very much, kind of gives me the shivers."

"Probably a good idea, not the safest place to visit."

I grinned slightly when Thomas entered the shop. Several customers browsed the shelves in the back and Nyles helped a woman find "something exciting" for her sister.

I placed the afternoon correspondence out of the way under the counter. "How is your day thus far, productive I hope?"

He smiled. "Informative, which will be of interest to one of my clients. This place is busy, good books have a way of stirring the imagination."

"Always pleasant to serve the . . . oh, bother, that man

again!" Mr. Clegg entered,   removed his hat, and looked around.

I sighed and went to meet him. "My uncle is not here, he probably won't return until much later after the shop closes."

"That is unfortunate, I'm sure he doesn't realize how important it is to come to an understanding regarding this property."

"Mr. Clegg, the place is not for sale, so please stop coming round."

As I turned away the fellow grabbed my arm . . . a grave mistake on his part. Before I knew what was happening, Thomas had Mr. Clegg's wrist in one hand and the back of his neck in a vice like grip in the other. Thankfully none of the customers seemed aware of the drama unfolding near the front.

My protector whispered something to the frightened man, who nodded vigorously, when released, scrambled out of the shop.

"He won't bother you again, at least, if he values his life."

I refrained from making any comment; Mr. Brandyce was seething beneath the veneer of calm. "We should take a walk, or perhaps go upstairs and have tea," I said softly.

He nodded, and took a deep breath. "A brandy would be preferable, that is, if you have something like that."

"Come with me . . . and, yes I have a very nice French apple Brandy Calvados."

We climbed the stairs; I settled him in a comfortable

chair in the sitting room and poured two drinks. We sat in silence and sipped the smooth, pale golden spirit until he was ready to talk.

"Who is Mr. Clegg?"

"An estate agent representing some large company who wishes to buy this building and other places on Henrietta Street. He has been here several times and told we have no interest in selling."

Mr. Brandyce had regained a bit of composure and ingested more brandy. "After today he should be convinced the place is not for sale."

"I'm sure he is quite aware of that now and probably scared witless."

"The fool shouldn't have touched you."

Thomas was correct about that, very bad form, on Mr. Clegg's part. It was also a certainty that Thomas Brandyce was a dangerous man when it came to my welfare.

What was I going to do about this person?

I had realized quite early he didn't wish to control or want to separate me from family and friends. He was a constant, a condition that wouldn't vary in any situation . . . what was wrong with that, rather marvelous to be truthful. I had thought on it a great deal.

"We were interrupted before you could ask your usual question."

He swirled the brandy, drank what was left and placed the glass on the table.

"Olivia Varrus, do me the great honor of becoming my wife."

I set my almost empty glass next to his on the small table positioned between our two chairs. "I accept."

He stared at me, then rose slowly, took two steps in my direction, and held out his hand. "Two are stronger than one, some days won't be especially good, but certain to be better with you in my life."

I grasped his hands, which were large and warm. We stood together, the blue eyes held mine. "Perhaps you should have dinner with us tonight. We have to inform Uncle Arch of our intentions."

"I say this at great risk to my well being, why the change of heart . . . your heart, not mine."

I placed one hand on his chest. "You are an exceptional man, and possess qualities I admire. There seems to be no logic to my consent but sometimes the heart desires what the mind aspires to."

"Don't understand anything you said, but you'll never regret your decision."

I chuckled slightly. "My life thus far has been rather mundane . . . that is until we met. Since I don't plan on rushing to the alter there should be time to learn more about you. Of course, you will want to become acquainted with my peculiarities too.

Shall we sit, and you can tell me more about your parents and how your father persuaded your mother to leave her position as governess."

For the next half hour I listened to a tale that was beyond belief. Mr. Brandyce Senior was married to the shy, sweet and fragile Lady Francis, who after the birth of a son retired to the country estate and preferred to live quietly.

As the years passed, Senior spent a good deal of time in London, only visiting his reclusive wife every few months. The son, Benjamin, was sent off to school and the parents lived mostly divergent lives.

Senior met, became obsessed with, Anna, the governess, and the two of them made the decision to have a life together. A divorce was next to impossible and would cause a scandal; he also had great respect for Lady Francis.

In essence Mr. Brandyce decided to live two separate lives . . . Nicholas Brand, Baron Hoverton became Owen Brandyce.

A lovely house in Mayfair was secretly purchased; they married, and lived happily with their children Thomas and Thea. Senior made sure the Brandyce offspring were provided for since his eldest son would eventually assume the title of Baron.

Before his parents died, Thomas was told the story, which was astounding, but rather amazing too. This couple had managed to live a secret life for over twenty- five years, a feat that required courage and strength of will.

The first thing I asked after this revelation was if Thomas already had a wife. Fortunately, he was a single fellow with no encumbrances. Always a good thing to know, I wasn't prepared to follow in his mother's footsteps and become involved with a bigamist.

"Have you met your half-brother, Lord Hoverton or Brand?"

"No, but I've made it my business to find out about

him. He is married, has three children, lives mostly on the Hoverton country estate consisting of over twelve hundred acres of woodland and pastures.

The place has been around since 1336, hidden away in the Surrey Hills, a patchwork quilt of fields providing fruit, vegetables, meat and poultry to the markets of London."

"Do you think his Lordship has any inkling he has other siblings?"

"Don't have the slightest idea, never received any correspondence or an attempt to contact me."

"Probably just as well, no need to bring up the past, what was done is done."

"That is how I feel about it, I had a wonderful childhood . . . now it's your turn Miss Varrus."

"Can't compete with your story, nothing comes close to what you have disclosed. Parents died when I was five, so don't remember much about them, my uncle has provided the best possible life and I shall always be grateful.

If you haven't already guessed, I'm rather independent and often speak my mind, probably due to the liberal education I received."

I took a deep breath and gathered my thoughts on how to divulge my unusual ability. Not that it would make any difference to him, so forged ahead.

"Thomas, there is something you should know but difficult to explain . . . ah, how should I put this . . . for some reason I seem to know what people are feeling."

The expression on his face didn't change all that much, he rubbed his chin and his eyebrows went up slightly. "Go on, you have my full attention."

"I can't read minds, and don't have any idea what a person is thinking per se. It's more like if one is lying, or sad . . . even angry, have bad intentions, or good objectives in mind. That is why I've never been afraid of you and your obsession."

He tapped his fingers on the arm of the chair. "You can tell when someone isn't telling the truth?"

I nodded. "More often than not. I do have a concern about what might happen to the unfortunate person that might want to harm me in some way."

His eyes seemed to grow a little darker. "Let's just say such an "unfortunate person" would never have the chance to offend again.

I clasped my hands tightly together. "Thomas you can't go around damaging or worse, those who offer an offence toward me."

He smiled brightly. "Of course not . . . one should never let their natural instinctive feelings run wild."

That was a blatant lie . . . something to work on . . . if possible. I'd think on it.

Chapter Seven

If Uncle Arch was surprised, he didn't let it show when we announced the news. After we were alone he would share his concerns. He asked the traditional questions about Thomas's ability to provide for my well-being and comfort, as any responsible parent would do.

We learned of a residence in Mayfair, it had to be fashionable; one doesn't live in a hovel in that area of London.

A trust provided a modest living and the successful private agency assured of financial security. Uncle Arch was fascinated in regards to how the organization functioned.

Thomas carefully explained he performed a service to people who needed help. Resolving various personal conflicts, unraveling a mystery of missing relatives, or finding a blackmailer to end the cycle of remittance.

I had an idea there was something more in regards to this agency but refrained from expressing such a notion. Thomas Brandyce was a master at hiding in the shadows and deliberately ambiguous about his profession.

After saying goodnight to our guest, my uncle and I went to the study to talk and enjoy a glass of sweet tawny port.

"My dear, are you sure about accepting this proposal?"

"I have given a great deal of thought about Mr. Brandyce and think this is the right thing to do. He is a good man, mysterious, but competent and clever."

"I didn't hear the word love mentioned."

I sighed and closed my eyes for a moment. "Love can be overrated, and I don't want to confuse the issue with such an emotion. All I can tell you is this man truly cares about me, and I like and respect him, which is enough for now."

"Just don't rush into anything, use that excellent brain, which has served you well."

"Don't worry; you won't see me running away anytime soon, there is still much to learn about Thomas Brandyce. So . . . how is the research on Hartlepool coming along?"

His eyes danced and he rubbed his hands together. "As you know there is a town called Hartlepool in the north. A small village began to grow around the religious houses already established in the 600's.

The abbey was unusual because it was a double monastery with both monks and nuns. The place was prosperous because of its metal work, ceramics and illuminated gospels."

"Did you find out why it was important enough to be given a Vulgate Bible?"

"Still working on that little mystery, but shall continue to chase after slivers of information."

"Oh, I discovered that Edward Selby was the deceased individual who lived in the house where the stones were found."

Uncle Arch furrowed his brow. "Edward Selby, the name isn't familiar, but shouldn't be too difficult to find out if the fellow was a collector of some kind. I'll add his name to my notes."

❧

Norton Engle, the solicitor, who had approached Cecily Lydstrom about her long lost granddaughter, had a rather unsavory reputation. The Law Institute had removed him from their roles a few years ago.

There were problems involving interesting beneficiaries of wills and trusts. Legal documents and distribution of real and personal properties of small estates were often suspect. Mr. Engle must be branching out into finding lost heirs.

Danny and Rob, Thomas's friends and partners in skullduggery, would search the counselor's office tonight; see what interesting items might be discovered. Brandyce planned to locate the fellow's residence and discover the best way to gain entrance during the early morning hours.

He had no qualms about absconding with valuables from people who preyed upon others. He reasoned this kind of justice compensated for the failure of those in authority to prevent criminals from preying upon the citizenry with impunity. He was a believer of evening the odds a little.

He reflected once again that it had been mere hours since Olivia made the decision he constantly dreamed. A heavy burden had been lifted, but he must be careful with his words and actions if her strange ability was real. The only thing for it was evasion and misdirection; of which he had plenty of practice.

A little deception was necessary to keep her safe from his sometimes-nefarious activities . . . otherwise, he would be absolutely straightforward . . . most of the time.The cab dropped him by the dimly lit street corner; he could walk the rest of the way to Engle's house. Thomas had driven past twice . . . once during the day, the other time at night. The neighborhood was quiet; the houses were of the detached variety, no shared walls, and had small gardens in the back.

The majority of places were two stories the lower part of stone; the upper level tile, and had three windows on each floor.

Shouldn't have much difficulty getting inside unless the jurist installed new locks, people didn't go to such lengths unless they had been burgled a time or two. Even then most locks were simple to figure out, some just took a little more effort.

Nearly all of the houses were dark this time of night; one house across the street had a light showing through the gap in the drapery on the second floor. Thomas watched from the shadows for a few minutes before circling around to the back and climbing over the short brick wall.

The garden was predictable, narrow paths and short hedges surrounded beds of roses, sweet William, hollyhocks and lavender. Honeysuckle grew along the wall and over an arbor on each side of the house. Thomas was quite happy the paths were of wood chips instead of gravel, kept the noise to a minimum.

He tread softly upon the stone terrace and studied the door . . . impressive and solid, however, the lock would take less than a minute to open. Once inside, stood quietly for several moments to let his eyes adjust. It became apparent this was a sitting room, with sofas and chairs, a large fireplace and tables of various heights.

The study must be around here somewhere. It would be nice not to traipse all over the house looking, but sometimes things didn't work out as expected.

Thomas moved slowly toward the door, making sure he didn't fall over any furniture in the dimly lit room. He was always happy when a place had gas lighting, much easier to see due to the flicker of the gas pilot element.

Hopefully the door to the hall didn't squeak, creak, or grate when he tried to open it. There was only a slight sound when he slowly maneuvered the door and peeked into the hallway. He allowed himself a deep breath and stepped into the passage and made his way to the next door, which was a dining room.

The house wasn't especially large, the study had to be around here somewhere, one last door near the stairs must be the correct room. Thankfully . . . it was. He didn't relish wandering around in the dark, wouldn't want to encounter a servant or Mr. Engle. Might be difficult to explain his presence.

Once inside, Thomas went quickly to the desk and studied the papers stacked in neat piles. Nothing worthwhile, a few documents about legal matters, another small stack of letters from various places of business. One from a tailor about the arrival of material from Italy, Thomas thought the fellow must be devoted to style, a natty dresser.

The loud banging from somewhere at the front of the house made his heart rate increase ten-fold, a few moments later he could hear someone coming down the stairs.

He quickly made the decision to get out of the room, the dining area would be relatively safe, at this hour of the morning no one should be having a formal meal. When he heard voices near the front door he peeked out, then dashed across the hall.

Thomas could hear the conversation as the people moved closer. Seems Mr. Engle had forgotten his key, the other voice was female, probably the housekeeper. The man spoke a little too loud and kept apologizing to a "Mrs. Dawson".

Thomas thought the fellow had been drinking, which was a good thing for him, hopefully the guy would tottle off to bed and sleep till noon. It would be nice if the housekeeper would trudge back to her room and do the same.

Brandyce leaned against the wall and waited for a considerable amount of time, didn't want to meet anyone going into the kitchen for some warm milk.

His thoughts turned to Olivia; he was still in a mild state of shock about her decision to accept his proposal. If it were up to him they would be married in the morning. He wasn't sure he could wait however long she might decide was appropriate. But for right now, he wasn't going to ask any questions.

The house was now quiet, time to resume his activities. After another furtive look down the hall he made his way back to the study. Nothing very important on the desk or even in the drawers, the locked one on the bottom had about twenty pounds inside a leather packet, which he left untouched. Didn't want Mr. Engle to know anyone was tampering with his belongings.

Thomas wandered around the room, nothing extraordinary, no safe behind any of the pictures. The bookshelves were not built into the walls; just stand alone, with a few books that looked rather dreary.

He sat on the corner of the desk, then decided to check under it, could be a hidden compartment. No compartment, instead found a trash bin pushed into the corner.

One could find very interesting items in the trash. There were several crushed up pieces of paper that Thomas carefully unwrinkled and spread on the desk to read.

It looked like Mr. Engle was practicing writing someone's name, the signature was written over and over again. Well, well, seems as though the lawyer was indulging in a little forgery, why else write a name so many times. Interesting! Thomas would do a little checking; find out who this person might be.

After tucking one of the sheets of paper inside his bag, and crumpling the other items back to their original condition they were returned to the bin. He made his way to the sitting room and out the door, through the garden and over the wall. It wouldn't take too long to get home, rather pleasant walking in the cool of the early morning.

After about fifteen minutes, walking at a brisk pace, he felt a presence moving behind him hiding in the shadows, probably not a good thing. At the next corner he would wait, keeping his back to the wall to avoid an attack from behind in case there was more than one assailant.

The furtive individual hurried along not wanting to lose sight of his target; upon turning the corner collided with the intended victim. The impact was an unpleasant surprise, the knife clattered to the ground when his wrist was grabbed with a powerful hand.

The snap of bone breaking and subsequent cursory scream was silenced when Thomas threw his attacker on the walk and ground a knee into his throat. "Stop struggling, it won't take much effort to add more pressure, break those little bones in your neck." Brandyce threatened softly.

Thomas could feel the man going limp. "I should put you out of your misery, you rat-bastard, but this is your lucky night, wouldn't want to shock the good people in the neighborhood by finding your stinking corpse when the sun comes up."

The fellow was breathing with difficulty and moaning when Thomas continued on his way after picking up the knife... and removing the creature's shoes.

Walking barefoot to wherever the miscreant lived should prove uncomfortable. A few blocks later he tossed the shoes over a fence, the knife he would keep until he got home.

Olivia had just opened the store when Mrs. Sullender rushed in. Tears ran down her plump face. "Something awful has happened to Andrew Portman, he was attacked in his shop, lots of leather goods were damaged as well."

I hustled the distraught woman to a chair. "Would you like some water?"

"No, nothing, it's just too horrible, something like that happening in this neighborhood is unbelievable."

"How badly was Mr. Portman hurt?"

"The doctor was called, don't know any more. Just thought you and your uncle should know. The police were sent for, no idea when they will arrive," she panted between sobs.

Nyles was hovering a few feet away. I asked him to fetch some water and a damp cloth to help sooth Mrs. Sullender; she was bright red and breathing much too fast.

I patted her shoulder, talked softly, and tried to calm the distressed woman. It wasn't long before my assistant returned. I offered the water and gave her the moist towel to wipe her face.

When she was a little less ruffled, I walked her back to the bakery. Her husband was at the counter with a customer. After the shopper left, I asked Mr. Sullender if there was any more news from the leather goods shop.

He rubbed the back of his neck and shook his head. "The coppers finally showed up, spoke to Paul and walked around the place to looked at the damage."

"Any word on Andrew Portman?"

Mr. Sullender shook his head. "Haven't had a chance to talk to his brother, saw the doctor leave a while ago."

Mrs. Sullender looked quite pale. "Perhaps you should sit down, try and rest, before going back to work." I suggested.

"Yes, I'll try to stop thinking about poor Andrew, but it's very upsetting."

I looked at her husband. "Is there anything I can do to help?"

Mr. Sullender shook his head, "Don't think there is much anyone can do right now, but as soon as I hear anything, I'll let you know." He put his arm around his wife and guided her into the back of the bakery.

I walked slowly back to the shop, thinking about what had happened to one of my neighbors. Hopefully Andrew Portman wasn't badly hurt, he was a sweet man, shy and quiet. Uncle Arch would be terribly upset when he learned about it.

I turned around to look down the walkway before going into the store and caught a glimpse of that annoying man, Mr. Clegg. He went inside the milliners, I was sure the very outspoken, Miss Larkin, would not be pleased to have the persistent fellow cluttering up her hat shop.

Nyles was waiting when I moved inside. "Anything more about Mr. Portman?"

"Not at the moment, I'm sure there will be information later in the afternoon. I'll have Jennie take over some food later."

A customer wandered in, she smiled, said she was just browsing and walked slowly toward the back. I had seen her before and knew she would make herself comfortable on one of the sofas and read for about a half hour . . . sometimes purchase something.

I began to work on a new display in one of the windows, something traditional, a few Shakespeare . . . *The Taming of the Shrew, Much Ado About Nothing, The Comedy of Errors.* Then throw in some Jane Austen . . . *Sense and Sensibility* and *Pride and Prejudice.* These books were a little more lighthearted I'd stay away from the dismal right now.

As I was working saw Mr. Clegg walk by, he stopped and looked in the window, when he saw me hurried away. One had to admit after his encounter with Thomas, the fellow didn't enter the shop anymore, but it didn't stop him from bothering the other property owners.

The morning post arrived, Mr. Harmon, the postman, handed over several items of mail, we chatted briefly before he continued on his way. A few things for Uncle Arch, *The British Chess Magazine,* and *Knowledge: An Illustrated Magazine of Science.*

A letter from a company called West End Brokers grabbed my attention. This was the second such correspondence. The first one about a month ago was an offer to buy the bookstore. The price put forward was laughable; Uncle

Arch thought such a ridiculous amount couldn't be taken seriously even if he was interested in selling.

I was curious to know what this brokerage group wanted, but could wait until later, right now there were more books to add to the window display, and of course the daily visit from Thomas to look forward to.

Chapter Eight

Thomas faced the window and looked across the street toward the bookshop. He watched Olivia with the baker's wife and wondered what was going on. He had also seen the odious Mr. Clegg making a nuisance of himself, going in several places of business. He noticed the man avoided the bookshop . . . if the fellow had gone inside, Thomas would have dashed across the street and made sure the little toad wouldn't bother Olivia again.

He grunted and thought the irksome man would have difficulty wandering around the neighborhood with a broken leg. He sighed and listened as sounds on the stairs drew his attention.

The outer office door opened, and then a moment later Danny and Rob made their way into his office.

"So . . . how went the foraging in Mr. Engle's place of business?"

The two men deposited themselves on the leather sofa and stretched their legs further into the room.

"The fellow has very low standards of cleanliness." Danny grumbled.

Rob ran a hand through his dark hair and rested his head on the back of the sofa. "Not much of a filing system either, papers stashed in drawers of cabinets in no particular order, the idiot wouldn't be able to tell if anything was missing if he wanted to." Rob reported.

Thomas sat behind his desk and toyed with a glass paperweight. "So you didn't turn up anything interesting?"

Danny yawned and rubbed his eye. "In the desk was a folder with cuttings of newspapers from years ago regarding the Baron what's-his-name and the wayward girl that ran off from the school in France."

"That would be Cecily Lydstrom's daughter."

"There were several more folders with newspaper articles about other people in similar situations, all having to do with missing relatives."

Rob smirked. "Seems our friend, Mr. Engle is hoping to obtain a finder's fee by tracing lost family members."

Thomas leaned forward and rested his elbows on the desk, then shoved a wrinkled sheet of paper across the top.

"I found this and several more just like it in Mr. Engle's study. Looks to me as if he's trying to copy someone's signature."

Danny struggled to his feet and picked up the paper. "Richard Duncan, wonder who this person might be?"

Thomas steepled his hands. "No idea, but plan to find out. If our lawyer friend is putting such effort into writing his name, Mr. Duncan probably has or will have money and Engle would like to get his hands on some of it."

The conversation stopped when a soft snore was detected from the sleeping Rob.

Thomas chuckled. "You two had better go home and rest, night prowling is rather tiring, and somewhat vexatious."

Danny ambled over to his friend and kicked the bottom of his boot several times. Rob muttered a few unintelligible words, then squinted through half closed eyelids. "What . . . I'm listening, just resting my eyes."

"Time to go my snoring hedgehog, we'll take a cab, doubt you can find your way home." Danny teased.

"I'll see you two this evening at my place, we have some letters from potential clients to look over." Thomas announced.

***

Olivia gathered the mail and went upstairs, to inform her uncle about Andrew Portman, not something she was looking forward to. Uncle Arch was quite friendly with most of the business owners on the block. He would be upset and probably want to dash over to see what he could do.

This was not the best time for such a visit. She and Jennie would drop off some dinner later on; maybe Paul could give them a little more information about his brother.

"So you are saying a crazy person wandered into the leather goods shop, beat upon Andrew, then went on to destroy some of the merchandise?"

"Paul doesn't think anything has been stolen, just damaged in some way, gouged and sliced. One can't sell blemished goods . . . and there were two ruffians." I murmured.

Uncle Arch sighed, then removed his glasses and pinched the bridge of his nose. Tell me once again about Andrew."

"A dislocated shoulder, broken ribs, a tooth knocked out, split lip and black eye. Thankfully he won't lose the sight in his eye, and going over and over this topic won't change what happened."

Uncle Arch huffed a little and replaced his glasses. "I know, but if one puts his mind to it, the almost hit and run of Mr. Johansson by a team and wagon seems suspicious."

I sipped a little more wine and brushed a few strands of wayward hair away from my face. "I hadn't given that incident much thought. I mean some operators of vehicles can be reckless, one can see many heedless drivers dashing through the streets. Pedestrians are always at risk."

My uncle shook his head slowly. "True enough, but both incidents happening to people that live on the same street just two days apart is rather dubious."

"Let us not jump to conclusions." I changed the subject to the contents of the mail.

"What did those West End people want?"

"Another offer to buy the shop, this one seemed a bit aggressive, almost intimidating, see what you think," and handed over the letter.

I studied the communication, taking my time before giving it back. "Might be a vague economic threat, and a suggestion that other property owners are selling out."

Uncle Arch folded the paper several times and placed it on the side table. "I haven't heard of anyone selling out, just the opposite."

"If everyone received something like this, they might think others are actually in the process of doing business with this company."

"I had the same thought, I'm going to speak with everyone on our block starting tomorrow."

"Excellent idea, take the letter along, see if others have received such postings."

*****

Thomas waited for the customer to leave before approaching Olivia. "Care to take a walk, it's a fine morning."

I smiled and looked around. "I think the place will be in good hands, Nyles is quite capable. Just give me a moment to let him know I'm leaving for a bit."

Locating my assistant wasn't difficult, never too far away when Thomas came calling. I think he was a little intimidated and possibly admired my consort at the same time, understandable. Thomas Brandyce had that effect on most people.

We walked toward Cavendish Square; it was quiet, not many people about as yet. The air was fresh; a soft breeze ruffled the trees.

Thomas held my arm firmly as we strolled. "What was going on with the baker's wife rushing about? Then the police milling in and out the leather goods place."

"One of our neighbors was attacked; some of his merchandise damaged. Uncle Arch is convinced that another resident, who was almost hit by a team and wagon a few days ago, is somehow connected."

Thomas frowned. "Why does your uncle think these two things are linked? What would be the underlying reason?"

"I don't have the slightest idea."

We stopped near the fountain and watched the water trickle over the statue of a girl with an umbrella. "Has anything untoward happened, something out of the ordinary going on?"

I reached down and dipped my fingers in the water and thought about the question. "The only thing I can think of that might concern the neighborhood is some company wishes to purchase all the businesses on Henrietta Street. We have received letters with ridiculous offers, and bothered by that Clegg person."

Thomas produced a handkerchief to dry my hand. I was in the process of returning his damp cloth when I noticed his face had become, for lack of a better word . . . vacant. I could feel his mood changing.

"What is the matter?"

He smiled brightly and folded the handkerchief and placed it back in a pocket. "Nothing worth mentioning, just thinking about what you said."

"Thomas Brandyce, what is going on in that efficacious mind of yours?"

"I have no idea what efficacious means. Have I told you how lovely you are, and that I can't wait to marry you? We really should set a date . . . soon."

"Changing the subject won't make me any less suspicious of what you were thinking."

"My thoughts were about your uncle, perhaps we should have a discussion regarding these offers from someone wanting to appropriate multifold properties." He leaned closer. "I can use big words too my darling."

"Your vocabulary is impressive, but doesn't alter the fact that you have something more on your mind than imposing words."

He grinned and gathered up my hand. "Shall we take the long way back?"

Uncle Arch was looking through the several pages of notes he had taken on his visit to the various places that housed archival documents. He shuffled the papers into a haphazard pile as we approached his desk. "Olivia, Mr. Brandyce, delighted to see you."

I patted his shoulder and looked at the messy papers. "Have you found anything worthwhile, or just fond of looking at old books and documents?"

Uncle Arch smiled. "As much as I enjoy immersing

myself in venerable works, I have been gathering infor- mation about Hartlepool and the abbeys. Shall we adjourn to the sitting room, about time for tea and some of Jennie's de- licious cake? I have been teased by the aroma for the last half hour?"

After the remains of our tea were removed, we settled into our chairs to listen to Uncle Arch recount his activities.

"King Ecgfirth of Northumbria gave the land to found the monetary in 674. The town grew around the religious houses of Hartlepool Abbey. By the way, the name Hartle- pool comes from the Old English for 'pool of the stags'.

"I don't think the king was particularly propitious in the romance department. After several years of marriage his wife, Aethelthryth, entered a convent and eventually became an Abbess, possibly of Hartleool.

Ecgfirth was a great supporter of religious endeavors, giving land and the financial means to build several more abbeys. Besides, Hartlepool, he sponsored the twin monas- teries of Jarrow and Wearmouth. You might remember the other names of these places as St. Peter and St. Paul . . . the place where the arch probably came from."

I was delighted with this information and interrupted his narrative. "So you think the writing on the stones can be as- sociated with the king and his abbess wife?"

"That is exactly what I believe. Reason enough for the good brothers of Jarrow and Wearmouth to create a bible to honor the support of the royals."

Thomas was looking a little confused. "Olivia men- tioned something about the translation written on the stone arch. I still don't understand the importance."

"It could be of great importance if there was another Codex Amiatinus, the earliest version of the Latin Vulgate version of the Christian Bible. The long-held belief has been that only three Bibles were written . . . one resides in Italy and fragments of the other two in the British Museum. A fourth copy would be mind boggling."

Thomas tapped his fingers together several times. "Now I understand how important a discovery this might be, not to mention valuable."

I chuckled. "Some might say such an item was price-less. An in tact Vulgate Bible could be considered a national treasure, such a uniquely British codex would be almost as important as the Anglo Saxon Chronicle or The Doomsday Book."

Uncle Arch rubbed his chin. "Everything you have said is probably true, but finding this tid-bit of information doesn't even start to discover a location The book could have been lost, destroyed or ravaged and pillaged hundreds of years ago."

I nodded "That is undeniable, but you and I have always loved a mystery, I think we need to learn more about Hartle-pool Abbey, and Aethelthryth, the Abbess."

Thomas rubbed his chin. "Mr. Varrus, I was wondering if you would allow me to see the letter from this company wanting to purchase the store?"

Uncle Arch leaned forward in his chair. "I don't think it important enough to bother with Mr. Brandyce, just a little annoying. Seems the other property owners have received similar communications."

"If you would permit, I would like to do a little investigating, learn something about this group, perhaps find out who is behind the rather aggressive tactics. Olivia says that Mr. Clegg, the estate agent, is in their employ."

"Uncle Arch you mentioned that the recent doings with our neighbors seemed suspicious, couldn't hurt to look into this company, it might have something to do with what is going on." I announced.

My uncle tapped his fingers on the arm of the chair, then fixed his gaze on Thomas. "I wouldn't want to put you out, I'm sure you have more important matters to occupy yourself."

"I have capable associates in my employ to help with business activities, making a few inquiries about this company shouldn't take much time. I'm curious to find out if the attacks on your neighbors have anything to do with offers to buy your property."

"In that case, I'll be happy to pay for your effort, go ahead and see what you can discover about the West End Brokers."

❧

Ruben Hodge watched the two men who stood in front of his desk. He folded his hands together then, twisted his large gold ring slowly. "I'm not entirely pleased with your handling of Mr. Johansson, I don't pay for near misses. The man should not have been able to go about his business as if nothing had happened."

Ellicot scratched his neck then squinted dark olive colored eyes at his employer. "The bloke was fast, got clean away he did. Wern't nothin' we could do about it, right Jingo."

Jingo Rush nodded furiously, his lank brown hair flapping into his eyes. "Thass right nothin' a'tall. Aimed them horses right at him. Now that leather goods fella, he didn't put up much of a fuss, easy pickin's he was. Squalled like a stuck pig." Rush grinned and showed his yellow, broken, front teeth.

Hodge gave the men a withering glare, then narrowed his eyes. "Thus far your efforts have proved less than adequate. I want those people frightened enough to sell. If necessary hire more help!"

The two men looked at each other. Ellicot began to nod his head rapidly. "We was just doin' what you said . . . ruffle their feathers a bit. It's certain sure we can do more, ain't that right Jingo."

"I suggest you do just that. The bakery or the bookstore might be a place to start. If your efforts prove a disappointment, you will be replaced." Hodge opened his desk and tossed a small bag toward the two men. "This is the last you will see of my money if those business owners don't decide to sell."

Ellicot snatched the pouch and the two backed away from the glowering estate magnate, and hurried out the door. They hastened past the intimidating secretary, Mr. Fiske, who glared as they went by.

Burt Ellicot muttered to his friend when they reached the sidewalk outside. "That Hodge be a mean one, makes my insides shake just a tad."

Jingo nodded furiously and wiped the sweat that trickled down the side of his neck. "Nasty son-of-a-bitch. We better do somethin' to make him happy. Couldn't hurt to hire on Packy and Donnie Brown, real handy, work cheap too. Now let's have us a look at them two stores like he said."

The morning started out nice enough, but by afternoon gray clouds appeared and Thomas knew it wouldn't be long before it started to pour. He stood outside the red brick building advertising the West End Brokers on the first two floors.

The third floor was a law office of Turner, Cartwright and Granger; forth floor belonged to Hopwood and Lovett, architects.

Thomas pulled the wrought iron handles to open the heavy wooden door and entered a well-appointed lobby. On the left side were wide stairs and to the right double doors painted a shiny black with large gold letters. The West End Brokers were not reticent about proclaiming their presence.

Chapter Nine

Before entering the office, Thomas pressed firmly on the fake sideburns and moustache to make sure they were securely in place. Then adjusted the thick round spectacles on his nose and opened the door.

The room contained three desks occupied by clerks who looked quite industrious. Finally one fellow glanced in his direction. "May I help you sir?"

Thomas offered a slight smile. "Indeed you may, I wish to speak with the manager, better still, the owner, a mister Hodge I believe."

The clerk rose and walked around his desk. "Do you have an appointment?"

"No, but it is imperative I speak with either the manager or the owner."

The clerk looked a little hesitant as if unsure of what to do. "I'll see if Mr. Fiske, the executive secretary, is available . . . your name please."

"My name is Albion Pertwee, of Pertwee and Witherspoon, Thames River Insurance."

The employee regarded the impatient looking man and frowned. "Insurance? I don't think ...".

"I assure you the matter is vitally important." Thomas interrupted.

The office worker nodded, said he would notify Mr. Fiske, and hurried up to the next floor. A short time later he returned and announced that Mr. Hodge's assistant could see him for a few minutes and pointed toward the stairs at the back of the room.

Thomas approached the desk of a rather sour looking individual. "If you are selling something, the West End Brokers is not interested. We have quite enough coverage from another agency," the small man intoned and finally made eye contact.

"Then you might not be aware that your previous company has been sold, and the policy is now being administered by The Thames River Agency. My partner, Mr. Horton Witherspoon, and I are contacting all of the former customers of Bridgeport Insurance about this change of ownership."

Mr. Fiske looked unsettled. "What are you talking

about! There has been no communication of such a change?"

Thomas managed a concerned look. "I don't understand, your company should have been notified . . . but I'm not surprised, we have found many irregularities. That is the reason Mr. Witherspoon and I are making the rounds in person."

Thomas deposited his briefcase on top of the desk with a resounding thump and pulled out a few papers to study. The already agitated secretary didn't look pleased at having a bag placed on his workspace.

"There have been many glaring mistakes found in the policies issued. Items that must be addressed, such as inaccurate square footage, building usage and so forth."

Thomas quickly moved toward a door that had 'Ruben Hodge' scrolled across

the entrance. "Hopefully this is not a storage room containing fireworks, wouldn't be a surprise if it were."

Mr. Fiske leapt out of his chair and hurried to stop this rather presumptuous man from entering his employer's office. "Now, just a moment, you can't barge in here! I assure you this area is private and belongs to Mr. Hodge and has nothing to do with fireworks or any other type of explosive."

"I'm expected to accept your word for it . . . believe me Mr. Fish, The Thames River Insurance Agency, can't afford to take anything for granted. Doing such a thing would be a grave mistake, might even put us out of business just like the previous company. If you don't allow a quick look inside, then such an action on your part might result in a cancellation of the policy."

The self-important secretary was beginning to look apprehensive. Thomas continued. "After a cancellation, it is often difficult to purchase new coverage from another company. Insurance agencies are suspicious about such things."

Mr. Fiske reluctantly opened the door. "Such impertinence! I will be watching, don't touch anything! Mr. Hodge is very particular about his possessions."

Thomas strode into the opulent room. The desk was mahogany, expensive and highly polished. The bookcases had glass doors and contained leather bound volumes that were difficult to read from a distance. A silver Chinese double inkwell with the head of a dragon was prominently displayed on top of the desk. Brackets holding two pens were featured on the horns, the object was costly and probably a collector's item.

"As you can see, there are no fireworks or anything else of that nature hiding in here." As an after thought the disgruntled man announced. "I would like to see some form of identification."

"Of course." Thomas smiled and reached inside his coat pocket and produced a card with the name of Albion Pertwee, Thames River Insurance. "I have a few policies in my case, but owing to confidentiality can't divulge any names. I do have a blank form if you would care to peruse."

Mr. Fiske studied the card carefully. "I will make sure Mr. Hodge receives this, he will want to look into the matter personally."

"Let's hope so . . . Mr. Witherspoon and I will do our very best to provide quality service. Thank you Mr. Fish, pleasure meeting you."

"The name is Fiske, not Fish . . . I'm sure you can find your way out," he replied with a huff.

Once outside Thomas chuckled to himself and thought this adventure might unsettle Ruben Hodge. It hadn't taken long to find some interesting things about the businessman. The fellow was considered ruthless in procuring properties for his clients. There were rumors of underhanded practices, the terms cutthroat, savage and vicious had been voiced.

Thomas was fairly certain that the two incidents involving the merchants on Henrietta Street were tied to Ruben Hodge and the hired help he employed.

Olivia and Archer Varrus must be warned, as well as the rest of the property owners. There was a good possibility that more trouble was coming.

The thought of something happening to Olivia made his head begin to throb and his insides churn. He must control himself and think rationally, but had to see that she was all right.

He waved down a cab, once inside the vehicle inhaled deeply several times . . . sound reasoning was needed, not some hysterical person jabbering away.

By the time he arrived in front of the bookstore he had achieved a modicum of

calm, it wouldn't do to upset Olivia. After paying the driver he casually meandered into the shop.

I looked up from filling out the order form. It took a moment to realize the person standing in front of the counter was Thomas Brandyce. My eyes widened in recognition, he looked to be some creature that came out of the woods, his wonderful face hidden behind lots of fur.

"I have the feeling you've been up to mischief Mr. Brandyce, or should I address you by some other name. There is a faint resemblance to the hairy countenance of Charles Dickens or Darwin perhaps."

Thomas brushed a hand over his face and took a deep breath. "I was trying to decide if growing a beard would make me look fashionable. Facial hair winnows out smoke and dust, besides shaving is a painful and useless custom."

Underneath the casual banter I felt a current of disquiet that made me uneasy.

"What's wrong!"

"Perhaps we should find your uncle and have a conversation."

"Uncle Arch has gone out . . . more research on Hartlepool I imagine."

Thomas fiddled with his sideburn. "I need to remove this hair, starting to itch."

I sighed, then went to find Nyles who was working in the back, said I was going up stairs and he should mind the store.

I waited in the parlor while Thomas retired to the washroom to divest himself of all that hair. To say I was curious as to what he had been doing was an understatement. Whatever occurred had unsettled him, and I found it difficult to sit quietly and wait.

Finally he appeared, his face a little red in places. "Much better, does it hurt to remove such a disguise?"

"Not really, a few places took some extra rubbing to get rid of the glue." He sat next to me on the sofa and took my hand.

"Want to tell me what happened . . . something has upset you."

Thomas sighed, then raised my hand to his lips and kissed my fingers. "I'm not upset, one might say I'm concerned."

"Concerned about what?"

"I have made an interesting discovery about the company who wants to buy the properties on Henrietta Street. The West End Brokers is owned by one Ruben Hodge. He has quite the reputation for being ruthless even brutal to get what he wants . . . and he wants this whole block for some client. I'm not clear what this purchaser has in mind to do with these properties at the moment, but I'll find out."

I studied his face, then leaned closer. "So you think this Hodge person is behind the beating of Andrew Portman and Mr. Johansson almost being run down?"

"Yes . . . and it will probably get worse . . . that means you and your uncle are vulnerable."

Now I understood why Thomas was unsettled, my safety seemed to matter above anything else.

"But you don't know for sure that anything will happen to me, Uncle Arch, or the shop do you."

"Not for certain, but I have a feeling bad things will continue. Perhaps you and your uncle could go away for a short while, close the store."

"What about Nyles and Jennie? Jennie has no place to

go and Nyles needs his weekly salary to help out at home."

Thomas brushed his fingers across my cheek. "Let me reflect on this for a while, we can discuss it further when your uncle returns." He enfolded me into his arms and kissed me softly. It was wonderful being sheltered this way; I could feel his heartbeat and the heat of his body.

I hadn't expected to have such a profound emotional reaction to this man. Perhaps I was feeling something more than respect and a deep admiration for his concern for those less able to defend themselves.

I drew away. "We should try to remember where we are, Jennie or Uncle Arch could wander in at anytime."

He grinned slightly. "More than enough reason to be married as soon as possible. Our intimate conversation wouldn't be surprising at all." He leaned forward and kissed me again. "Tomorrow evening you and your uncle are invited to my home for dinner."

Considering that we saw each other almost every day I hadn't given much thought about his place in Mayfair and that I had never been inside. "I accept and sure Uncle Arch will be delighted as well. We sat in silence for a few moments. "All of this sounds serious, any particular reason to have dinner at your place other than to enjoy my company."

"Not really just an excuse to be with you, which gives me pleasure."

"Thomas . . . this man, Hodge, do you really think he will continue to harass the people around here?"

"From the information I have garnered, there is little doubt in my mind he will be coming after those who refuse to sell. Unsavory things have happened to many others, beatings, fires, destruction of merchandise and property seem to be the way he achieves what he wants."

"Why don't the authorities do something about it? Surely people have complained."

"They probably have, but these acts of violence are done by hired thugs, can't prove Hodge has anything to do with it. Most of the time no one can identify the perpetrators anyway. Then there is that element of fear . . . fear is powerful."

I grasped his hand. "So do you have something in mind to help us?"

He grinned and pulled me closer. "I have some ideas, but right now I want to try and convince you to set a wedding date, if not tomorrow, how about the next day or even next week."

I kissed him lightly on the cheek. "You are single-minded in your quest. But I promise to have an answer tomorrow at dinner."

Ruben Hodge turned the card from the fraudulent insurance company over several more times. He had been to see Mr. Shasteen at the office of Bridgeport Insurance; the meeting had taken a good portion of the morning. He was now back in his office contemplating what to do.

What was going on, and who was this Albion Pertwee . . . not the new owner of Bridgeport Insurance. There was no new owner. So why would anyone want to do this, nothing could be gained by such a pretense.

An uneasy feeling niggled at him as he regarded the card once again. He would have to find this Pertwee fellow, but right now he was expected to have lunch with Engle. The lawyer had a new client who wanted to sell a house, seems this Duncan person inherited a rather large property and several other pieces of real estate from some relative.

⁂

Ellicot and Rush strolled past the shops on Henrietta Street; sometimes they stopped to look in windows. Most of these places didn't have much in the way of security; large casements that displayed merchandise and easily shattered.

They would amble around to the alley later, look at the doors and locks. Mr. Hodge mentioned the bakery and bookstore . . . places to investigate. Best time was at night, no one around to disturb or identify them.

Jingo Rush enjoyed his sweets, the aroma of fresh bread and sticky buns drew him back to the bakery. It was only when Ellicot shoved him down the walk that prevented him from going inside.

"We gots to move along don't want them people to remember us lurkin' about, ain't zackly dressed fer this neighborhood."

Rush grumbled, but moved away from the bakery and the two men meandered toward the bookstore. Inside the windows were pictures and books of knights, horses and armor.

Malory's *Le Morte D'Arthur,* Tennyson's *Idylls of the King, Ivanhoe* by Sir Walter Scott, and *Sir Gawain and the Green Knight* were just a few of the volumes on display.

"Look at all them fellas with swords and whot-nots, sometimes I whished I could read some." Rush announced.

"Wot you want to do that, nothin' in them books we care to be aknowin'. stuff and nonsense if you ask me", muttered Ellicot.

"Didn't ask you now did I . . . we best be a goin' . . . sure do like them swords tho."

Uncle Arch reported on his newest findings about Hartlepool Abbey later that afternoon. No trace remained of the buildings after all these years. A monastic cemetery had been found near St. Hilda's, a church that had been built in the 1200 hundreds.

In a few written records about Saxon churches the abbey was described as small rectangle wooden buildings grouped together into clusters separated by fences and boundary ditches.

The abbey had gained importance because of the literature produced and archived. There was also some kind of metal working, as well as animal husbandry. The site was abandoned in the late 700's probably because of the on going political problems and the Viking invaders.

"So there is nothing left of the place, no standing walls?"

"Just the cemetery that has been incorporated into the grounds of St. Hilda's Church." Uncle Arch replied.

I tapped my fingers on the arm of the chair and concentrated for a moment. "If the place was abandoned and not destroyed, then it would be reasonable to assume any valuables would have been removed to another location."

Uncle Arch nodded. "Don't think the move would have been too far away, so the next task is to locate another religious site close by. There are several areas that might require investigation."

"We need the map of Northumberland. The atlas should be around here somewhere, in fact there are several if I'm not mistaken."

Uncle Arch relocated to his study and soon returned with a very large and weighty book. "We can start with this, it will give us the location of towns close to Hartlepool. I can go back to the archives and see if any towns had large churches. I think the new place would probably be substantial and built of stone rather than wood . . . more secure."

Chapter Ten

The house of Thomas Brandyce was located on Half Moon Street, Mayfair. A white brick residence spanning four floors, with three reception rooms, eight bedrooms, and an east-facing roof terrace. The home was impressive, elegant and quietly understated.

Thomas mentioned that Flemings Mayfair, a small, sophisticated hotel was down the street, the place opened in the early 1850's and was quite popular with those who could afford the shocking prices charged for a nights lodging.

I didn't feel out of place being the only female in attendance at dinner. Daniel St. Jules and Rob Landis, Thomas's friends, were amusing and interested in what Uncle

Arch had to say about his book collecting. There was also good natured teasing directed toward Thomas and his ability to keep our relationship so quiet.

All and all the evening was lovely. I did casually mention that late August would be a nice time of year to be married; we could select the actual date later. That announcement called for a celebration, which consisted of several bottles of champagne and heartfelt congratulations.

I had discussed my decision with Uncle Arch before hand, he seemed happy, but felt sure there was a small twinge of sadness at all the changes that would take place. I guess it was to be expected, children grow up, leave the fold and start a new life . . . an age-old process.

Thomas, on the other hand, had difficulty maintaining any semblance of unbridled joy. Rather amusing for someone who usually displayed an unreadable countenance.

My husband-to-be escorted us home. Uncle had indulged in slightly too much wine and was having a small problem navigating the stairs leading up to our living quarters. Thomas assisted with getting him into bed after removing his shoes and coat. I spread the quilt over the sleeping form and turned down the light to a flickering glow.

"Thank you for the help, Uncle Arch doesn't often over indulge. He will probably sleep until noon or later."

We wandered into the sitting room and settled on the sofa. Thomas pulled me close and kissed me gently. I felt the warmth of his hand on my arm; it was a comfort to be held, to know this man cared.

"I have something for you." He reached into the inside

pocket of his coat and produced a small box, opened it and presented an exquisite ring. Even in the soft light the large diamond glistened.

It was a challenge to breathe, much less speak. "If you don't like it I can take it back and find another." Thomas anxiously exclaimed.

"No . . . no, it's beautiful, wonderful and unexpected . . .

"I wanted you to have something to celebrate the occasion, this trinket is nothing compared to the gift of having you in my life. I wasn't sure you would make a positive resolution about us . . . about going through with the marriage, but wanted to be prepared." He placed the ring on my finger, it was a bit large, nevertheless, I was delighted.

I rested my hand on his cheek. "Everything about you is unconventional, but to be honest, I wouldn't have it any other way. I'm happy with my decision, our life will be unquestionably engrossing, perhaps even intriguing.

A thought has occurred, a subject to be discussed. You would be mistaken to believe I plan on sitting in that huge house sewing or painting flowers on porcelain cups."

Thomas smiled and offered a sigh. "I can't imagine anything of the kind . . . though it would set my mind at ease . . . but something I shall have to work through."

"I intend to continue in the shop, I enjoy what I do, and Uncle Arch needs my help. I'm relieved and happy this little bit of business is out of the way." I wound my arms around his neck, pulled him close and kissed him with fervor.

He mumbled something about appreciating my thanks and perhaps we might engage in this type of "business" more often.

To suggest we adjourn somewhere more confortable was probably not a good idea. Eventually we managed to shamble down stairs. It took a while to get him to leave despite the inventive excuses. I promised that soon we wouldn't have to shelter in dimly lit rooms . . . something to look forward to.

After practically shoving him onto the sidewalk and assurances of locking everything securely, I leaned against the stout oak portal and smiled. A few months ago I never could have imagined how my life would be altered.

For the most part I was content with the day-to-day world of books, customers, and the occasional estate sale to hunt for a bargain. Now, in little more than a month I was to be married. One had to marvel how unpredictable life could be.

Thomas Brandyce had certainly changed the direction of my existence and would probably continue to do so. Dealing with his emotions was demanding at first, but I was learning to sort things out.

I couldn't be sure, but the feelings that washed over me could be construed as love . . . whatever that might be . . . how interesting. I have to think on it.

❧

Ellicot and Rush took their time making their way to Henrietta Street, it would be foolish to arrive while people might be around to witness their activity. They had decided the bakery would be the place to bring fear and destruction to the stubborn business owners.

Jingo Rush grinned in anticipation at how the front windows and glass shelves inside were going to splinter and crack. Display cases were probably expensive so the owner just might decide to take the offer to sell.

The men kept to the shadows for several minutes casting a last look around the quiet street. Nothing stirred, no lights could be seen from any windows, time to get started.

Ellicot brought out a mallet with a heavy metal head, while Rush made do with a post maul. The front windows shattered instantly, which allowed the men to dash inside and continue their demolition. The glass display cases disintegrated into fragments upon impact.

Everything happened so rapidly there was little time for anyone to stop the rampage. The ravagers were gone before the family managed to find clothes, turn up the lights and rush downstairs.

⁓

I stood beside the tearful Mrs. Sullender and stared at the ruined shop. The baker's three children were sweeping glass into piles.

"I don't know how I can afford to fix everything that needs fixin'. Mr. Sullender muttered. "The windows will be costly all by themselves. Can't say how much the cases will be. I guess lots more than my grandfather paid forty years ago."

Mrs. Sullender wiped her eyes with the hem of her apron. "Who would do such an awful thing, can't think why this happened, we have never harmed anyone."

I put my arm around the distraught woman's shoulders.

"I'm just happy the family is all right. Hopefully the police will be able to find the monsters responsible. In the meantime there are shelves in our storage area that can be used to put the baked good upon."

Mr. Sullender walked over and offered a slight smile. "Thank you, that will be greatly appreciated."

"I'll send Nyles to help board up the front windows. It shouldn't take long to be up and running again."

Late that afternoon Uncle Arch came from the bakery to announce the windows would be replaced in a couple of days. Mr. Sullender had accepted the offer of a small loan in order to expedite matters.

He sat in his favorite chair and rested his head on the padded cushioned back. "I doubt this latest brutality is a coincidence. After what Thomas reported about the tactics of the West End Brokers, it's evident the business owners on Henrietta Street are being intimidated.

"Doubtful much will be coming from the authorities, especially since there is no proof this company has done anything more than send letters with offers to buy our properties."

"When Thomas arrives, we must formulate a plan to keep our shop from being an easy target. We could be next!" I announced.

How could we protect ourselves, the front windows were easily broken. The thought of fire in a place full of paper made me cringe.

"We use our brains and try not to panic, won't do any good to give in to hysteria. Once we come up with something, we gather the other shopkeepers on the block and find where they stand. Frightened people often make irrational decisions."

Even though it was warm inside, a coldness was creeping through my body. I had a horrible feeling this situation would result in something more than damaged property. Whether by accident or on purpose someone would come to great harm.

Thomas frowned and leaned against the counter. "I saw the boarded up windows of the bakery. More property damaged to try and induce people to sell."

I nodded and stacked another book on the pile. "What can we do to prevent us from being next?"

"I have been working on a new concept for the front of your store. It's not exactly a new idea, more like barrowing from the past."

I stopped shuffling books. "I'm listening."

"Actually this device is just about finished."

I went around the counter and stood in front of my fiancé. "What on earth are you talking about?"

Thomas grinned. "I plan to fortify the shop."

Words were not readily available for a few moments. "Fortify the shop, as in erecting a stone wall with slots to shoot arrows perhaps?"

"Something like that, not a stone wall, more like a portcullis . . . an iron gate used to protect castle entry ways."

I blinked several times in disbelief. "Wonderful idea, we can winch the gate open to let customers inside after lowering the draw bridge over the moat."

He took my hand. "Let me explain, the barrier will not be solid, more like a grate that folds. It can be unfolded and pushed to the side when the shop is open for business and pulled back together and locked after hours. The slots in the grate will be too small for a villain to throw something large enough to break a window or ram open the door."

"Thomas Brandyce, you are a bloody genius." I gasped out between bursts of laughter.

"Thank you my lady for such a compliment . . . I think!" And offered a deep bow.

"When will the "portcullis" be installed?"

"Perhaps later this afternoon."

I moved a step closer and reached for his hand. "Thank you for all the efforts on our behalf. I know you have had men watching the street at night. I was sure someone was lurking about, which was a concern at first, but soon realized the person or persons were not up to anything other than observing in the shadows."

He shrugged and grinned. "I was wondering when you would notice my men. I put them in place the night after the bakery was damaged. Couldn't take the chance anything untoward happening to you or the shop."

Two women walked in and headed in our direction. Thomas squeezed my hand then quickly made his way to the door, he waved as he passed by the front windows.

I turned my attention to the customers, answered their questions and guided them to the area where they could find something that might be of interest. Business was good, not much time to think about anything more than selling, ordering and stocking items in their proper places.

After lunch I walked to the newsagents on the corner for the afternoon papers. While perusing the magazine selection found a periodical that featured women's fashions, I should probably look for something suitable for my wedding. Not that the event was going to be anything extraordinary. The ceremony would take place in the register office, with a small celebration afterwards at the Mayfair house.

Uncle Arch wished to invite several of his associates and there were two distant cousins that should be included. Thomas's friends, neighbors from Henrietta Street, Nyles and Jennie would round out guests for the brunch. The plan was to keep everything simple, afterwards take a train to the south of England, to the small coastal town of St. Ives in Cornwall.

Thomas was enthused about the place with its charming narrow streets, warm summer climate, and a lovely sandy beach. I was looking forward to our week away from London and the recent unpleasantness. Hopefully the West End Brokers would become interested in some other location and leave us alone.

Mr. Tully, the shopkeeper rose from his usual chair with some difficulty and brushed a hand through his thick white hair. He had been the proprietor of this place for as long as I could remember. The man must be in his late seventies, his lined face was a little pale, but the blue eyes were bright as always.

"Good afternoon Olivia, you look as right as ninepins."

I smiled and set the papers and magazine on the counter. "So nice to see you up and about Mr. Tully. Sophie said you were not feeling well."

"My daughter worries too much. Just a touch of the rheumatiz, a little twinge in me back now and again, can't keep a body down fer long."

I counted out several coins for my purchases. "You take care, lifting bundles of papers won't help your back get better."

"Been doin' that fer more years than I can remember, just part of a days work."

"I know, but perhaps take it a little easier for a while. See you soon Mr. Tully.

I stopped, and looked inside the bakery on my way back unable to resist the aroma of bread baking. The door was open and there were a variety of goods displayed on the old bookshelves retrieved from our storage room. Mr. Sullender had pounded a few more nails to make the shelves sturdier.

Soon the front windows would be installed and the place would look whole again. So far the monsters responsible for the recent spate of trouble hadn't been back. Perhaps the night patrols discouraged any more raids. One could only hope this was true.

A wagon was parked in front of the bookstore; I could see Thomas's bright head towering above the other men standing around. The new security gate must have arrived. I was curious to see the structure or whatever this "portcullis" might be.

Thomas brought the fellow he had been talking with and introduced him as a Mr. Matthews, the person in charge of installing the new security gate.

"As I was saying Mr. Brandyce, we fasten the grill guides and brackets directly to the walkway and joists above. The metal rods and link panels slide back and forth. and the locking posts secure the curtain to the sides."

I had no idea what the man was talking about so just nodded and tried not to look as stupid as I felt. I didn't care about bolts and whatever as long as the contraption kept the vermin from damaging the store.

Hopefully Thomas had a vague understanding of how the thing operated. When Mr. Matthews stopped his explanation I smiled and murmured how interesting all this was, but should really get back to work.

I hurried inside to find Nyles and Jennie peering out the windows. "I wonder how long it's going to take." Nyles asked.

"Don't have the slightest idea, might be quite a while." I set the newspapers and magazine on the counter and wandered to where my helpers watched the wagon being unloaded.

Jennie sighed. "Shame all this has to be done . . . better this than what might happen if those vile creatures decide to attack us. Makes my blood boil to see the mess at the bakery and poor Mr. Portman all banged up.

Lucy Sullender says her mum is scared all the time, can't say as I blame her, my heart jumps when I hear sounds at night."

I didn't admit I felt the same; I wasn't sleeping very well either. "Come look at the magazine I brought, there might be some interesting ideas for a wedding dress." A small distraction was needed right now, anything was better than dwelling on the bad things that had happened.

Chapter Eleven

Ruben Hodge slammed his fist upon the desk several more times. The news from those two idiots, Ellicot and Rush, wasn't as expected. The bakery didn't close at all; instead it was business as usual.

In addition, there was some sort of barrier in front of the bookstore. What kind of rubbish were they talking about? He would drive past this afternoon and take a look for himself.

All of these delays were making him uneasy. His clients wouldn't wait forever; there were other estate agents offering sites these people might consider.

It was critical to deliver Henrietta Street, the most important site in the area.

He was also invested in less significant properties elsewhere. It hadn't taken too much effort to convince those owners to sell; one small fire and a few bashed heads did the trick.

Right now he was stretched a little too far, his plan was to sell the newly acquired properties at a substantial profit to speculators-investors. But this lot wanted the area directly behind Oxford Street . . . the nobs.

It rankled him the arrogant toffs thought they were so much better than he. More often than not he was more affluent than they, most of the so-called socially elite didn't have a pot to piss in. Their holdings mortgaged to the hilt, much of their land sold off to pay long-standing debts.

It was only because of his wife and brother-in-law that he was invited into their homes for the elegant dinners and parties.

Ruben strode to the bookcase and unlocked the glass-enclosed shelves nearest his desk, the one featuring his beautiful collection of jade. Each item was created or purchased for good luck. Koi fish, a small dragon, turtle, crane and a gold cat that always seemed to calm the tension cursing through him.

He held the dragon in his hand and softly caressed the cool green stone. These beautiful objects were just a small part of his collection; the majority was at his house in the display room under lock and key.

This little creature was almost insignificant compared to

the much larger emerald green dragon at home. Ruben carefully returned the objet d'art to its place and locked the cabinet.

The ache behind his eyes would likely continue until the pain overwhelmed, which eventually required confinement in his darkened bedroom. Laudanum, numerous opium powders, and a cloth soaked in vinegar and opium helped. He might be able to contain the throb by downing a substantial amount of Gower's Mixture kept in the desk drawer.

He wouldn't give into the pain there was too much to do. A stack of bills from the refurbishing of the country house required his attention. Just one more "must have" his wife insisted upon.

The old monstrosity might have been something special a hundred years ago, now it was a pit to throw money into. Roanne asserted it was necessary to have a country estate to entertain friends and family.

Ruben took another swig of the tonic, replaced the cap and returned it to the drawer. Then looked at the statement for the new roof. It boggled the mind, how could a roof be almost five hundred pounds? This was just the beginning; there were floors, walls, the enlarged kitchen and so on and so forth. He needed some air to clear his mind and think about what he should do with Henrietta Street.

The walk from his office didn't take long and helped relieve the pain in his head. He approached the bookstore and stopped to examine the metal panel folded neatly beside the window.

What the hell was this, he had never seen anything like

it. When closed the gate would do a masterful job in protecting the windows and door from any kind of vandalism. It was a clever idea, and he wondered who had devised such an apparatus.

No reason not to have a look inside, his face wasn't known, and could survey the store without arousing suspicion.

He strolled through the open door and gazed about the pleasant space.

"May I help you find something?"

I approached the gentleman studying the room. His manner appeared casual but I could feel something more calculated. His clothes were quality and fit perfectly. The dark hair was thick and styled in the latest fashion; one might consider him handsome with his well-trimmed mustache and goatee.

For some reason I found him to look a bit sinister . . . probably due to his deep-set black eyes.

"Are you looking for something in particular?" I inquired.

"Not really, I was passing by and thought the place might have some entertaining reading material."

His remark was not entirely true. "Please look around, we have a good selection to choose from."

"I will, thank you. Are you the owner?"

"Yes, along with my uncle . . . if you have any questions, just ask."

He stared at me for several moments. "I do have a question about the interesting looking gate out front, I don't think

I have seen anything quite like it before."

That was a true statement; in fact his interest was acute. "The gate or probably a better name for it is a grate was just installed. There have been several businesses on the block vandalized recently and hopefully this will prevent our shop from being damaged."

"How unpleasant, it would be distressing to have such an incident happen to this lovely place."

The comment was almost the exact opposite of how he really felt. This person was making me uncomfortable and I looked around to find Nyles. I could hear him conversing with someone in the stacks.

"We carry new as well as used books which are located near the back. Please excuse me." I wanted to distance myself from this man.

He took a step toward me, which was one step too close causing me to move aside.

"Could you tell me who is responsible for the grate?"

"I don't remember his name, but the fellow is quite talented, it didn't take too long for the portcullis to be assembled. Now if you will excuse me I must speak to my assistant."

"Of course. You said the used books are in the back?"

"Yes, through the archway over there." He turned to where I indicated and ambled toward the rear of the shop.

I took a deep breath, happy to be away from his piercing eyes and the questions about the new security measures. The man had no interest in books . . . no his concern was elsewhere.

Cecily Lydstrom listened intently as Thomas provided information gathered on Norton Engle.

"The solicitor, and I use the term loosely, was reprimanded and removed from The Law Institute, and not known for his integrity. It is my understanding he has been contacting other families in similar circumstances such as yours."

The lady ran her fingers over the carved wood cane leaning against the chair. "I assume you refer to people with estranged relatives."

"Yes, that is part of his practice, he also does wills, estate management and liquidation. The reason for his censer from the Law Institute was about questionable practices in regards to those mentioned activities."

"In other words, Mr. Brandyce, the man is a scoundrel and probably involved in other underhanded activities."

Thomas smiled slightly. "My thoughts exactly Mrs. Lydstrom. But if you think there is something to the story about your granddaughter I will look into the matter. Mr. Engle could have come across information that might be true.

One thing I know, the lawyer seems to have a talent for forgery, so any written paperwork should be considered suspicious."

The lady sighed and leaned back in the chair. "Thank you I will consider your offer and let you know of my decision. I'm sure if there is a grandchild wanting to find me they can wait a little longer."

Thomas looked around at the shelves of books in the library. "This is quite the collection."

"Most of it came from my husband, he was a accumulator of books, new and old, also quite a few manuscripts from the distant past. The family was avid about such things."

"My future in-law, Archer Varrus, has acquired an inventory of similar items, rather a specialist in early history. Perhaps you have heard of him."

Mrs. Lydstrom pursed her lips and drummed her fingers on the arm of the chair. "Archer Varrus . . . yes, doesn't he own a bookstore, I seem to remember my husband had some dealings with him."

"That is very possible, Mr. Varrus has provided many clients with vintage works. He would probably enjoy your collection."

The lady looked toward a large cabinet. "My husband was somewhat of a hoarder, he often piled his old items rather haphazardly all over the house. I gathered most of it together after he died and put it in that chiffonier. Perhaps Mr. Varrus might suggest someone interested in cataloging everything, it would be nice to know what I actually have."

"It would be my pleasure to make an inquiry on your behalf." Thomas stood. "If you should require something more Mrs. Lydstrom, please don't hesitate to contact me." He presented another card.

"Indeed I shall Mr. Brandyce . . . Letty will show you out."

Thomas was fairly sure he would be hearing from the lady again. The lure of knowing about her daughter, Julia, and her circumstances was too important to ignore. He or one of his men would probably be off to the town of Keswick to investigate.

He walked to the next street and hailed a cab and headed to the bookstore and Olivia.

The last customer was gone; it was quiet for the moment. I placed the magazine on the counter and turned to the page with the bookmark. The drawing of a dress had caught my attention because of its simplicity. The cut followed the body's natural shape, a sleek, tailored design. An overskirt could be added to give the garment a completely different look if one desired.

I envisioned the gown made of cream colored silk with an overskirt of pale yellow velvet. A cream-colored lace shawl that trailed almost to the floor would complete the ensemble. It was uncomplicated and reserved, rather than bold, with wild colors and ostentatious fluff and flounces everywhere.

The small shop off Regent Street shouldn't have any trouble producing such an uncomplicated gown. The design wasn't difficult, endless yards of material weren't required. I would take the sketch and walk over first thing in the morning.

It was a relief to have that decision out of the way, just the wedding dress and possibly another for traveling. There was no need to go mad and purchase a complete new wardrobe, I had a nice selection of serviceable dresses, and the thought of endless fittings made me nauseous.

Thomas had yet to make his daily appearance. I wanted

to tell him about the overly curious man that had been in the shop. The fellow wasn't interested in books and when he left stood outside and contemplated the portcullis for an inordinate amount of time.

I had peeked from behind a bookcase to observe as he ran his hands over the metal grate. Immediately after his departure hurried to check the back door to make sure it was still locked.

Uncle Arch had returned from whatever archives he was investigating about an hour ago. It had been a while since he'd found time to work on the mystery of Hartlepool.

Locating towns close by the abandon religious site with a substantial church or abbey might prove difficult. Especially if such places no longer existed. Many small villages over the last few hundred years disappeared for various reasons, civil wars, crop failures and plague.

The Black Death, or the bubonic plague, was estimated to have killed up to sixty percent of the population of Europe in the 1300's. All over England smaller towns lost much of their population, the people that survived often moved away leaving entire villages deserted.

The task to find the fourth Vulgate Bible might be an exercise in futility. But sure my uncle would have a wonderful time looking through the archives. He planned to compile a list of towns within a twenty-mile radius of Hartlepool. Perhaps ten possible sites, including Durham, not many would be large enough to have a substantial stone church.

"Not particularly busy at the moment," stated Thomas.

I hadn't heard him enter the shop, my mind miles away.

"Many things to think about, an upcoming wedding, my uncle . . . and a very strange man."

Thomas became more alert. "How do you mean strange?"

"He was overly curious about the portcullis and the name of the inventor, not a bit interested in books as he proclaimed."

"I don't suppose he is lurking around anywhere?"

I huffed a little. "Not hardly, he left some time ago . . . just made me uncomfortable, could have been his cold eyes and the way he examined the grate."

"Describe him?"

"Well dressed, expensive, but that isn't unusual, many customers wear such clothes. The fellow was of average height, dark hair and eyes, mustache and goatee. Another thing, once he was outside inspecting the gate he massaged his temple on the right side. I got the feeling he might have been in pain."

Thomas moved to the window. "Our security device is a curiosity, this person might have been interested in how it was constructed."

I joined him at the window and looked toward the street. "You're probably right . . . so what have you been involved in today?"

"Spent time with a client, engaged in some tedious reconciliation of accounts, and helped Danny follow a servant suspected of purloining trinkets gone missing from his place of employment."

I grinned. "In other words just another day in the life.

Dinner is at seven, Jennie has been baking, I know because of the delicious aroma wafting through the air and the grumbling from Uncle Arch being denied dessert. He has been to the archives and I'm sure he wants to share his findings."

"Somewhere I imagine an invitation to dine is hidden in your statement."

"If you have another engagement ignore the overture."

"I accept the chance to be in your company . . . always a great pleasure."

Thomas went to the door and looked outside in both directions. "I'm going to take a quick look, perhaps the gentleman you mentioned is still around somewhere."

"He has been gone for quite a while, I doubt he's skulking on street corners."

"I'm sure you're correct, but I'll walk around anyway, stop at the newsagents for a paper."

❧

Archer Varrus hadn't accomplished much in the pursuit of a possible area the inhabitants of Hartlepool Abbey might have relocated. Not many old Saxon churches survived the ravages of time, weather, and the Norman conquest.

He didn't even know what to look for, a thousand years was a long time for a book to remain hidden, even if it had survived everything else. Nothing, as far as he could determine from the old works hinted at a fourth Bible ensconced in some out of the way place.

Surely if it survived, the church or whatever, would have publicized the fact. Having something like that was a draw for pilgrims, and persons with wealth wanting to support such a place. Relics were thought to have healing powers or to perform miracles, saving towns from being ravaged in war, and crop failure or the plague.

The bible couldn't be classed as a true relic such as baby teeth from Jesus, a sliver of wood from the true cross or pieces of the Virgin's veil. But such a book could be advertised as the direct word of God, or some such thing.

Archer studied the bucolic painting on the wall. Perhaps he should be looking for a religious institution touting the acquisition of a new artifact. Something of that nature occurring in the 800's just might be a place to focus his attention.

Chapter Twelve

Thomas walked briskly away from the bookstore. He kept his eyes peeled for the person Olivia had described, there was little doubt it was Ruben Hodge. He had made it his business to observe the fellow on several occasions.

Not only did he know what Mr. Hodge looked like, he knew quite a bit more, including where the man lived in London and his recently acquired country estate.

It wouldn't be difficult to find out what private clubs, if any, the fellow frequented. Ruben Hodge was not a person who sat at home in the evenings, he was an aggressive business man interested in contacts or acquaintances that would improve his standing in society. A social club was almost a necessity.

At dinner tonight he'd again bring up the subject of closing the shop for a while. Olivia and her uncle would be safe at his place; Jennie and Nyles were included knowing how important they were to the Varrus family.

If Hodge was snooping around instead of his henchmen then the situation was serious, the bookshop probably moved to the top of the list. Making the place more secure increased the possibility of a physical attack on any of the four people connected with the store. It was a damned if you do, damned if you don't, position.

Those thoughts were heart wrenching. It meant during business hours anyone could walk in and do whatever harm intended. How long did it take to bash in a head or slash someone . . . such a deed could be done in an eyewink.

Thomas reached the end of the block, stood at the corner, scanned both directions, then turned to walk back. He should purchase a paper since this was the reason given to be wandering about, the newsagents was only a few steps away.

The small shop was chocked full of newspapers, magazines, confections and tobacco. Glass jars contained boiled sweets, liquorice discs, various colors of pulled candy sticks, pink pear drops, fruit pastilles, and peppermint Hambugs.

The elderly man sitting behind the counter nodded as Thomas entered.

"Good afternoon Mr. Tully."

"And a fine afternoon it is Mr. Brandyce. Haven't seen you around for a bit."

"Not much of an excuse other than business as always.

He pointed to the jar of candy. "Ten pieces of liquorice and this paper please."

Mr. Tully placed the round black sweets in a small bag. "That will be four-pence."

Thomas counted out the coins, put the candy in his coat pocket, and the paper under his arm. "Thank you Mr. Tully, see you again soon."

"So you will be searching for a church that features a relic?" Thomas inquired after Archer admitted his lack of progress on the Hartlepool mystery.

Uncle Arch chuckled. "Most churches of any size had a relic of some sort. Such items bestowed honor and privilege upon the possessor. I would imagine if one counted the slivers of bone from the Saints those places professed to have had, there would be a dozen St. Cuthbert's, St. Patrick's, or St. Jude."

"My uncle will enjoy every minute of the hunt." I turned my attention toward Thomas. "You mentioned a concern you had in regards to the shop?"

Thomas compressed his lips together then frowned. "It has occurred to me that in making this building more secure it could invite an attack of a personal nature. I think moving to my house would be a practical solution, the invitation includes Jennie and Nyles of course."

I stared at Thomas for several moments, then looked at my uncle. 'I don't want to close the shop, it would be giving in to scare tactics but perhaps we could compromise, stay elsewhere at night."

Uncle Arch took another swallow of brandy, then carefully set the glass on the table next to his chair. "I promise to make a decision about this matter soon."

⁂

Packy and Donnie Brown scuttled in the shadows toward Henrietta Street. It wasn't in the wee hours of the morning, but late enough for all the stores to be closed.

Burt and Jingo wanted the newsagents on the corner to suffer enough damage that the place wouldn't be open for business anytime soon. The brothers had come prepared with hammers, matches and lamp oil to get a fire started once inside the shop.

Donnie was in a hurry; he'd arranged to meet a lady friend now he had the means to show her a good time. He felt the coins nestled in his pocket and grinned.

Good old Jingo, always a pal, giving him and Packy this job. Shouldn't be nothin' to break a few windows and set some newspapers on fire. Well, Jingo didn't say to light anything on fire but he didn't say not to . . . fire was real good at puttin' a place out of business.

Maybe after this little bother they could do some work for Lida Devore. That's the reason Jingo and Bert were busy tonight, old Lida had them collecting. One didn't want to miss any payments to that crazy bitch; she'd hunt ya down if'n it took forever.

They crossed the street and hurried into the alley to stay hidden. After a few minutes, ventured out, dashed around the corner, took a last look around and smashed the window. The men began to splash lamp oil on a display of magazines when they heard a piercing whistle and feet pounding in their direction.

There wasn't enough time to do anything but drop the can of oil and run. The brothers headed toward the small park, to get lost in the bushes.

Donnie could hear his brother wheezing, gasping for breath. Packy was falling behind . . . not good, if they got nicked again it would be a long time before either one of them walked free.

Packy was thrown to the ground, his head shoved into the prickly bushes. A heavy weight on his back made breathing even more difficult. He tried to roll onto his side, get some room to take a swing at his attacker. The attempt failed, his face was thrust once again into the brush.

"Keep on wiggling you worm, more reason to break your neck, " a voice muttered. The pressure increased on his back, a broken stick stabbed into his cheek. Where was Donnie? His brother should be able to get this dolt off, use the knife! Donnie was good with a knife!

Packy was grabbed up by his hair and punched in the stomach several times before everything went black.

Donnie turned around once to see his brother being dragged away by two men. He should have gone back, tried to help, but saving himself was uppermost in his mind. Right now he had to get somewhere safe and think about what to do. He didn't know if the bloke's that had Packy were bluebottles they didn't have uniforms.

Thomas gazed at the disheveled man tied in a chair. The fellow was blindfolded didn't want the bastard to recognize anyone.

"You have a name?"

The man grunted and turned his head in the direction of the voice.

"Don't really care about that . . . who hired you?"

It was a long moment of silence, then the prisoner smirked and shouted. "Sod-off!"

"As you wish, I'm sure you will have plenty to say later on." Thomas turned to Danny and Rob and spoke softly. "Take him to the hole, he can meditate in peace and quiet."

The hole was a tiny stone pit under an old boarded up factory not far from the river. A contrary guest might be thrown down into the twelve-foot burrow; a more cooperative one could use a ladder that was pulled up and out of the shaft.

Thomas found this method worked quite well to gain information, one didn't need to inflict pain, the dark, silent hole was very effective. A couple of days without food and water changed minds and loosened tongues.

I was seething beneath the veneer of calm. The small shop had been cleaned, the lamp oil mopped up, shards of glass swept and the damaged magazines tossed away.

The front window boarded and secured until new glass could be installed. I brushed the hair off my face and took the last bucket of water outside to pour into the street.

The thought of what could have happened kept running through my head.

Uncle Arch and Mr. Tully had been upstairs playing chess when the windows shattered. If the monsters had been successful, both men probably would have died in the fire.

The guards Thomas employed caught one of the arsonists. Being a law-abiding citizen before all this mayhem occurred I would have turned the miscreant over to the police. But there has been a glaring lack of interest from the authorities to find the culprits responsible for the acts of violence.

In the past I had admonished Thomas not to go about willy-nilly inflicting damage upon those individuals involved in nefarious acts of . . . whatever. Now I wanted to get my hands on these vile creatures and inflict a great deal of damage . . . my mind was filled with ways to get some sort of retribution.

I knew many quotes about seeking revenge, mostly not to ever do it. "He who plots to hurt others often only hurts himself." "Vengeance is mine," says the Lord.

Right now I prefer. "Forgive our enemies, but not before they are hanged."

Sophie, Mr. Tully's daughter, took a last look around the shop, then leaned on the doorframe. "Thank you for the help Olivia, it could have been so much worse . . . my father and your uncle…"

"I know, but the worst didn't happen."

"When is this going to end? When we get so frightened or hurt we practically give our property away?"

"I can't tell you much about future plans, because I don't really know anything, but there will be a reckoning in the near future," I said with more confidence than I felt.

Donnie Brown sat in a dark corner of the dimly lit pub. What was he going to do about his brother? It had only been a day since Packy was taken away, surely by now someone would have heard something, especially if he'd been nicked. He'd walked by the police station, but didn't go inside.

What was he going to say? "My brother and me was watchin' some blokes set a fire when you rozzers chanced by, wasn't doin' nufink wrong, ran cause we wuz afraid we'd be blamed." No tellin' wot Packy might of said, the stupid arse.

Donnie hoped Ellicot and Rush didn't want their money back, it's not like they didn't do some damage, the window got busted out so there's that. Wasn't much left to give back anyhow . . . and wot about Packy? He'd just have to wait and see.

⁂

Norton Engle listened to his client prattle on about his dearly departed relative. His mind mostly devoted to how much profit he would make from the sale of Mr. Duncan's properties. According to Hodge, convincing this naïve young man that real estate was in a slump wouldn't be difficult.

"...finding the translation from the old abbey was fascinating, well it was only a partial rendering. Should have kept the stones and found an expert in Old Saxon or whatever to finish the message. Uncle Selby wouldn't have bought those things as a lark. The old gent was always looking for a long lost treasure, you know, a message from the grave so to speak."

The lawyer offered a vague smile. "Oh yes the engraved rocks from Northumbria."

"I became curious when the names St. Peter's and St.

Paul's were mentioned in the same breath as Bibles. So I did some investigating and historically there is only one Bible still in existence from back in the 600's."

Engle cut another slice of meat and savored the tender morsel. "Your uncle collected antique Bibles?"

"No, but from a notation in his journal he thought there might be another Bible besides the one in Italy. But seems he was too ill to continue.

Lord this man could put a corpse to sleep, who on earth cared about such drivel.

"Well, I guess one will never know about such things."

"I'm fairly certain Uncle Selby was on to something. He was good at finding lost things of value, that's what he did for a living and how he managed to afford all the property I've inherited."

That last statement made an impression. "This Bible you speak about, would it be valuable?"

Richard Duncan poured more wine into his glass and took a hearty swallow. "The

Codex Amiatinus, the oldest surviving Vulgate Bible, is considered priceless."

Engle placed the knife and fork down and wiped his mouth with a napkin. "Correct me if I'm wrong, but you are saying there could be another such book somewhere."

Duncan grinned. "Seems like a possibility, but since the notes my uncle left were not finished, one can't be sure."

"Where are the stones now?"

"Gone, sold with the rest of the stuff no one wanted."

Engle was trying not to appear as excited as he felt. "Do

you know who purchased them?"

"Haven't the slightest idea."

"Surely you could find out, might be fastenating to have the inscription fully translated."

"I guess I could contact the group who ran the estate sale."

"Yes, excellent idea, you should do that."

"Are you interested in artifacts Mr. Engle?"

"Not really, I was just thinking it would make an amusing historical footnote, set the scholastic world all a twitter."

Engle finally extricated himself from the talkative Mr. Duncan and went home to think about what the fellow had said about a Vulgate Bible. Once in his study made the decision to gather more information, it shouldn't be too difficult, after all, the book was supposed to be famous.

Mr. Duncan said he would try and find out who bought the stones.

The newspaper was neatly folded on his desk. He hadn't bothered reading anything for the past few days most articles were about politics. The Liberal party defeated by the Conservatives, editorials on London prostitutes, ongoing troubles with Ireland, such matters were tedious.

After pouring a drink he picked up the paper, skipped the first few pages and turned his attention to a small article about a visiting son of the Maharaja of Varanasi.

Engle mumbled the visitor was probably one of fifty children from numerous wives. No doubt the fellow wanted to get out of the clutches of a strict father and came to London to indulge in whatever a Maharaja indulged in.

He continued reading about this Vijaya Shinde person, seems there was to be a display and auction of a considerable amount of jewelry. The man certainly picked a grand place to show off his gemstones. Claridge's was a luxury hotel, one had to have more than a few coins to rub together in order to stay for any length of time.

Might be interesting to have a look at the jewelry, probably run into Ruben. Roanne was passionate about pretty sparklers and her husband was passionate about keeping her happy . . . for now.

⋅⋅⋅

I looked at the clock, just about time to close. The very elegant and elderly Mrs. Popwell had been in and I was writing down the books hidden away in her large bag. Her maid had slipped me a note with the names of the three books. I would send the bill to her son in the morning.

The lady came in several times a month; we would have a lovely conversation on various topics. Invisible creatures in her garden, the best cheese, the horrible name given to one of her friend's grandchildren and what taste the color blue might be. We decided it probably wouldn't be spicy.

One had to admit the woman did make me think unconventionally which was rather amusing. Of course there was never a mention of purloined merchandise, I couldn't decide if she did it for fun or couldn't be bothered to pay.

Nyles was in the back and Jennie should return from the greengrocers soon. I climbed the stairs to search for more of the good writing paper stored in the desk when a blood-curdling scream shattered the air.

My heart began to pound. Jennie was shrieking, then heard footsteps running up the stairs; I stood in place, terrified. What seemed hours, but more like seconds I remained rooted to the floor, the screams came closer and Jennie dashed past.

A moment later a man appeared at the top of the stairs he shouted unintelligible words and waved a cudgel.

My eyes frantically searched for something to throw or fend off this animal; nothing was available except the large atlas Uncle Arch had been reading.

The creature paused at the top of the stairs; his head slowly swiveled around to look at me, he seemed to be in a trancelike state. The feral eyes focused despite the twitching of his body, there was no mercy in that face . . . if he could reach me I would die.

I grabbed the book in both hands and ran toward him with one thought in mind . . . hit him hard and keep on swinging.

Chapter Thirteen

I watched the man tumble down the stairs, the club still clutched in his hand as his arms flailed in the air. He landed on the last step with a thud and didn't move. I was afraid to get close, so stood at the top and grasped the railing.

Nyles started toward the motionless figure but was pushed away by a very large individual. Panicked thoughts were how to protect myself, Nyles and Jennie, if the man started up the stairs, when he spoke.

"You are safe now Miss Varrus, my partner has gone to find Mr. Brandyce."

The only words that made any sense were "safe" and "Brandyce".

I leaned against the railing then slid down to land with a

jolt on the top step. "That man . . . be careful he has a club."

"Not to worry, been knocked out, don't suppose he'll be up and around very soon." The fellow pried the club out of the unconscious assailant's hand.

Nyles was pacing back and forth as Danny St. Jules hurried through the door. He ventured to the foot of the stairs and studied the unmoving form. Then murmured quietly to the other man.

Danny looked up and smiled. "Are you all right Miss Varrus?"

I took a deep breath and let it out slowly. "Yes . . . I'm not hurt."

"Good to know, I'll get this person sorted, you stay upstairs. Thomas should be here soon."

I could only nod and rest my head on one of the rails. Jennie! I remember Jennie. Was she hurt! It took some effort to stand, although to sit and not think about anything would have been nice.

I hurried down the hall; peeked into the sitting room, then heard faint sobs from the kitchen.

Jennie was huddled in a corner on the floor. I knelt down and gently stroked her hair. The frightened girl gasped and let out a squeal. "It's all right Jennie . . . are you hurt?"

"Miss Olivia, he was crazy . . . I didn't even know he was there, just rushed up and grabbed my basket as I was entering the shop." Jennie whimpered.

"Take a deep breath, come . . . sit in a chair, I think we need a drink, some brandy perhaps."

The carafe was on the sideboard in the dining room. My

hands shook as I poured the caramel colored liquid into the short-stemmed glasses. It didn't help much to remind myself to be calm; it was up to me to give the appearance of being in control even if I wanted to dissolve into tears.

I took a deep breath let it out slowly, clasped and un-clasped my hands together several times, then picked up the glasses and went to the kitchen.

We sipped the woody sweetness. Jennie coughed and scrunched up her nose after the first swallow. "The stuff kind of grows on you after a while," I said.

"Can't see why a body would drink it more than once, give me a good ale anytime."

"Some people call it the nectar of the gods."

"Just as well I don't get too fond of it, wouldn't want it said I displeased the gods."

The girl's face had gained some color, and she'd stopped shaking. I noticed her dress was torn along the shoulder seam. "Were you hit?"

"No, the man grabbed my arm, but I twisted away and ran into the shop. Where did he go!" and looked toward the door.

I grasped her hand tightly. "Not to worry, people who work for Mr. Brandyce are taking care of everything."

The frightened look faded a little and she settled back in the chair, then took another sip of brandy.

We talked quietly for a time then told her to wash her face, change the torn dress and rest for a while, hopefully she would feel better.

At least I thought it would make her feel better. I know

I could do with a lie down and a cool cloth on my forehead, it might help to forget the crazed man and the wild look in his eyes. I wondered fleetingly what was going to happen to him, but didn't really care all that much, just as long as he never came back.

I suddenly remembered Nyles, hadn't thought about him in all this madness. Before I could drag myself out of the chair Thomas entered the room. The look on his face was harrowing; his facial muscles were tightly clenched.

He wasn't doing especially well in controlling his fear and anger. If I went to pieces he would probably be out of control . . . not a good thing.

"Are you all right?" he inquired in a deathly calm voice.

"Yes, I'm fine, or will be later. Sit down Thomas, finish this brandy," I said with more authority than I felt and pushed the unfinished glass his direction.

He folded himself into the chair across from me, his eyes were icy and his body rigid. "Tell me what happened."

I tucked the straggling strands of hair behind my ear and began the tale. Jennie screaming and running up the stairs, the unintelligible gibberish the mad man shouted, the crazed look on his face . . . and how I slammed him in the head with the atlas. I thought I detected a shadow of a smile on Thomas's face . . . maybe.

"He was at the top of the stairs and fell backward when I hit him. Right after that one of your men ran in and told me to stay where I was and sent his partner to find you. A few minutes later Mr. St Jules arrived and announced he would take care of everything."

"We have it all sorted out, you don't need to worry."

"What about Nyles, is he all right?"

"Nyles is fine I sent him home and closed the shop. How are Jennie and your uncle?"

"Uncle Arch wasn't here had taken himself off to the archives and Jennie received a fright but will recover.

What will you do with that man, Thomas . . . he really wasn't right in the head, seemed almost in a trancelike state, a blind rage."

"When he comes around I'll have a little chat, perhaps he was drunk, sometimes alcohol makes people act crazy. Right now, I want you to come with me into the other room, we can sit more comfortably on the sofa and recover a bit."

Dinner was brought in from a restaurant that Thomas frequented. The chicken was tender the potatoes roasted and well seasoned. Uncle Arch managed a second helping of everything while Jennie, Thomas and I pushed the food around the plate in an attempt to eat a few bites.

"I should start packing, won't need much right now." I murmured. We were going to Thomas's place for the night; it hadn't been hard to convince us to leave. If I'd refused, I'm sure my fiancé would have carried me away without hesitation.

My uncle broached the subject of who was responsible for the assault. "I have little doubt the West End Brokers are to blame for what happened."

Thomas nodded but made no comment, in fact he said very little except that we should stay at his home.

Uncle Arch reached for another piece of bread and

147

slathered it with butter. "I'll accept the invitation to be your guest at night but feel it important to keep the shop open. Jacob Tully, the news agent, is doing the same; he will stay with his daughter and family at night, business as usual during the day."

I placed the napkin on the table and leaned back in the chair. "The whole thing is ridiculous, I'm sick and tired of it all, we can't keep on like this."

Thomas rested his elbows on the table and steepled his hands. "I have a few things in mind, its time to send a message to Mr. Hodge . . . quid pro quo."

Uncle Arch tugged on his ear. "Something for something, if my Latin is correct, would you care to elaborate?"

"Not at the moment, but the gentleman in question will sit up and take notice. Now, we must finish eating and pack up, the carriage will be here soon."

My accommodation was lovely, conveniently located next door to Thomas; a large wardrobe closet connected the two rooms. I had placed my bag on the chest at the foot of the bed. The chamber featured pale blue walls and bright white trim. The curtains were a darker shade of blue with silver threads woven into the fabric, which seemed to emit a soft glow.

An abundance of crystal glassware shimmered around the room, muted light from the gas sconces made everything sparkle. The marble fireplace surround had blue and white china vases at each end a beautiful porcelain clock and cut glass figurines in the middle.

The inlaid table near the window held a large urn full of

white roses, bluebells and cornflowers.

"Do you like it?" Thomas asked. He was leaning on the doorframe of the connecting entryway. "I wasn't sure if you favored blue, so took a chance. If you hate it . . . it's an easy fix."

"I feel like a princess, it's enchanting, and yes, I love blue. Oh Thomas . . . " I was trying not to cry and blinked back tears.

In a few strides he was at my side and enfolded me in his arms. "Don't cry, I can't stand to see you cry."

"I'm not really crying, tears of joy don't count as crying."

"I'll try and remember that in the future . . . how will I know the difference?"

"Oh, you will know the difference, my face will turn red and blotchy and my vocabulary contains words a proper lady shouldn't know."

He kissed the top of my head then chuckled softly. "And where does a proper lady learn such words?"

"That my dear fellow is a secret." I rested my head against his chest. "Lord everything is such a mess, a little more than two weeks until the wedding, perhaps we should postpone."

He drew away, then placed his hands on my shoulders. "Not a chance in hell will that happen happen, if anything, we move it up!"

The man looked fierce and anxious at the same time, if such a thing were possible. I couldn't help myself and giggled. "I take it back, wedding as scheduled."

"Now that we are in agreement I will let you settle in. As you have probably noticed our rooms connect, my door will be open and I'll be looking in throughout the night."

"So if I see someone lurking about I shouldn't scream? How will I know the difference between you and one with vile intentions?"

"Such an odious creature must get past Danny and Rob and two more rather large individuals wandering around the garden. And then there will be me waiting in the shadows."

"In that case I shall have no trouble falling asleep."

I lied. It was difficult to sleep; first I was cold, then too warm. When I managed to drift off, awoke with a start a few minutes later. Two pillows made my neck ache; one pillow was like sleeping on a board.

Left side, right side, both uncomfortable, same with sleeping on my back and forget finding a decent resting place on my stomach.

Since I was never without a book the only thing to do was read. The overstuffed chairs near the fireplace looked confortable enough. I would have to turn up the lights, which might wake Thomas, considering the connecting doors were open.

I had no idea if he was a light sleeper . . . a distinct possibility but I hadn't heard anything from him not even snoring.

Uncle Arch made such huffing and chuffing sounds one had no problem finding his sleeping quarters.

It couldn't hurt to peek into the room next door. I promise my intentions were innocent, take a quick look then quietly close the door on my side and read for an hour or two.

The bed was empty, not even an indication of anyone having slept or laid a head on the pillow. Perhaps he was prowling around looking for something to eat, he hardly touched his food at dinner.

Could be having a drink and chat with Rob and Danny, whatever he was doing wasn't my concern.

Hopefully after meandering through a few chapters of my book I'd be able to sleep. Tomorrow would be business as usual.

❧

Thomas wasn't scrounging for food or chatting with Rob and Danny. The three men were in the offices of Ruben Hodge. It was easy enough to gain entrance, not much thought had been given to security precautions. Managing the dead body was a little more difficult.

The cretin who had attacked Olivia and Jennie was dead. Suffered a broken neck in the fall down stairs. Thomas felt a certain satisfaction that the blow delivered to his head contributed to his demise . . . nicely done Olivia! Not that he would ever mention such a thing to her.

After Danny discovered the fellow wouldn't be available for questioning there was no reason to tell Olivia anything other than the moron was unconscious.

A cart was procured, the body taken to the storage room in back of the shop, out the alley door, loaded into the cart and driven to the warehouse.

Thomas was going to take the game Mr. Hodge was playing to the next level, time to turn the tables so to speak.

Let Ruben Hodge figure out how to get rid of the body.

Earlier that evening their guest in the hole at the warehouse had bubbled over with cooperation. Mr. Packy Brown was a fountain of information about his brother Donnie, and two bastards named Bert Ellicot and Jingo Rush. Seems Rush and Ellicot hired the siblings to break-up the newsagents place. He didn't know Ruben Hodge by name, other than a "toff estate bloke" who used the services of Bert and Jingo to convince many a "poor sod" to sell his property.

As for the dead man, the description of a short man with black hair and eyes, scar down his neck, and possibly foreign was a person called Spanish. Packy indicated that "Spanish" was crazy even without smoking tobacco mixed with henbane leaves. With henbane he was a lunatic.

The door into Hodge's private office was opened without difficulty. Thomas looked around the elegant room; he remembered the silver dragon desk set. The beautiful item was removed and placed in a bag. Should bring quite a nice sum. The body was dumped into the leather chair and artfully arraigned.

Thomas wanted a better look at the books in the glass-fronted case, might be something worth removing. The last case, middle shelf, didn't have any reading material; it contained several figurines and was locked.

Must be something old Ruben considered special enough to keep locked away. Shattering the glass probably wasn't necessary, but Thomas couldn't resist making a mess.

The items inside proved to be worth the effort. Jade . . . beautiful jade trinkets begging to be relocated.

Rob decided the rest of the glass in the bookcase doors should be shattered. Might as well be consistent. The three men took a final look around before making their way down stairs. Ruben Hodge was in for a rather unpleasant surprise when he opened his door.

Thomas had rummaged through the desk belonging to the weasel-faced secretary, Mr. Fish or Fiske. As anticipated the names of several gentlemen's clubs Mr. Hodge frequent-ed were easily located.

Not surprising most were social rather than political. The London, and Marlborough Clubs where places profes-sional businessmen mingled, and the Portland Club was for a serious game of cards. At the Portland one could win or lose a fortune, both had happened over the years.

Thomas carefully opened the dressing room door. He quietly moved toward the bed and was ready to panic when he found it empty. His eyes darted around the chamber in search of Olivia.

In a chair by the fireplace his gaze rested on the sleep-ing form. He could breathe again and allow his heart rate to slow. A book was in her lap, the beautiful thick auburn hair spread across her shoulders.

This was the woman he needed and longed for . . . intel-ligent, witty and whimsical, she kept him grounded . . . au courant, for lack of a better word.

He watched the gentle rhythm of her breathing; she would be more comfortable in bed but probably wouldn't relish being disturbed. Just let her be, it was not much longer until light.

A couple hours of sleep were in order, it had been a busy night and he was tired. What he wouldn't give to see how Ruben Hodge handled the surprise in his office. If Thomas were lucky the manky sod would suffer a heart attack and die. Couldn't possibly be that fortunate . . . damn.

Chapter Fourteen

The dining room seemed to overflow with large men. In addition to Thomas, Danny and Rob, there were two other gentlemen sitting around the table. They stood when I entered the room.

Thomas moved to my side. "Mr. Simon McQuade and Mr. Alec Gibson, may I introduce my fiancé, Miss Olivia Varrus." The men greeted me with smiles and appropriate words when being presented.

The aroma of breakfast wafted from the direction of the sideboard. Platters of bacon and ham, eggs, kippers with grilled tomatoes, chunky cinnamon applesauce, scones, plum jam and clotted cream were displayed upon the tabletop.

Jennie hurried through the door with a silver carafe.

"Fresh coffee gentlemen." And proceeded to refill their cups. "I will keep a plate warm for Mr. Archer when he comes down." Jennie whispered as she came to my side.

My uncle wasn't an early riser, his usual habit of reading until after midnight, meant he'd have breakfast around nine or later.

"How are you feeling this morning Jennie, better than last evening I hope."

"Much improved Miss Olivia. My quarters are pleasant, and I've been helping Mrs. Reed. She is very nice and her daughter, Lizzie, has been showing me around."

One had to smile at such enthusiasm. "I'm glad you're not suffering any ill effects from yesterday."

She bobbed a slight curtsy. "I must get back."

I looked across the table at Thomas. "Jennie seems to be settling in nicely. Mrs Reed is . . ."

"Mrs Reed is the cook, she doesn't live in. Her daughters, Lizzie and Florence are here part-time to keep the place clean. I haven't a need for more domestic workers such as butlers, footmen, or valet. Something we shall discuss later if you like."

I hadn't given much thought to servants. Never had a personal maid. Jennie came to the rescue when I required help and Vi . . .Violet Howard before she retired. Vi had been my nanny for years, a surrogate mother of sorts.

More staff was something to think about, but right now I was famished and wanted to engage in conversation with these interesting and amusing men.

Ruben Hodge was not the least bit amused. Terrified was probably a more apt description. After the shock of finding a dead man sitting in his chair, came the rage in discovering the jade objects and silver desk set stolen.

Mr. Fiske was cowering outside the door while his employer screamed obscenities and threw books around the room. When it was quiet the little man ventured in but stayed well away from the body.

"What should we do Mr. Hodge!"

"Do . . . what do you think we will do . . . you . . ." Hodge bellowed, then took a deep breath and started to pace in front of the desk. Even though the eyes of the dead man were sightless and cloudy they seemed to follow the angry man as he moved back and forth.

"Perhaps we should call a doctor or the police."

Hodge looked at his secretary and sneered. "I think it's a little late for a doctor and the police will have questions I can't answer . . . then there is what a scandal would do to my reputation. Should make front-page news in all the rags.

No, no, police or doctor . . . contact Mr. Engle, I'm sure he will know how get rid of this thing . . . for a hefty price no doubt."

Ruben had to get out of the room; it was closing in around him. Who the hell was doing this and why? Nothing much frightened him until now . . . a dead man in one's office was beyond terrifying especially since he knew him.

He had hired Spanish to intimidate anyone connected with the Varrus bookshop. The last time he had seen the man alive was in his office two nights ago.

Spanish was an ex-bare knuckle fighter. Even though small in stature he was a wild man when doing battle. The little guys usually didn't stand much of a chance when paired with a larger brute. If one wanted to engage in pugilistic contests you fought all comers regardless of age, size and weight. Spanish had been good until he wasn't.

Fighting was illegal, if caught by the authorities the participants were arrested and fined, but for the most part such activities were ignored.

The general public loved to see what amounted to a barroom brawl . . . kicking, gouging, head butting and biting made for exciting entertainment. Many times the crowd became violent if the favorite didn't win . . . the place erupting into a free-for-all.

Hodge was trying to think what might have happened at the bookstore. There were only the two females, the young assistant and the old man, none of them likely to trouble Spanish . . . so what the hell had taken place!

Trying to figure it out would have to wait. He had to get rid of a dead man, not something he had ever experienced.

Then there were his missing possessions . . ., he wanted them back! One could make a tidy sum, even when paying substantially less than they were worth. Not many people in the stolen merchandise business could afford such items.

Most traffickers dealt with trinkets nicked by robbers who were paid some trifling amount. Shouldn't be difficult to find the more high-end dealers in London, Engle could again be helpful with locating such people.

Norton Engle folded the note from Mr. Duncan in regards to the etched stones. The estate liquidation manager for his uncle's house-hold items couldn't recall much about the person who had purchased the unusual pieces. But did remember the company who had carted them away . . . Walters Brothers Hauling.

The lawyer smiled and creased the letter several times, then placed it in the desk drawer. Shouldn't take much effort to find the haulers. Engle had become very interested in locating the new owner of the stones, especially after his research.

The Vulgate was a fourth-century Latin translation of the Bible by St. Jerome and became the official Latin Bible of the Catholic Church. The Codex Amiatinus was renowned as a single-volume and most accurate copy of the Vulgate translations. The books were quite large . . . almost twenty inches in height and seven inches thick. Unusual for that era as books were costly and time consuming to produce.

Only three copies had been created, or so it was thought. One went to Italy as a gift for the Pope, the other two were at the twin monasteries of Jarrow and Weremouth.

The British Museum had to make do with a few pages that survived from the rare books. It was said that those in charge of that august institution were consumed with envy that the quintessential English tome was in foreign hands.

The thought of a fourth copy caused Mr. Engle to become almost giddy. A discovery like that could be worth a fortune . . . but he shouldn't get ahead of himself. There was much to do, starting with locating the stones and translating what was written in its entirety.

Afghanistan! The Second Afghan War was where these men had served together. A war with no purpose, no benefit, and a rather sobering experience for those involved.

They were attached to the 3rd Mounted Division. But if I was correct in reading between the lines and the not so well hidden emotions flowing between these gentlemen, there was something more.

The breakfast table wasn't the place to delve into whatever it was. Eventually I would find out if I really wanted to know more.

So settled back and listened to the good natured banter, laughing at teasing comments such as "Things like that didn't ever happen where I come from" the reply "Where you come from they still eat their young." Or "He ran from under a leaking roof and sat in the rain." A reference to lacking intelligence was suggested by "Poor iron won't make a sharp sword."

Jennie was kept busy refilling coffee cups and baskets of scones. As she swept by Simon McQuade I noticed a subtle look pass between the two. We had been at this place less than twenty-four hours and a possible romance was brewing?

I would make inquiries about Mr. McQuade, not because I was nosy, more like investigative . . . investigative sounds better than snooping.

As much as I tried to dismiss all thoughts of what was happening in our neighborhood, and specifically the bookshop, apprehension tinged with fear was present.

A new face to the shop brought anxiety . . . not something I enjoyed. Nyles was on edge too. It was a relief when Alec Gibson casually strolled through the door. He wandered around the store, selected a book from the history section and sat down on a sofa off to the side. From there he could see who came and went.

Simon McQuade replaced him a few hours later. Thomas made his daily appearance; we had a chat about trivialities . . . before leaving he checked the back door.

Uncle Arch pottered about up stairs, he planned to stay close for a while. Announced there was plenty to keep him busy as he searched for estate sales in the accumulated newspapers.

Later this afternoon I was to have a fitting for my wedding dress, something I wasn't looking forward to. That was the last thing I wanted, to stand around while someone poked pins into my skin. To be fair that didn't happen very often, maybe twice over the years.

Danny St. Jules would accompany me to the dress shop it shouldn't take long. The gown was a simple design no elaborate tucks, flounces and different lengths of skirting to adjust.

***

The hauling company was located on a large lot, enough room to park various types of wagons and carts. Mr. Engle waited in what was probably a small parlor before being used as an office of sorts. There were two battered desks separated by an old bookshelf that held wire baskets full of papers.

Engle sat on a faded sofa in front of the window. The young woman who had been working at one of desks eventually returned with an older man.

"This is Mr. Engle papa. He wants to know if you remember a client who wanted some rocks hauled away."

The man frowned and scratched at the stubble on his chin. Rocks! Don't recall moving no rocks."

The lawyer offered his most charming smile. "Not rocks sir. No these were stones moved from a house near Mayfair, they had writing, or marks etched on them.

My friend is the nephew of the diseased, the owner of the house. He wants to contact the person who bought the masonry to see if the fellow would be interested in similar items recently discovered."

"Them stones is they valuable?"

"Not valuable in terms of money, more like historical records from hundreds of years ago. The markings are written in Old Saxon which should be preserved since the monastery they came from is mostly tumbled down."

The fellow looked at Engle for a time then shrugged." Don't recall the name of the bloke what hired us, but they was taken to a book shop in Westminster on Henrietta Street. I remember cause we don't often haul such things, mostly furniture and trunks and such."

"Thank you Mr. Walters." Engle pressed several coins into his hand. "Pleasure to meet you." then hurried out the door.

A bookshop on Henrietta Street . . . rather a coincidence. Hodge had been going on about problems he was having with the storeowners near Cavendish Square. Couldn't convince any of that lot to sell their businesses for the paltry sum he was offering.

Not that he would question Ruben about his dealings, Engle found their association much too lucrative to ruffle the man's feathers. After all, the lawyer was trying to become indispensable to the estate promoter. It was no easy task to make documents seem to say one thing but the fine print means something different.

The bookstore should be open. No time like the present to drop by and have a chat with the owner. Perhaps this person managed to translate the writing.

He would have to be careful not to seem overly excited about things, act like a scholar not a fortune hunter. Offer a helping hand, finding such a codex would be a tremendous historical boon and all that rot. Ruben would be amused when he told him about this development.

But he was getting ahead of himself again. Take it slow, appraise the situation and the people at the store.

The ride across town was almost pleasant not much traffic for some reason. After paying the fare made his way to the park to sit and think of how he should go about this situation.

One didn't just barge in and insist on examining the stones. Staying as near to the truth as possible kept one from making mistakes and getting caught in a lie. Obviously try not to appear desperate, mildly interested would do.

He circled the fountain then meandered toward Henrietta Street. Crossed Old Cavendish Street, passed several shops and stood looking at the display of books in the window.

The young man writing something in ledger looked up as Engle entered the shop.

"Good afternoon, may I help you find something?"

Engle smiled and removed his hat. "I'm looking for the owner of this fine establishment."

Nyles glanced briefly at McQuade sitting near by. "Mr. Varrus is not available at the moment, perhaps I could help you."

The lawyer sighed deeply. "I really should speak to him, the reason I'm here is a rather long story." He reached into an inside pocket of his coat and drew out a card.

"Please give this to Mr. Varrus."

It looked expensive; the paper was of good quality, the lettering an elegant scroll. Nyles examined the card to see if this person was some kind of estate agent. He was relieved to find the man was a solicitor. "I will see that Mr. Varrus receives this."

"Thank you. This shop is charming; perhaps I'll find something appealing, I'm always looking for anything historical. A glimpse into the past gives one a perspective into the future, don't you agree?"

Nyles grinned and nodded. "On the wall to your left you will find a selection of books that might be of interest."

"Thank you . . . don't forget to give Mr. Varrus my card, I'm keen to make his acquaintance."

Packy Brown wasn't in the best of shape. The thought of dying in this small, fetid, dark place was a distinct possibility. The chunks of bread and flask of water twice a day had become the focal point of his existence. Shouting for help was futile, it only made his throat raw, the tears of frustration and fear didn't accomplish anything either, just added to his suffering.

It was the silence and darkness that was making him crazy. He didn't know how long he had been here, there was no way to tell, the blackness was total. He knew he was getting weaker, because he had no energy to inch around the walls more than twice or three times.

Counting the steps from wall to wall was the only thing that kept him from complete madness. It took thirty-two steps to make a circuit. There was a small jagged edge of stone his fingers brushed over as he toured his limited space.

The craggy verge was the starting and stopping place of each lap.

Packy had never given much thought to a higher power, his mum had taken him and Donnie to church once in a while, not to hear a sermon, but to get something to eat.

He dreamed of hot, thick soup, thought about God, if there was one, and Donnie and mum. They all blurred in his head as he rocked back and forth and hummed a mindless tune.

The sound of the lid opening far above made his heart thump incredibly fast. He thought he saw shadows moving . . . maybe so, maybe not, then the sound of a voice.

"Mr. Brown, the ladder is to be lowered, but first a hood

will be tossed down, please put it over your head. Do you understand what I'm saying?"

Packy struggled to stand. "Yes, yes I understand, you lettin' me go? He shouted hysterically.

"Put on the hood, let me know when it's secured, then the ladder will be lowered. Don't be a fool and try having a look-see, if you do anything stupid, it won't take much to put you back down there . . . this time it will be for good."

A few minutes later Packy Brown was out of his confined space, hood in place hands tied behind his back. "When are you gonna let me go? I told you everything, don't know nofink more." He managed to rasp.

"If you cooperate you won't be harmed. My friend has a job offer, who knows you might find a new career opportunity."

Chapter Fifteen

Thomas stood inside the doorway of a warehouse talking quietly with a man. They discussed the fate of Packy Brown. Mr. Shaw was in the transportation business, he provided crewmembers for merchant ships. Many times departing vessels were missing able-bodied men to fill out a ships company.

Usually Mr. Shaw recruited willing participants but if necessary found a replacement by rather dubious means. He was notorious as a "crimper" someone who kidnapped men by serving them opium-laced whisky, then hauling the unconscious sod to a ship awaiting an incoming tide.

As proprietor of a boardinghouse and two pubs the supply of participants were abundant.

By morning Packy Brown would be on his way to some foreign port of call. Thomas wanted the fellow dumped far away, preferably a place that didn't speak English. If Mr. Brown were lucky, he might get back to England in a year or two, or not at all.

Since encountering Olivia, Thomas endeavored to conduct himself in accordance to her wishes. For the most part tried to restrain his more base instincts. There was an impulse to chuck rat bastards into the Thames and let their lot be decided by the river. Often before being relegated to the turbulent water they suffered a bang-up of some kind.

Such an activity was still an option; especially if anything untoward happened to Olivia, he would be devoid of any rational behavior. The accidental death of the rotter called Spanish had taken matters out of his hands, can't kill a dead man.

Ruben Hodge was a muddle. The bloke didn't get his hands dirty, he hired the rough element of London to do it for him. Mr. Hodge craved money, social status and most of all power. Thomas wanted to take it all away, do the same thing the fellow had done to many other people . . . after that . . . not really sure.

❧

The gown was beautiful, for the first time in my life I was mesmerized by something as silly as a fashionable dress. The cream colored silk hugged the body; there were no restrictive sleeves or miles of material hanging off my backside. The lace shawl could be draped over the shoulders and threaded through the arms to hang almost to the floor.

The whole look changed when the pale yellow, velvet overskirt was attached and the yellow, silk, long-sleeved bodice buttoned in place. The gown was worth the expense and promised by the end of the week.

I was tired after a busy day at the shop and the appointment with the dressmaker, so sitting by the fire in my room was lovely. The solitude calmed the mind.

It was late, the house pleasantly quiet, the rain had been light but steady all day. August in London was always unpredictable, most of the month had been relatively warm in the afternoon but the evenings were getting cold. The fire that had burned brightly an hour ago was now a warm glow.

Even though I couldn't hear him, I could feel his approach. It was always that way when Thomas was near, sometimes the impression was turbulent, almost raging. He was good at hiding those feeling, but not good enough.

Tonight the presence was soft and gentle. I turned away from the fire and leaned over the arm of the chair. "Not able to sleep tonight? The rain usually makes me drowsy."

Thomas moved past my chair and stirred the fire then added more coal. He sat in the chair next to mine. "I have a little gift, something for the blushing bride."

"I didn't realize that brides blush any more than usual."

"It's probably more appropriate to say blush than nervous."

I grinned and smoothed my tousled hair that was free from the prim bun I usually wore. "Can't say I'm especially nervous either . . . now you know . . . I'm rather shameless.

Thomas brought a small velvet bag from his pocket.

"You said your wedding gown was yellowish, simple yet stylish. Hopefully these will add a little sparkle to the ensemble."

I poured the contents of the bag into my hand and gasped in surprise. Then held one of the gorgeous yellow diamond earrings toward the light. "Beautiful . . . absolutely beautiful."

"They are called "Fancy" yellow, and in better light one can see an orangy color swirling around like a flickering flame."

I hurried to the dressing table, turned up the gaslight above the mirror and fastened the gold and yellow jewels in my ears. The orangy-yellow gemstones dangled and danced when I turned my head.

"Thank you, thank you a million times, perfect, more than perfect . . . splendid, beyond compare." I babbled.

Thomas chuckled softly. "I gather you think they will be acceptable."

I tried to look serious. "I suppose I could be persuaded to wear them, but it will be a chore."

He took me in his arms and kissed me softly, then gathered my hair in his hands as if afraid I would run away then kissed me again. It wasn't soft and fluttering any longer, hungry, lustful, almost overpowering, and I realized how much I loved this man.

"I'm sure we would be more comfortable over there." I nodded toward the bed.

He briefly looked in that direction. "No doubt it would be wonderfully soft and possibly restful. But I don't want to rest, I prefer to be near the fire, where we can talk."

"Isn't that akin to setting up camp and sleeping under the stars?"

"I don't think we shall be sleeping, I rather like the idea of a quilt in front of the fire, its warm and we can listen to the rain on the windows."

Thomas was correct it was warm, very warm, but we didn't talk much or listen to the rain and the quilt was more comfortable than one could possibly imagine.

Ruben looked with distaste at the body folded inside the trunk. He shuddered to think how ghastly it had been to handle a dead man . . . and inhale the unforgettable stink of death.

Engle hadn't come around until very late in the afternoon, much to Ruben's ire. After looking at the body lounging in the chair the lawyer determined the fewer involved in this problem the better. So it had been decided to put the corpse in a trunk and toss both into the river.

Driving around in a cart with a crate wouldn't draw anyone's attention even after midnight. Engle knew there were quite a few abandon buildings along the waterfront that had a dock built over the river. Shouldn't be any trouble to dispose of the diseased.

Of course, as Ruben predicted this little adventure had proved costly. There was the rent of the cart and horse, purchase the chest, pay Norton Engle's time, and one must not forget Mr. Fiske.

When, not if, he found who had done this to him, they

171

wouldn't breathe the smoke-filled London air for very long. The dead man was one thing . . . the stolen jade another.

Engle said he would start asking about in the morning at several shops specializing in loans to the posh and receiving merchandise to secure such loans. The acceptance of natty stolen goods was often a sideline in those places.

Quality items such as the jade and desk set would fetch a goodly amount and easily identified. Getting anyone to admit a transaction involving the stolen trinkets was more difficult. Difficult but not impossible, offering a healthy bribe to the right people often proved advantageous.

This mess was proving to be expensive, Engle wouldn't investigate for free. Now more than ever he had to acquire the properties on Henrietta Street. There was enough reserve to purchase most of the businesses, but required a quick turn around, buy and sell as soon as possible.

The country house was a drain. Now Roanne insisted upon a conservatory, which would add thousands more to the already bloated price tag. Every time his wife mentioned the word "Smithfield" the name of the monstrosity, he cringed.

Another reason he had grounds for unease was the rumor of a curse as why the place had been left to rot. But if one listened to gossip most of the centuries old castles and manor houses probably had curses, perhaps haunted . . . nothing but rubbish.

He wasn't going to let tittle-tattle bother him . . . but the missing jade pieces had been purchased to bring good luck. Which, of course, had nothing to do with anything . . . stupid superstition.

Engle straightened and rubbed his back; the trunk was heavier than he thought it would be. The scowl on Ruben's face was almost laughable, he looked as though he wanted to kill anyone and everything.

"Not much farther old stick a few more feet and we'll be rid of it."

Ruben didn't offer more than a low growl and a swift glance toward the end of the dock.

"Look on the bright side, it could be freezing cold and slippery as hell." Engle stated.

"Pick up your end and move, I want this over and done."

Engle took a deep breath and grabbed the handle. The men staggered toward the end of the pier, stopped, then shoved the chest into the water.

I examined the card Nyles handed me. "What did this person want with my uncle?"

"Didn't really say, just seemed disappointed Mr. Archer wasn't available and anxious to get in contact with him as soon as possible."

I looked at the card again. "Don't suppose he was someone representing those estate people do you?"

Nyles shrugged his shoulders. "Didn't mention anything about buying or selling, seemed interested in historical books, but not enough to purchase one."

"I'm sure he will call again if the matter is important."

Nyles gestured toward the windows. "We should

change the display soon."

I looked at the exhibit. "Since you mentioned history, perhaps we should do something like that. In fact I'll leave it up to you, just make it eye catching."

Nyles grinned and hurried over to the history section. The young assistant was quite capable of selecting a variety books that might induce people to learn more about the Greeks, Romans, Saxons or whatever.

Uncle Arch had finished his second helping of pie when I entered the dining room.

The afternoon had been quiet so I was upstairs for lunch. The mail was spread over the table. "Anything interesting?"

"A collection of books and manuscripts from a very large estate in Gloucester

is for sale. Might discover a long lost literary work stashed away in a drawer."

I ladled some soup into my bowl. "One can only hope, but I'm sure the family has had experts comb through everything, or this collection can't be sold piecemeal. An entire library is expensive."

"Can't hurt to take a look, doesn't take long to get there by train."

"When is the sale?"

"Three weeks from today, after the wedding and your trip to St. Ives."

"Sounds like an excellent way to spend a day, you should be ready for an outing since you'll be running the shop while I'm gone."

Uncle Arch put aside the brochure and searched through the mail. "Did you see the card from a Norton Engle."

"Yes, do you know this person?"

"Don't recall the name, Nyles said he was rather anxious to meet with me."

I enjoyed another spoonful of vegetable soup. "I'm sure he will come back if the matter is important. The card said he is a lawyer, maybe someone left a fortune to their favorite bookstore owner."

Uncle Arch looked over his glasses. "Don't count on it my dear girl."

I added more salt to my soup. "The meeting with the shop owners is tomorrow night. Did Thomas mention he would like to attend."

"Yes and yes, he wants to see if the other shopkeepers are interested in having metal grates installed over their windows and doors. If so, might be able to get a price reduction."

"Can't hurt to ask, our protective covering wasn't cheap. But neither are windows, doors and the replacement of damaged goods. Might make them feel a bit safer if they decide to have something similar to ours.

೭ಾ

Donnie Brown didn't know what to do about his missing brother. He'd actually been to see the coppers at the station house in Westminster. They had no record of Packy being arrested. So what had happened to him? A person can't just disappear; he had seen his brother taken off with his own eyes.

Then there were the two blokes coming into the Hanged Man asking for Rush and Ellicot. Finn, the barkeep, said he'd give them a message when they came around.

Must be something important no one ventured into the Seven Dials without a good reason. The place was a notorious slum, grimy, stinking, a breeding ground of misery, and more than enough poverty to go around.

He needed money; he'd have to do something about that. No money, no gin or a place to sleep, could be those fellows looking for Ellicot and Rush had some job that needed doing. He knew that Bert and Jingo were hired like that; a short time later they came back with a few coins to squander.

Maybe he'd sidle up to Finn and find out. Might as well be him, he was just as good as them other two.

Donnie was out of breath after his walk. the dock area was silent and a little scary this time of night. But it's where Finn had told him the two blokes said they would wait a couple of nights for Rush and Ellicot if they were interested in a bit of work. He'd just hang around see what was going on.

Even though his skin prickled and his mouth was dry he continued walking toward the third building on the left. Donnie kept looking over his shoulder, his eyes straining to see into the shadows. He'd feel better if Packy was here, not so frightening.

Were those footsteps! Did that shadow move, or was he acting like a ninny? He stopped and placed his back against the rough side of the building and slowly looked around. Nothing moved . . . maybe this wasn't such a good idea! A door opened up ahead, he could see the soft glow from inside the building.

Donnie exhaled several times before making his way to the light. This wasn't so bad, he allowed himself to think of how good a few slugs of gin would taste after he got paid . . . before everything went black.

His hands were numb, the rope cut into his wrists. The blindfold prevented him from actually seeing the men nearby. He was gripped with fear, his head throbbed and the bindings were too tight.

"What is your name?" came a voice close by.

Donnie turned toward the sound, then stuttered. "W-W-Who are you?"

"What is your name?"

"Let me go, I ain't done nofink!"

"I will ask one last time for your name before I cut off a finger, you'll have nine more chances to answer the question."

The frightened man was sweating; and struggling with the ropes without success.

"Donnie Brown . . . names Donnie Brown." He whimpered.

"Any relation to a worm called Packy?"

There was a long moment of silence before Donnie answered. "My brother, he's my brother, I want to see him."

"That might be arranged if you answer a few questions."

"What questions?"

"Who hired you to set fire to the newsagents?"

"What newsagents? Don't know what yur talkin' about!"

"Sorry to hear that Mr. Brown, your brother was very helpful."

"My brother is a stupid sod, talks crazy most times."

The voice went on to explain about the pit, ladder, and the possibility of his return to supply food and water when Donnie was more forthcoming with information.

Thomas was a little disappointed that Ellicot and Rush hadn't accepted the invitation to come to the warehouse for a job. But removing Donnie Brown from causing harm to unsuspecting people wasn't such a bad thing; catching the other two was just a matter of time.

Chapter Sixteen

"Rickards must have really wanted that jade. Didn't quibble much over the price." Rob stated.

Danny continued counting the money as he listened. "You don't look especially knackered after your travels."

"Chepstow isn't a bad place for being in Wales, besides I had a nice compartment on the train, very restful."

"Might be enough here to help the people on Henrietta Street with repairing their property. If not, there is probably more good stuff in old Ruben's house."

Rob drank some brandy and rested his head on the back of the chair. "Rickards mentioned he would be interested in more jade if the quality was as good as what he just bought. He did mention that all the pieces had something to do with luck. Wonder if Hodge is superstitious and feels the need for magic charms or whatever."

Danny secured the money in a large leather wallet and put it in the safe. "Thomas will want to know that bit of information. Could be useful."

"It was a good idea to do business in Wales, the items could easily be traced in London. Those little good luck charms will be on the Continent in a few days, Rickards says the French can't get enough of quality gems and whatnots. Where is everybody?"

"Jennie is with Mrs. Reed in the kitchen, Thomas, Olivia and Mr. Varrus are at a meeting with the property owners. Should be here later this evening.

Rob grinned. "Speaking of Jennie, how is the romance going?"

Danny poured brandy into a glass and sat down. "Simon doesn't say much, but smiles a lot more than usual."

"Jenny is a sweet girl, Simon could do a lot worse."

Danny stretched out his long legs. "Early days, my good man, early days."

The bricks crashed through the milliner's shop windows knocking over the model heads. The beautiful hats fell to the floor; a few were crushed beneath the heavy stones. Before they could access the shop Ellicot and Rush saw two men running in their direction and panicked. The thugs were not foolish enough to hang around waiting to be identified or even caught.

The containers of paint were tossed aside as they turned the corner and headed for the next block. Their pursuers weren't far behind, but not close enough to apprehend the two villains who scampered down an alley and over a fence.

Jingo and Bert continued to run toward Regent's Park, which was a convenient place to hide.

When safely away discussed what had happened. Who were those blokes, they came out of nowhere! This incident should be reported to Mr. Hodge, it could be the shopkeepers had hired guards. Bert doubted ordinary people would have given chase; most citizens were like sheep, easily frightened.

Maybe Donnie and Packy Brown had encountered the same thing, that's why they hadn't seen the brothers loafing around The Hanged Man Pub.

Ellicot had a glimpse of Donnie from a distance seemed like he was avoiding them since the brothers were hired to fit up the newsagents. However, the Brown's were rather gormless and worked cheaply, which meant Ellicot and Rush pocketed the majority of funds.

Mr. Hodge wasn't going to like the news; they could just imagine the prat waffling on and on. After being chased it might be a good idea to stay away from Henrietta Street and even Ruben Hodge for a while. It wasn't his head that would be bashed if caught.

There was a job offer according to Finn, the barkeep, couldn't hurt to do a little work for someone else like they had for Lida Devore.

The property owners meeting ended abruptly when Alec

Gibson slipped into the room to report the damage to Miss Larkin's shop. Simon McQuade was keeping watch outside the milliners.

Mrs. Sullender, her daughter Lucy, and I tried to mollify the shocked Mildred Larkin, while the men inspected the damage.

"The windows are gone but most of the hats are in decent shape." Uncle Arch announced.

Mr. Portman stated they would have the place boarded up in no time.

"Lets get your lovely hats situated and sweep up the glass . . . perhaps you shouldn't stay here tonight." I said.

Miss Larkin studied the ruined storefront then unlocked the door and went inside. She carefully stepped around the broken glass and adjusted the lights.

After looking at the damage, picked up a hat and smoothed out one of the ribbons along the side. "No one is going to drive me out of business, I haven't worked myself into exhaustion for over fifteen years to let some nasty little gannet scare me away. Mr. Brandyce, count me as interested in a grid for the windows after the new replacements arrive."

Thomas smiled slightly then went to speak with Alec and Simon. "What happened?"

Simon leaned in close. "We were at the other end of the block near the bookstore when the windows were smashed. It took a bit to get down the street; by the time we reached the hat shop the two guys were on the move. At least they didn't manage to throw paint all over everything."

"I saw the cans in the street. Miss Larkin could have suffered a greater loss if you hadn't been there. Glad you were able to chase them away."

Alec frowned. "Just sorry we didn't catch the bastards."

"Can't be everywhere at once . . . your main job is to watch the bookshop. If those two mutts are who I think they are, we might have the pleasure of their company soon enough."

Miss Larkin would stay with the Sullender family for the night. We women swept up the glass and settled the hats on the model heads while the men put boards over the broken windows.

Everyone was jittery, but went home feeling a little better after Thomas said there would be people watching through the night.

Thomas and I sat in front of the fire in my room after the incident. I was angry, sad and tired.

"I know there have been men watching the shop, I thank you for that, but guarding the entire block is impossible. It would take a troop of soldiers twenty-four hours a day to protect everyone, not to mention the cost.

"Perhaps I have a troop of soldiers to do just that."

I tapped my fingers on the arm of the chair and smirked just a tad. "You have a contingent of men at your command."

"Perhaps I should explain, it's a rather long story."

"You have me hanging on your every word my darling man."

Thomas sighed and gazed into the fire. "As you already

know I spent time in Afghanistan. I was young, reckless and incredibly stupid. Our unit fought bravely against the so-called rebels, the Afghans, defending their country. Those of us going out each day to engage the enemy soon realized it would be difficult to win, much less survive, unless we did something different.

The old ways of charging up and down waving sabers and shooting from a formation didn't work. The rebels used hit and run tactics and sabotage. The old guard officers complained and huffed about 'these uncivilized people didn't behave like gentlemen and it wasn't the way to fight a war.'

War is a horror, men die or are maimed and crippled in body and mind. War is not a game, you fight to win . . . there are no rules. The British Army eventually succeeded but at a great cost and little to show for the effort.

Some of the men and younger officers wanted to do things differently. It took a deal of convincing but was finally decided that a small group of us would be trained in a different way.

Many of the warlords that controlled the country were paid handsomely to "befriend" the British Army; we were permitted to "join" a contingent of marauders.

There was constant fighting between the scores of petty tyrants, which allowed our little band to learn the techniques of how the rebels fought successfully against a much superior force.

In time we gained a certain expertise. The old rules didn't apply when using ambush and sabotage. Confrontations with large units were avoided, the art of surprise, secrecy and taking advantage of the terrain were utilized. Harass the enemy when they camped at night, retreat, scout and spy, became the best way to fight.

Our little group did survive for the most part, three of the ten were killed, one was wounded but can function with the use of a cane. You know most of them, Rob, Danny, Alec and Simon. Brian Murray and Warren Downing are the other members of the clique," Thomas paused and took a deep breath, then continued.

"We roamed the area around Qandahar in the south. Can't say much for the climate or the terrain, mostly hot, flat and arid, hard packed desert, low brushwood plants and frequent dust storms. Not a place one might wish to holiday or even pay a short visit.

The one bright spot, historically speaking, was the ancient Silk Road caravans had traveled through the area. The towns we frequented still offer the same type of goods for sale. Because of the desire to do business despite never-ending war, our little group formed a partnership with several silk merchants.

I would imagine that many of the more successful dressmakers in London, Manchester and Birmingham buy our goods. The product we provide is a fine silk with unmatched color, especially purple, cerulean blue and vibrant red. We also sell felt cloth, and quality hand knotted silk rugs. Needless to say such merchandise is exquisite, expensive and very profitable."

I didn't know how to respond to what Thomas had confided. The story was like some wild adventure novel. This unconventional man sitting next to me, the one who probably stalked me for months and now never far from my side was a professional . . . what?

It didn't really matter and couldn't get much better. I actually had my own heroic, idealist, defender of the downtrodden . . . determined to be my husband.

I knew he was waiting for me to respond, perhaps become a little emotional about what he had divulged. Maybe offer some profound statement on going off to war. I doubt he expected what was uttered.

"I have always wanted a purple silk scarf, but the color doesn't complement my eyes."

He was silent and looked rather perplexed before making a quick recovery. "Per haps another color, I'm sure I could find something suitable."

We laughed and I took his hand. "Thank you for confiding about your time in Afghanistan. War is not pleasant. Unfortunately, it's often romanticized. There is nothing romantic about killing others or having comrades die . . . its truly dreadful about the friends who didn't come home.

I had wondered how your agency could afford to pay a living wage to so many. The volume of business doesn't match."

"You are very astute . . . for a woman."

I smacked him on the arm for that remark, which made him laugh. "Stop, I take it back. Well . . . the silks, felt cloth and carpets furnish a tidy sum, my little service provides an outlet for excess energy, a chance to engage in more exciting activities."

I could imagine what those activities were, but refrained from asking, he probably wouldn't tell me anyway.

We were silent for a time before I spoke again. "I would like to suggest that we postpone our trip to St. Ives for a while. Leaving would be a mistake right now. After the wedding celebration we can spend the night at one of the posh hotels . . . what do you think?"

Thomas inhaled deeply. "Thought you were wanting to call off the marriage, but since that is not going to happen I agree we shouldn't leave. A night at Claridge's Hotel will be fine, we can go to St.Ives later."

"Excellent idea . . . so you have a store that sells wonderful silk fabrics."

"Not really a store, more like a warehouse."

"Who runs it for you?"

"A member of our little troop. Warren Downing, the one who was injured. He still manages to get around fairly well with a cane."

"So, you all share in the profits?"

"We do, Warren is paid extra since he manages the day to day operation."

"I would love to see it some time, especially the carpets."

"I'll be happy to show you around, introduce you to Warren."

We sat in quiet contemplation and watched the flames change color. "Thomas what are we going to do, every one is so sick of being afraid and waiting for the next attack."

He raised my hand to his lips. "I see no harm in letting

you know what we have planned, it should prove entertaining, and truly satisfying to us . . . not so much for Ruben Hodge."

Alec Gibson was in his usual place on the sofa. He stopped reading when a man entered the shop and approached the counter.

"May I help you?" I inquired.

The fellow smiled and offered his card. "I was here recently to see Mr. Varrus, is it possible to speak with him?"

I examined the card, then looked carefully at the gentleman. "My uncle is upstairs, may I enquire why you wish to see him?"

"It's rather involved, perhaps I should be discussing this with Mr. Varrus, he might find the subject interesting."

The man was being deliberately vague, probably because I was an empty-headed woman. I smiled sweetly and resisted fluttering my eyelashes. "If you speak in short sentences and repeat important topics I'll try and remember to tell my uncle why you are here."

Norton Engle furrowed his brow and gazed intently at my face, he looked somewhat confused. "Ah . . . yes . . . ah, it has to do with the stones he purchased some time ago."

Now what motivated a lawyer to have an interested in the stones from Jarrow Abbey? I was keen to find the reason. "Please feel free to look around while you wait Mr. Engle."

I'd send Nyles to fetch Uncle Arch; I didn't want to take this stranger upstairs. So far I hadn't detected anything untoward, but I was very curious about the visit.

Alec had moved off the sofa to observe Mr. Engle as he

examined the books on the display table. I waited near by for my uncle.

A few minutes later Uncle Arch lumbered slowly down the stairs followed by Nyles.

I spoke softly. "The gentleman over by the display table is Norton Engle, the lawyer who came in earlier. For some reason he would like to discuss the Hartelpool stones."

Uncle Arch scratched his chin. "Humm . . . Hartelpool!

My uncle walked over to the lawyer. "Mr. Engle, you wanted to speak with me in regards to the Abbey Stones?" I sidled closer to listen.

The man smiled, exuding an abundance of charm. "Indeed Mr. Varrus, it has come to my attention that you purchased some antiquities. Artifacts that could be of interest to academics, or those like me, with a passion for England's rich history."

Not entirely true statement. Mr. Engle wasn't much interested in 'England's rich history'. I looked at my uncle and slightly shook my head to indicate a falsehood.

"May I inquire how you know of this purchase?"

"Oh, my . . . I should have mentioned that I represent the nephew of the person who recently expired, the former owner of the estate where the artifacts were bought. The stones were a topic of conversation and since I'm terribly eager about such things wanted to know more."

The man was no more eager about historical things than I am about shopping and dealing with crowds. "Have you come to make an offer on the stones Mr. Engle?" I asked.

"Oh dear me no. But I'm intrigued about the inscription

written all those many hundreds of years ago. As I understand the writing is Old English and Latin?"

"Yes, a mixture of both and difficult to read because of
the condition . . . fragments in some places." Uncle Arch
explained.

"My friend, Mr. Duncan, the nephew of the former
owner said he had found a partial rendering in his relatives
notes. Something about a Bible that was written over a thousand years ago."

"My uncle has had difficulty in translating all the script,
too much damage. I doubt if anything more can be deci-
phered." I intruded.

Mr. Engle narrowed his eyes slightly. "Would it be possible to see the stones?"

I leaned against the counter and tried to look casual.
"Been packed away, they were taking up needed storage
space."

His smile was no longer charming, more forced. "Do
you think there might be something of historical value revealed in the scribbles? Valuable in an antiquarian sense of
course?"

Uncle Arch shook his head slowly. "No nothing at all.
Just names of religious places that were important a thousand years ago . . . now heaps of rubble."

Chapter Seventeen

Where the hell were those idiots? Ruben had sent several notes to Ellicot and Rush. He knew they couldn't read but the barkeep in that god-forsaken hole of a pub

had a basic knowledge of the written word.

Mr. Fiske wasn't fond of venturing into the Seven Dials area, who could blame him, the place was a sewer. Making one's way during the day was much safer; no one in their right mind went at night. But Ruben did offer an incentive to his assistant, he could leave early on Wednesday . . . a loss of a few hours of Fisk's time was better than going himself.

If he didn't hear from those dolts by later this afternoon he would find others eager to take his money. There was the rough element frequenting the boxing exhibitions willing to knock a few heads or bust up a place for a price.

That was where he had found Spanish. Ruben shuddered a little at the thought of maneuvering his body into the trunk.

He reflected upon the chair in his office that had been replaced. Sitting on something a dead man had sprawled upon was revolting.

Time was money and he couldn't afford to waste either. He had investors wanting results. Ruben had refrained from setting fire to the places on Henrietta Street because of the danger to the adjacent Oxford Street stores. These were the merchants who wanted to expand across the alley to the buildings on Henrietta Street.

Once a fire got out of control it could spread and consume everything in its path, fire wasn't particular as to what it destroyed.

George Clegg, his estate agent, would be sent around again to see if the property owners were more in the mood to sell, there had been several more places that experienced problems. The replacement of windows and damaged goods wasn't cheap; and of course fear was a main ingredient in convincing people to listen to reason.

He would be off to one of his clubs in a few hours; and could usually find boxing enthusiasts wandering about, they always knew when and where a match was to take place.

"I have a appointment to see your friend Cecily Lydstrom about her collection of old books and manuscripts." Uncle Arch said between bites of roast pork.

Thomas looked somewhat fuddled. "Cecily Lydstrom . . . oh yes, of course. So you are going to do what exactly?"

"I've decided to help with putting things in order, might be fun."

"I thought you were going to suggest someone, not do it yourself." I questioned.

"The more I thought about it the more interested I became."

"What about Hartlepool?"

My uncle speared a piece of carrot and waved it around. "Hartlepool isn't going anywhere and I'm rather tired of looking for relics right now. There are just so many finger or toe bones, severed heads, nails from Jesus' crucifixion, ashes, sacred vessels and alter linen one can stand."

I couldn't help but laugh at that statement. Then remembered to tell Thomas about Mr. Engle, the lawyer, who visited the shop.

The look on his face was puzzling. "Tell me more about this visit," he said in a deceptively calm voice.

After our explanation, Thomas remained silent for a few moments. "This is not the first time the gentleman has come to my attention. In fact one of my clients had a concern about the man.

I know lawyer Engle has a questionable reputation. As you mentioned Olivia, I too am curious about his interest in the writing on the stones. Archer, it was quick thinking not to mention that you translated the entire message. Mr. Engle seems to be fishing for information and I doubt you have seen the last of this person."

Wonderful, how absolutely wonderful! Now there was something more to add to my uneasiness. I should be thinking about my wedding, but no . . . right now getting married was relegated to an afterthought.

I could say my "I do's" in between crazy people wanting to bludgeon me into oblivion, vandalize the store, and trying to uncover the whereabouts of a long lost book. Well twaddle that, I needed a drink, make it three or four drinks!

I pushed my plate aside, slowly levered myself from the chair and tossed the napkin into the air and watched it float to the floor. Uncle Arch stopped eating; Thomas almost knocked over his chair trying to stand. "What's wrong!"

"Wrong, what could possibly be wrong, everything is bloody marvelous!" and marched out of the dining room. But not before snatching the decanter of brandy and a glass.

I cast more coal into the fire and viciously stabbed the poker about to encourage the flames to burn higher. The decanter of brandy had decreased somewhat in quantity and sat on the small side table beside my now empty glass.

There was no excuse for my behavior Thomas and Uncle Arch had done nothing wrong. I'd apologize in the morning, right now I wanted to forget about vile, greedy people and let my mind drift away on a brandy soaked cloud.

A soft tap on the door caused me to open my eyes. I looked at the mantle clock it had been an hour or more since I stomped out of the dining room. "Olivia . . . are you all right?" Uncle Arch called through the door.

I thought about ignoring him but really shouldn't be so rotten. "I'm fine, just tired, please don't worry, tomorrow I will be ready to face the world again. My behavior was appalling, I apologize."

"Can't say I blame you, we have all been upset, get some rest."

"I will . . . good night,"

I poured a generous amount of the caramel colored liquid into my glass and sipped it slowly, feeling the slight burn as the brandy passed over my tongue. I wondered where Thomas was . . . probably having second or maybe third thoughts about why he had become involved with a mad woman. There was still time to run like hell and not look back. Perhaps that's what I should do, run like hell . . . and where would I run to exactly!

A tropical island might be just the place, I could sit by the ocean in the sun, consume fish and coconuts, although I don't especially care for fish and never encountered a coconut.

There must be something else to eat on a tropical island . . . fruit, yes, fruit of some kind.

"How is the brandy?" a disembodied voice asked.

I was a little surprised that I didn't feel his approach, but considering my state of mind, understandable. "I'm going to a tropical island and eat fruit."

Thomas examined the contents of the crystal container. "May I join you?"

I squinted my eyes and gnawed on my bottom lip. "Do you really want to go with me to the tropical island?"

"Of course, but I meant I'd join you in a drink."

"How long will it take to sail to an island?"

Thomas picked up my glass and took a sip. "Depends on where, the Caribbean is closer than the South Seas."

"Do you think we will see a mermaid, I've read about sailors pursuing mermaids. If such a creature appeared before your very eyes would you be tempted?"

Thomas sipped a little more brandy. "Not really, couldn't hold a candle to someone else I know. Besides mermaids probably don't read minds."

"I can't read minds, just tend to know how a person feels sometimes . . . maybe."

"And how do I feel?"

I studied his face carefully. "Can't tell right at this moment you always try to hide what is going on in that devious mind of yours."

A slight smile briefly appeared on his handsome face. "Devious! Never!"

I reached for the glass, which seemed to be eluding me for some reason. "I have to admit you are skillful in the use of underhanded tactics . . . good, but not that good dear boy."

"You think you know me so well?"

I shrugged. "No . . . but I do know me very well. Right now you are trying to decide what to do with your inebriated fiancé. Let's see . . . humm, toss me in a bath of cold water, pour gallons of coffee down my throat or let me drink a few more glasses of wine, rum or whatever is in that lovely cut glass bottle."

"None of the above, how about I carry you to bed, curl up beside you as you fall asleep in my arms."

I closed my eyes and inhaled deeply. "Safe and warm,

no bad men allowed."

Thomas moved closer and brushed his fingers through my hair. "No bad men allowed . . . promise."

Thomas left the sleeping Olivia and headed downstairs and out of the house to Victoria Station. Danny and Rob would be waiting for him in Croydon if things went according to plan. The train ride would only take a half hour. Ruben Hodge's country house was another mile and a half from the last terminal.

Danny had been in Croydon since yesterday to reconnoiter and secure horses at a local stable; it wouldn't take long to cover the distance from station to country estate. The men carried all the supplies needed in three kit bags.

Thomas had been to the estate several times. It was surprisingly easy to find information about who lived on the grounds and if someone such as a caretaker was close by.

It was convenient that the watchperson lived a short distance from the house. Thomas had even been given a tour of the place by the man in charge of the renovations, didn't question the presence of an insurance agent named Albion Pertwee from Thames River Insurance.

Getting through the side door was child's play. The men surveyed the dining room piled with lumber and the remains of shredded wallpaper scattered over the floor. Most of the other rooms were in a similar condition, scaffolding, scraps of wood and a plethora of sawdust conveniently heaped in corners.

All it would take for the place to go up in flames was a spark, which the men would gladly provide. Within fifteen minutes each room glowed with a small flame, which would rapidly become an inferno.

The friends watched from a distance to make sure the whole structure was engulfed before riding away. Thomas doubted Hodge had bothered to insure the place because of the condition . . . not a livable state. Nevertheless the fire would be costly and a drain upon resources.

After returning the horses they would catch the early train and be back in London for a late breakfast.

Norton Engle did not believe Archer Varrus or his contentious niece. Their story wasn't the least bit convincing, the old goat had probably translated the writing on the stones immediately after purchase.

Engle doubted whatever was written was anything like a treasure map, but the information might lead to something of value. So there lay the problem, how to get his hands on such a rendering. It wasn't likely he'd be invited into the old man's study and the shop was fairly busy during the day, so sneaking in unnoticed wasn't an option.

At night the place was secured from being burgled by that metal screen contraption. The back door might be easier, worth a try, he knew just the right fellow.

Unfortunately he didn't know what to look for or where such a document might be kept, so he would have to give this matter some more thought. Right now he had an appointment with another family, desperate to learn more about their estranged relative.

His friend, Carrie Carter, was invaluable in acting the

part of a long missing female child or grandchild. She looked so young and innocent and had the ability to become whomever the foolish relatives wanted her to be. Carrie didn't do this fine job of acting for free; she didn't do anything from the kindness of her heart.

In a few more days he would contact Mrs. Lydstrom again see if she had made a decision about her granddaughter and hopefully offer a goodly amount for him to investigate further.

Archer Varrus was in the process of separating the large quantity of papers, books, fragments of old documents and manuscripts into something manageable. Mrs. Lydstrom did have a journal her husband had kept for his acquisitions. At first the notations had been up to date, but then became more haphazard, but it was somewhat helpful and a place to start.

The problem was to find what or where individual leaves had come from. He was separating the different languages, a Greek medical text fragment, several pages of a Greek adventure story, and a poem about one of the gods.

Another pile contained a few pages in Latin devoted to the lives of Christian Saints. A 13th century Byzantine prayer book, a liturgical text from the 11th century, and an illuminated page of flowering flora from an herbal guide to medicinal plants.

The 8th century Latin insular script style pioneered by monks in Ireland, he found especially interesting. Couldn't refrain from pouring over a beautiful copy of *The Gospel of John* duplicated from a manuscript written about 125 A.D.

Archer removed his glasses and rubbed his eyes. He should stretch his legs, his back hurt from hunching his shoulders for such a long period. He was also getting hungry. Mrs. Lydstrom had told him to ring if he required anything.

When the maid appeared he told her he was leaving for the day and to make sure nothing was disturbed on the table. He had carefully divided the many stacks of old literary works by language, Greek, Latin and English.

He would return the day after tomorrow and continue trying to make heads or tails of a wonderful, but confused mass of antiquity.

Archer had left Nyles to handle the shop. When he departed after breakfast Olivia was still asleep, which was good, she obviously needed the rest. First he would check on Nyles, then go to Thomas's place if Olivia wasn't at the store.

His niece was the most important thing in his life. She had brought joy to his solitary existence from the moment he fetched her from his brother's house of sorrow. The five year old seemed to know her parents were never coming back and her world was to change forever.

The child asked questions about everything, her mind was quick; he developed the habit to look for answers to her questions in the wonderful supply of books at the shop.

"Why is the sea salty, where does the wind come from, why do people die, why are people's eyes different colors, were just a smattering of questions asked.

As for toys . . . forget dolls, they were politely accepted

and put away in the chest at the foot of her bed. Hoops, puzzles, wooden building blocks, chess and books occupied her time.

He had been quite taken aback when the girl announced that certain people were lying or not to be trusted. An example being a salesman touting the quality of his leather bound volumes. The sample he presented was as described, but on closer inspection the bindings were inferior and the book would soon fall apart.

The "nice" men who were collecting donations for the poor at Christmas had her tugging on his coat as she whispered not to trust their sad story.

A few customers were intent on something other than the selection of books; more often than not the aim was to steal. It was probably disconcerting for the thief to have a youngster following him or her around the store, the startling golden eyes observing their every move.

Far from being upset about this unusual ability Archer was enthralled and even encouraged the girl. He guessed both of them were different than most . . . he liked the diversity.

Just as Olivia's world had changed when her parents died, his world would be different after the wedding. He was thankful Thomas was such a worthy companion for the girl, even though the man was an enigma. At least he wasn't as daft as a donkey nattering about the place.

As long as Olivia was happy he would be satisfied. They would discuss the living arrangements after the wedding and when the damn underhanded criminal attacks came to an end.

Archer strolled into the shop. Off to the side Simon McQuade was leaning against the stair rail talking to Jennie. Nyles was helping a customer and Olivia sat at the desk looking through some papers.

"Good afternoon my dear, how are you feeling?"

I inhaled deeply, smiled sweetly despite a thumping headache, and turned to greet my uncle. "I am well, thank you. The sun is shining, breeze is calm and the mail sorted."

"Anything important requiring immediate attention?"

"Nothing, not even a mysterious, unsigned, invitation to dinner somewhere expensive."

Uncle Arch sighed. "That is disappointing."

Chapter Eighteen

Roanne Hodge couldn't hold back the tears any longer. She had remained stoic while listening to the notification. Smithfield, the country house, had been damaged by fire according to the telegram.

Ruben tried with little success to console the distraught woman. Eventually he calmed his wife with assurances he would take the next available train and find how much harm the house had sustained.

A few hours later he stood before the skeletal remains of an expensive pile of ash. The foreman and several workers strolled around with shovels and made half-hearted attempts at tossing dirt over places that still smoldered.

No one could explain what had happened, might have been a match from a careless worker, a jolt of lightening from the summer storms that appeared frequently, maybe a buildup of sawdust that sometimes burst into flames.

The muttered remark from the caretaker about the mournful baying of a dog before the fire was a rather nervous reference to the curse. A dog howling was always detected before something bad happened at the manor house, according to the locals.

The incompetent caretaker was a superstitious fool and should be fired. But Ruben had had difficulty finding this pathetic sod in the first place, plus the man lived near by and was only paid a few shillings a month. To be honest what could anyone have done to put out flames in such a large place so far away from town and a fire brigade?

Ruben was not especially sad about the fire, he had no desire to live, even part time, in the country, it would probably drive him mad. What did distress him was the huge amount of money invested with nothing to show for such expenditures. The only value left was in the land, which, if sold might pay off a portion of the loan.

He had taken a short-term debenture to cover the purchase and start on the renovations. His reserves, which came from investors, were for buying the Henrietta Street properties.

He only half listened as the builder twittered on about the loss of his scaffolding and pieces of equipment left inside the house. As far as Ruben was concerned the fellow could go hang himself if he thought he was going to be reimbursed for anything.

Ruben wandered around the remains and every so often kicked at a ruined piece of slate from the expensive roof, or a chunk of stone that had cracked from the excessive heat of the fire.

His head was starting to ache. Letting his temper get out of control wouldn't do anything but make the throb worse. My god, the ignorant sod kept warbling on about the curse, bad luck, and giant dogs lurking in the dark. There was probably a lady in white or a black mist too . . . bastard!

During the trip back to London he thought about his wife. He didn't like Roanne to be upset it always proved costly; when he left she was in a terrible state.

Perhaps he might convince her that a country house wasn't a good idea. Right now he couldn't afford to rebuild anyway, but Roanne didn't have much concept of money, she just enjoyed spending it.

She always exceeded her clothes allowance and almost every new gown needed jewelry, hats and shoes to go along with it. Perfume, flowers for each room in the house, and the new carriage, a bargain, according to her, at just sixty pounds was just a sample of her extravagances.

Pin money for her personal use on small items was gone in a matter of days instead of a month. The several pounds magically disappeared with little or nothing to show for it. It was maddening. He was beginning to regret the decision to marry, but the woman was a beauty and had many social connections. But he must curb her extravagant expenditures.

If Clegg were unsuccessful in his attempts to deal with the property owners in the coming days, he would be forced to employ drastic methods. Might even consider fire, as destructive as it was . . . things were getting somewhat urgent.

Ruben massaged his temple as he waited for a cab to take him from the station to his residence. He had to tell Roanne the bad news and try to alleviate her sorrow about Smithfield. Hopefully after that he could take some tonic for his head and rest.

❦

I smiled, tomorrow was my wedding and nothing was going to stop me, or rather us, from celebrating the occasion. The dress was hanging in the wardrobe, Mrs Reed and her daughters were busy in the kitchen at the house in Mayfair preparing for the party afterwards.

Thomas was hanging about, getting underfoot and being teased by his friends. Most of the neighbors had dropped in at some point during the day to wish me joy and happiness.

The shop would be closed tomorrow, the store should be safe enough especially with the new iron banded door in the back and the heavy bar that slotted into place.

Thomas had insisted this be done to make sure no housebreaker could get inside even if such a person managed to finagle the lock open. The door wouldn't budge when the inside bar was secured.

I was putting one of the display cases together. Different shapes and sizes of bottles contained an assortment of colored water placed on stands of varying heights. The chemists had provided wonderful colors like carmoisine red,

Prussian blue, saffron, Indigo carmine, violet, fast green and elderberry juice purple.

The theme was mysteries that featured poison to commit a foul deed. Stories about Mary Ann Cotton a mass murderess, Christina Edwards, Dr. Pritchard and several more villains who resorted to poison to do away with husbands, wives, and others who got in the path of these killers.

I found that sensationalism was of great interest to customers and such a colorful display should entice people to come inside to browse and purchase.

After arraigning a few more books I glanced through the window and watched Mr. Clegg, that estate agent person, stroll past. He stopped to look at the colorful bottles, then caught sight of me and hurried away. The man hadn't bothered us since the encounter with Thomas, but I had seen him stopping in other places.

Now he was back and it was troubling. The fellow wasn't troubling; it was who he represented that made me anxious.

I called Simon over. "See that man over there," and pointed to the left.

Simon went to the door and peered out. "The short, thin fellow?"

"Yes, would it be possible to observe him for a while?"

"I'll nip across the street, one of the boys will be in the office. Shouldn't be too difficult to have one of them see what this chap is doing and follow his movements.

"Thank you, Simon . . . and thank you and the others for helping. I know it's rather boring hanging about."

He chuckled. "Can't think of a better place to catch up on my reading, comfortable surroundings, great company and delicious food. Better get cracking and find Alec or Rob while the little bloke is in the stationary shop."

I sensed in the few moments Mr. Clegg had stared at me through the window that something was different, and not in a good way different. But refused to become carried away, for the time being I'd clear my mind of everything except finishing out the day, going to Thomas's house and preparing for tomorrow.

The look on his face was worth the effort. Thomas grasped my hand and escorted me down the last few steps.

His eyes traveled from my head down to my toes. With Jennie's help, part of my hair was swept up on top of my head and held fast by silver combs, the rest cascaded down the back in a mass of curls.

I rarely used cosmetics but this was a special occasion. I had carefully applied Venetian talc, tinted a very pale pink, over my face to produce a slight blush. Elderberry juice to create a fine line under the eyes and brushed across brows, a smattering of charcoal dust on my lashes and a tiny bit of beetroot to add color to cheeks and lips. One had to admit the look was quite nice, and from the way Thomas stared, and grinned, he thought so too.

"You are the most beautiful woman in the entire world, he said softly. "Venus and Helen of Troy would be envious."

"I don't think I would like to be on the bad side of either of those two women, they were not the most forgiving females . . . or so I've read."

"Nevertheless, you are lovely."

I brushed my lips against his. "Shall we go?"

The ceremony was brief and witnessed by Uncle Arch, Rob, Danny, Jennie and Nyles. If one actually thought about it . . . rather a waste of money to have such a beautiful gown but I wasn't going to complain.

Most of the friends and neighbors from Henrietta Street were in attendance for the lavish and bountiful buffet. A few hours later Thomas and I set off for the hotel and our one-day honeymoon.

As we crossed the lobby of Clairidge's, there was a sign indicating where a display of jewelry was on exhibit.

"Wonder what that is all about?" Thomas mused.

"This little affair has been advertised in the papers for some time. The Maharaja of Varanasi is showing a rather large collection of jewelry, which can be purchased for staggering amounts. I'd love to see what is being offered, might find a lovely trinket for a mere trifle."

Thomas guided me toward the stairs. "I'd love to see what you have to offer, my darling wife."

I couldn't help but giggle. "Why Mr. Brandyce you are positively leering!"

"I never leer Mrs. Brandyce, my expression might be considered suggestive with a touch of eagerness and heartfelt devotion."

"In that case we must sally forth and elevate such feelings of eagerness but retain the heartfelt devotion."

Thomas chortled and tried not to garner attention from other people on the stairs. We quickly found our room and stood looking at the gold lettering on the door. *Empress Eugenie Suite*.

"Our luggage was supposed to be delivered this morning and Rob picked up the key so we wouldn't have to deal with an overly helpful porter," Thomas stated and unlocked the door.

The room was magnificent, delicate silks and embroidered brocades, velvet and tasseled detailing in a palette of pink, grey and gold. The gold embroidered headboard was striking, as were the chandeliers of gold with crystal droplets.

When I stopped gawking in amazement and flopped on the bed, announced. "I guess this will just have to do, after all it's only for one night."

Later that evening we ambled down to the dining room for dinner then decided to have a look at the Maharaja's jewelry collection. An ornate reception area had been selected for the exhibition.

There were glass cases spread about the room. Not far away from the cabinets were massive men with turbans who looked rather formidable. One couldn't help notice the large knives tucked through the turquoise sashes around their waist.

People oohed and aahed at each case. "The jewels must be grand," I whispered.

We moved slowly toward the first display. Oh my goodness, a multiple strand necklace of diamonds and sapphires glittered on a blue velvet cloth. On each side of the necklace were earrings, rings and bracelets of the same beautiful stones.

The next case held emeralds and pear-shaped diamonds; the collection featured pendants, brooches, several necklaces, bracelets, and large solitaire diamond and emerald rings.

The third glass enclosure was devoted to diamonds and pearls. Ropes of pearls that could easily wind around a person's neck three or four times were draped over the black silk cloth. "What do you think the Maharaja is asking for those?" I said.

Thomas shook his head and smirked. "Probably more than I have in my pocket."

A moment later Thomas bent close and whispered. "We need to move over there," and guided me quickly to the other side of the room.

He stood in front of me rather like a shield. "What's happening?" I asked quietly.

Thomas turned slightly to look over his shoulder. "If you casually peek around and direct your gaze to the couple at the fourth cabinet you will see Ruben Hodge and wife."

I carefully did as Thomas requested. Mr. Hodge was the same man who came into the shop; his wife was a dark-haired beauty. They were both dressed to make an impression, which they seem to be doing. Someone had been summoned to discuss whatever the Hodges wanted to enquire about.

"Wonder what is going on over there. Mrs. Hodge seems adamant about something . . . and why are we hiding?"

"I think its better that old Ruben doesn't recognize you

as being from the bookstore."

"Why not, he probably wouldn't remember me anyway."

"Because I don't want him anywhere near you, and don't count on him not remembering who you are. Better to be safe and stay out of his sight."

I continued to watch surreptitiously as the two people conversed with the gentleman at the display case. Then quickly moved back behind Thomas. "The room is beginning to get crowded with people we don't want to meet."

Thomas looked at me. "What are you talking about?"

"Mr. and Mrs. Hodge have been joined by our lawyer friend, Mr. Norton Engle. Perhaps we should remove ourselves as unobtrusively as possible, I wouldn't be surprised to see that Clegg person creeping around too."

The reception room was moderately full of people so we managed to leave without drawing any attention. Thomas and I returned to our room and decided to settle in for the night, there was still a bottle of champagne to open, and I wanted to forget about Hodge, Engle and Clegg for a while longer.

Our wedding day and night had been glorious, one couldn't have asked for anything better . . . well, possibly a few more days to be alone would have been nice, but there was time for all that later.

Before we left the hotel I wanted to see the rest of the jewelry collection and especially the cabinet that the Hodges were interested in. The fourth glass case contained diamonds and rubies, a breathtaking array of gemstones and gold.

Something in that case had attracted their attention, which was understandable; such a compilation of ornamentation was amazing and rare.

Even though I wasn't wild about jewelry I was dazzled by the amount of beautiful items on display and the cost of such baubles, monumental.

There had been a lovely trinket that caught my eye. A brooch, made of pink and white diamonds, the delicate birds sat on a gold branch looking at each other. One could almost believe they would burst into song . . . charming and sweet and completely unaffordable . . . oh well.

Thomas could have stayed with Olivia in their opulent room for weeks or months but doubted he could convince his wife of such an idea. He couldn't isolate her from the world even though he was tempted to do just that.

Seeing Ruben Hodge at the hotel made his blood boil. The reason he didn't want Olivia to be seen in his company was if at some point he was caught doing the things he was determined to do, Olivia would never be associated with anything nefarious.

His activities would increase against Mr. Hodge and his associates. In fact, Rob and Danny had been busy last night in Ruben's office. If everything went according to plan the bastard would be unpleasantly surprised at what awaited.

Thomas suppressed a laugh when he thought about it. It had taken his abettor a few days to acquire the many embellishments needed to decorate the grand office in such an artful manner.

Why this décor might become all the rage to those with

an eye for a different kind of aesthetic sense, and the nose too.

Wilfred Fiske had been at his desk outside his employer's office for at least a half hour. He had carefully arranged the papers in proper order, filled the ink well, and tidied up the drawer containing pens and nibs.

Fiske separated the metal nibs into either broad or pointed in the small containers in the drawer. The broad nibs for thick strokes, pointed for the finest hairline strokes, which created English Roundhand, Copperplate, or Spencerian script.

Wilfred used mostly Spencerian Script for business correspondence but enjoyed the English Roundhand to form an open flowing type of writing. He had copied favorite poems in this form, which were hidden away in box at his flat.

He closed the desk drawer, eased out of the chair and walked around the outer office. Where was the faint unpleasant odor coming from?

Mr. Fiske wouldn't risk his job of entering Mr. Hodge's office. It was kept locked since the theft of his boss's jade and the . . . ah other unmentionable item had been discovered. No, he would look through the correspondence on his desk and make sure the ledger was up to date.

Chapter Nineteen

It was a bad idea, a really bad idea, but Ruben wanted them as much as his wife. He had convinced himself the jewels were to console Roanne for the loss of the country house, and the large expenditure would be quickly repaid.

One had to admit the ruby earrings were breathtaking. The gemstones large and blood red had an inclusion that formed a star. Inclusions usually made gems less valuable but not in this case. The star configuration was exceedingly rare and increased the value of the stone.

Roanne was wildly happy and talking non-stop about

ordering a new red gown to show off her latest acquisition. Hopefully everything would be ready in time for the dinner party at "Bunty's."

Ruben suffered Bunty and detested her condescending husband. But it might be worthwhile to have the earrings displayed and casually let slip the cost of such trinkets. He probably wouldn't have to do it himself, Roanne would tell Bunty and in a matter of seconds all of London would know.

The reserve account would be paid back as soon as possible, Clegg was making progress; at least the absentee owners of three properties were ready to sell. They were uneasy about the on-going problems in the area. There were adequate funds to cover such an expense.

Hodge would have Mr. Fiske prepare more letters, advising of this new development and strongly urge the other business owners to do the same.

He climbed the stairs to his office, his assistant stopped writing when Ruben arrived at the desk. "Come inside, I have letters to draft."

'Yes, Mr. Hodge, I'll be right in after I gather my materials."

Ruben unlocked the office door and strode inside. "My god . . . Fiske, what the hell . . . *FISKE*! Came a horrified screech.

The room was covered in rats . . . dead and dying rats in various stages of decay. The desk, furniture, bookcases, and carpet were garbed with vermin that oozed blood, entrails and maggots.

Fiske added to the revolting scene by spewing his

breakfast over the floor and dashing outside to get away from the stench and gore.

Ruben could only stand in place, look around the room in shock and grope for his handkerchief to press against his nose and mouth. Then he stumbled out, slammed the door shut and locked it with slightly trembling hands.

Who was doing this to him? Why was it happening! He couldn't think of anyone at the moment. Sure . . . he had enemies, who didn't. Of course his business practices were not especially nice, but nice didn't get results, and results were what mattered.

The more he thought the more it didn't make sense. He had to clear his mind and not panic, it wouldn't help to panic. Just take a deep breath and get control of the situation.

His assistant sat shaking behind the desk, his face pale, eyes darting about wildly.

Ruben leaned against the wall and mopped his forehead with the handkerchief

"Find someone to clean this mess and have the office cleared of everything."

Fiske's voice cracked in reply. "Yes Sir . . . yes Mr. Hodge, where do you want the furniture delivered?"

"Dump it all in the river, or burn it, I don't care, just as long as I never see it again, do you understand . . . *GET RID OF IT!*"

Danny sprawled on the leather sofa in the Privatus office. "What was the final settlement to old Wiggins?"

"Wiggins isn't that old, he just looks that way probably

due to his occupation. Killing or trapping vermin all day ages a man. Seventy-five rats came to a little over five shillings," replied Rob.

"Highway robbery! The old git must be laughing up his sleeve at our expense," Danny grumbled.

Rob grinned. "Don't really care, Hodge paid for those odious critters anyway.

All the expensive items such as the silver letter opener, gold pen set, a rather nice pair of enameled cufflinks, and the twenty or so pounds in the "hidden" compartment of the desk was worth the effort."

Danny stifled a yawn. "Thomas wants Mr. Varrus to deliver the money received from our devious activities to each business owner that sustained damage. Some story about an anonymous humanitarian should be good enough. I'm sure the folks won't quibble about where the funds come from anyway."

Rob looked out the window at the shops across the street. "These forays at night make me tired, and rats, even dead ones make me itch, despite a long bath."

Danny stretched out his legs. "If I were Ruben Hodge, I'd hire a guard, make that two or three guards, to patrol my place of business. Another expense for nothing, because it's doubtful there will be anymore nocturnal visits for a while, not much left to steal anyway.

Oh, by the way, Brian Murray has been gathering information for Thomas at his clubs. Don't have all the details, but should be something fun," he mused.

"Warren Downing mentioned that Brian might be settling down, behaving himself and acquiring a wife," said Rob with a grin.

"The Honorable Brian Murray settling down . . . not likely!"

Rob smirked. "His father, the Earl of Dunmore, would be grateful if such a thing were to happen. Never can tell, his brother isn't in the best of health, so Brian could end up with everything . . . happens all the time with second sons."

"Imagine "Dumpty Murray" a flipping Scottish Lord!" snickered Danny.

"I can see him now, lurching down the church steps, falling into the large wrought iron candle holders and setting his bride's lace train on fire," Rob chortled.

"One must admit he's poetry in motion astride a horse and one of the best long range shooters around, might be a tad better than Thomas."

"And a disaster at the dinner table or sitting on a chair, seems to fall out of them on a regular basis, probably because furniture is stationary, unlike a galloping horse." Danny added.

Norton Engle sat patiently in the drawing room. Mrs. Lydstrom was probably making him wait deliberately. He had found allowing a person to bide one's time was advantageous, made folks anxious and inclined to do business.

"Good afternoon Mr. Engle," came the cultured voice. "Your note said you had more information regarding this mysterious granddaughter."

The lawyer stood as Cecily Lydstrom entered the room.

"Not exactly more information, I confess having a desire to know if you have made a decision about wanting my services."

The lady seated herself in the rose colored, overstuffed chair. 'I'm still considering your offer; such an undertaking shouldn't be taken lightly. The possibility of opening old wounds and the consequences that might develop could prove unfortunate.

You have yet to mention the fee for this endeavor."

Engle folded his hands and smiled. "Of course there will be expenses, travel, food, lodging and my time. Tracing the coming and goings of people can be tedious, as well as the examination of church records and archives," he said smoothly.

"Tell me, Mr. Engle how did you come upon this information in the first place?"

"It is part of my business to locate people. I advertise in several newspapers about finding missing loved ones, thus a person will contact me to help with inquiries. The opposite also happens; I read the personal columns and take note of those who are seeking lost relatives or friends."

A servant appeared in the doorway. "Excuse me madam, Mr. Varrus is about to leave and would like to speak with you for a moment."

"Thank you, Letty, ask him to wait in the library, I'll be there shortly. Before you go, please show Mr. Engle out." The lady stood and grasped her cane.

"I still haven't made up my mind, but will ponder your offer."

Outside the gates of the Lydstrom place, the lawyer turned to look at the massive house. He wondered what Archer Varrus was doing there and quite relieved the two hadn't met in the hallway or foyer. He didn't think such an encounter would be prudent.

His visit with the lady didn't go very well, but sure the old bat was interested in his story of a grandchild, which might lead to finding the missing daughter. He would give it some more time, maybe come up with a document of some kind to help the woman make a favorable decision.

He still hadn't given up on the idea of gaining access to whatever Archer Varrus had learned from the stones, he was sure the man had important information. If Mr. Varrus and his perverse niece didn't want to collaborate, maybe one of the bookstore employees would.

There was that assistant fellow. It shouldn't be difficult to convince him to divulge whatever there was to be uncovered. Engle doubted the young man earned much, the promise of extra funds should be gratefully accepted . . . everyone had a price.

⁓

Thomas read through the letter he had spent considerable time composing. It was carefully crafted to make Roanne Hodge wild with anger and bring the wrath of a woman scorned upon Ruben's head or any other vulnerable body part.

This was in retaliation for the most recent correspondence to the business owners predicting dire consequences if they didn't sell.

The threat of placing articles in newspapers about inferior merchandise, and adulteration of food would make customers stay away. Eatables befouled by animal and human excrement, alum and lead in baked goods, chalk in milk and lice and bedbugs infesting fabrics were just a few of the bullying tactics mentioned.

The anonymous communication to Mrs. Hodge was far from subtle. It had detailed information about several females with whom her husband was involved. In fact, on more than one occasion a few of Roanne's possessions had been given to these women to prove his affection.

Thomas could describe such items because he was responsible for removing them during one of his early morning incursions into Hodge's residence. Trifles that he had found shoved to the back of a drawer in Mrs. Hodge's wardrobe closet. A ruby and pearl hatpin, pearl buttons, small silver perfume pendent and a tiny butterfly brooch were removed.

Nothing extremely valuable or notable, he didn't want the servants accused of stealing and dismissed.

It had been tempting to extract a few of Ruben's jade objects from the locked cases in his display room while prowling about. He, or one of his friends, would return at a later time to relocate the whole collection.

Thomas wasn't too concerned about making Roanne Hodge upset; he had heard that her family situation had been dire. Debt forced the sale of much of the estate, little left but the name and position in society. According to Brian Murray, Ruben Hodge acquired a wife as payment for keeping the family from being penniless and Roanne made sure she wanted for nothing.

Brian was acquainted with Roanne's brother, Charles Bartlett. The brother seemed to be doing well since his sister's marriage. The large mortgage on the estate had been paid off and Charles was becoming known for breeding fine horses and hunting dogs.

Mr. Bartlett had recently become engaged to a young lady with a substantial dowry. Soon worries about money would be over, which had to be a relief for the young man.

Not that those situations were rare by any means. The need for funds to keep the great estates afloat was an ongoing problem. Heirs had to marry for money, forget any notion of love and romance.

The upkeep of a place with fifty to eighty rooms and more was mind-boggling. The employment of as many as forty servants inside and out depending on the size of the house and grounds had to be expensive as well.

A trend developed, barter a title for much needed wealth . . . enter the American heiresses; Marianne Caton became the Marchioness Wellesley. Frances Work, now the Honorable Mrs. James Roche.

The beautiful Jeanette Jerome was grudgingly accepted to be the wife of Lord Randolph Churchill for an infusion of untold thousands of American dollars. The marriage would alleviate the almost empty coffers of the Dukes of Marlborough.

There were dozens more marriages of that ilk, so Roanne and Ruben Hodge were not anything special in the grand scheme of things.

The missive would go out in the afternoon post. How sad he couldn't be around to see the reaction of this anonymous tattling. The signature from "A Friend" was hardly that, a well meaning, real friend, wouldn't be so unkind. But kindness wasn't what was needed when dealing with the likes of Ruben Hodge . . . and there was more to come very soon.

Thomas stuffed the envelope in his coat pocket. His thoughts turned to his wife, their marriage didn't involve wealth for a title, and there was genuine affection. He was fortunate, Olivia could have reacted far differently . . . being stalked by a strange man wasn't exactly common. His overwhelming passion was bizarre, eccentric and probably some form of uncontrollable madness. But that was the way of things . . . nothing to be done just enjoy the results.

❧

"What are you reading Uncle?"

"A very interesting bit of history I found in Mrs. Lydstrom's library. A clergyman wrote it some seventy-five years ago. Seems the fellow was interested in Saxon churches that were still in tact and not a mass of rubble or had disappeared completely over the years.

I joined him on the sofa. "If I remember correctly most of the early churches were made of wood not stone. It wouldn't have taken too long for such places to rot away if no one made repairs and so forth."

Uncle Arch laid the book aside. "Absolutely correct. So the churches that are left had to have been constructed of stone. I'm looking for places in the north doing business in the 800's. Might find a likely candidate where the religious community of Hartlepool moved after abandoning their abbey."

I smiled. "So you haven't given up on finding a fourth Bible?"

"Not yet, always love a mystery, my dear girl. Speaking of a mystery, your husband has given me the task of presenting the shop owners on Henrietta Street substantial sums of money. Everyone who has suffered a loss of some kind will be compensated.

Thomas has explained such generosity as coming from a concerned citizen who wishes to remain nameless. Do you know anything about it?"

When it came to my husband and his toing and froing I was at a loss. It was obvious he was up to something . . . that was a certainty, but he had a talent for hiding behind a mask of innocence. Well, except for anything that concerned me, that emotion he had difficulty controlling.

I chuckled. "I'm sure it's fine, I wouldn't question where the money is coming from, just accept it and be glad there is a 'concerned citizen' somewhere."

Uncle Arch shrugged, adjusted his glasses and picked up the book. I leaned over and gave a peck upon his cheek, and quietly left the room.

The dusting wouldn't do itself; I really hated that task, just as I completed the last bookcase in the back it all had to be done again. The horrid grey soot affixed itself to hair and clothes and made one sneeze.

At least the chore was mindless; thoughts about everything imaginable from the plot of a mystery novel to the latest political upheaval could flit through my brain. But always intruding was the ongoing situation and waiting for something awful to happen.

I knew it wouldn't be much longer before things would blow sky high, I could feel it, and made me afraid. Especially since Thomas and his friends were right in the middle of it.

Nyles finished bundling the books for the customer, then nervously looked out the window for a few moments. He had to tell Miss Olivia what happened yesterday even though he'd been advised to keep things to himself. As much as he could use the money he wouldn't take it from that lawyer fellow.

Doing such a thing was stupid, and would leave him vulnerable for god knows what else.

He fiddled with the pen on the counter, then straitened the books on the sale table that didn't need to be adjusted.

This was as good a time as any, no one in the shop except for Alec who looked ready to fall asleep on the sofa. Nyles took a deep breath and walked swiftly to the back of the store.

I climbed off the step stool and flicked the feather duster away from my face. Should take the thing outside and give it a good shake, then go upstairs, wash my face and hands and put the dirty apron in the bin to be washed.

Nyles was lurking at the end of the stacks. "Nyles, do you need me for something?"

The young man slowly approached. From the way he

was biting his lip I knew he was upset. "Nyles, are you all right?"

"No, I'm not all right, I have to tell you something."

I placed my hand on his arm and squeezed a little. "All right, go ahead, what's the problem?"

He let out a deep breath. "You remember that lawyer fellow, the one who came looking for Mr. Archer?"

I nodded. "Norton Engle?"

"Yes, that Engle person . . . well . . . ah, he offered me two pounds to get the translation from those old stones Mr. Archer was working on. Said it would be easy money and you and Mr. Archer were hiding information everyone was entitled to know about."

I held my temper in check, didn't want the young man to think I was angry with him. "Thank you Nyles, you did the right thing coming to me. Don't worry, I'll take care of this matter."

Chapter Twenty

That evening at dinner I was so angry I could hardly eat. "What a vile thing to do!" I said with rancor . . . "That, that odious creature trying to involve Nyles in . . . some outrageous plot!"

Thomas gently enfolded my fingers in his. "Mr. Engle is a greedy opportunist and thinks he can make a deal of money."

"The man must find a fourth Vulgate Bible before that can happen. Giving him the translation won't help, can't say as I've been able to achieve much." Uncle Arch grumbled.

Thomas grinned. "So give it to him, or rather let Nyles

produce a copy of what was written. How much was Mr. Engle offering?"

"Two pounds . . . two pounds for turning thief!" I said indignantly.

"I'm sure Nyles could use the money and it won't make our lawyer friend any the wiser. What was the wording again Archer?"

Uncle Arch closed his eyes in thought. "Ah . . . something about blessing the works of thy servants to spread the word of God. Bibles distributed to St. Peter's, St. Paul's, the Pope and Hartlepool."

Thomas drank a little more wine. "And this was written in the 600's and Hartlepool Abbey was abandon in the 800's. Two hundred years is a long time to keep a written document especially during turbulent times. Now add another thousand years . . . not much possibility the Bible is still around."

I had regained a little more composure after listening to the men talk. "The fool is still an arse and deserves to be throttled. Perhaps we can do something devious in return?"

"Such as . . ." Uncle Arch probed.

I started to chuckle. "Such as a wild goose chase, somewhere far away, surely we can come up with a remote place in the wilds of Scotland, Wales, even Ireland."

"Archer, I'm sure you can make a few notes on places a Vulgate Bible might be hidden. Not where you actually may have thought about, Nyles can include the information along with the translation, ask another pound or two for good measure."

Uncle Arch reached for more bread. "The fellow isn't

stupid, he has enough wherewithal to know about a Vulgate, so sending him into the wilds of Scotland wouldn't be prudent.

I think a few notes suggesting that Hartlepool Abbey was a potential hiding place for the Bible should be enough, let the greedy lout make his own decision. I'm sure he knows the Abbey was abandon, if not, then he'll be surprised to find St. Hilda's Church was built on the old site. That is, if he decides to travel such a distance."

Nyles was feeling slightly nauseas as he waited for Mr. Engle near the fountain in Cavendish Square. He knew Thomas was lurking close but was still nervous. Miss Olivia and Mr. Brandyce had coached him and said being anxious was a good thing, made him look guilty for stealing.

He paced in front of the fountain, then sat down on a bench for a few minutes, got up and continued to traipse up and down the walkway.

Finally the lawyer scuttled toward him and they walked slowly to a vacant seating area.

"Happy to get your note. Let me have the document."

Nyles patted his coat pocket. "Not until I see the money you promised. I found more than the translation . . . jottings, Mr. Varrus wrote about some place in Northumbria. Should be worth another few pounds."

Norton failed to hide his annoyance, took a deep breath then tried to look friendly by smiling.

"Depends upon what the "jottings" reveal, maybe they have nothing to do with the translation. Let me have a look."

"First the money, then the rendering from the stones."

Engle's lips tightened. "Very well," and reached inside his coat and produced the coins.

Nyles handed over the first paper and waited. "This second one is about Hartlepool Abbey and some church . . . should be worth another two pounds."

The lawyer folded the transcription after a quick glance and tucked it away, he sat quietly for a few moments, long enough for Nyles to stand and walk a few steps.

"Fine, another two pounds, let's have it," Engle said with a withering glare.

Nyles held out his hand for the money before giving over the second piece of paper, then offered a curt nod and hurried in the direction of Henrietta Street.

He was tempted to run, but that would look ridiculous, besides his heart was pounding so fast he would probably swoon like a schoolgirl . . . not a good thing.

Back at the bookstore Nyles sat on the sofa and took several deep breaths. "He handed over four pounds . . . four pounds!" The young assistant reached in his pocket and produced the coins.

We couldn't help but laugh at Nyles expression and Mr. Engle's gullibility. "What are you going to do with your ill gotten gains," Uncle Arch asked.

"You mean I should keep it!"

"Of course lad, you earned it, deserve every penny for being honest."

Nyles examined the coins, then grinned. "Get me mum some wool material for a warm coat and my sister, Gemma, a pair of shoes.

I patted his shoulder. "What about you Nyles, isn't there something special you might want?"

"Not at the moment, I'll add what's left into my savings account, never know when you might need it."

"Excellent, my boy, got a good head on those shoulders," Uncle Arch declared.

Thomas strolled through the door and came over to our small group. "The boy is a natural, from where I was standing could see the entire exchange. Mr. Engle didn't look happy, but Nyles seemed sure of himself."

"For a fact Mr. Brandyce, I was shaking and wanted to run after getting the money, thought the man would snatch it away or something."

Every one was pleased and relieved at how things had turned out, Nyles was safe and well paid. Engle achieved nothing that would help him locate anything more than a forgotten monastic cemetery near the 12th century St. Hilda's Church in Hartelpool.

It was doubtful that Engle would try to dig up a cemetery or be allowed to vandalize St. Hilda's. Northumberland was over two hundred miles from London, as much as I wanted the toad gone, it probably wasn't going to happen. One must be grateful for small favors . . . four pounds for Nyles and nothing much for that sodding canker sore.

Roanne was sick with anger. Not because of Ruben's infidelity, more at being a laughing stock because of the bastard's inability to keep his pants buttoned.

She wasn't thrilled when her brother begged her to accept Ruben's proposal of marriage. In fact she was horrified, but his money would buy them out of the hole dug by her father and grandfather.

Duty to the family and all that rot was the only important thing, her feelings didn't matter. So she had made the best of the situation, and her favors came at a very high price. The grand home in London, jewels, clothes, and a country place now a pile of ashes.

Her husband provided everything one could want, but Roanne felt more like a possession than a wife. A bauble Ruben presented to the world then locked back inside the gilded cage. At times she thought he might be spying on her movements when leaving the house.

At least Ruben was decent looking, not some old, fat, bald, vile smelling creature with one foot in the grave. Come to think about it, being a widow was a delightful situation. No one could force her to do anything; she would have money and property in her own right, and best of all no husband who smothered like a heavy quilt.

Unfortunately, Ruben wasn't dead, but she didn't have to put up with his philandering, she would escape, travel somewhere. Above all get away from Ruben Hodge, and take her collection of jewelry, clothes and stash of money.

She would have to be careful, take a few days to make arrangements. It was a certainty Ruben would search and force her to return if at all possible, which wouldn't be pleasant, especially after the surprise she would leave. The thought of what she planned made her smile in satisfaction.

Brian Murray quickly moved forward until the chair settled on the floor. His habit of balancing on the back legs often resulted in disaster, as did becoming tangled in table-cloths, or stumbling into delicate side tables and sending vases of flowers crashing to the floor.

Most things moved too slowly for his liking, five course meals, sitting around drawing rooms trying to make polite conversation were agony. The only reason he managed to get through university was because of Thomas Brandyce.

Right now he watched Ruben Hodge make the rounds as he engaged the social elite in conversation. A few actually seemed interested in whatever the fellow had to say, but most nodded, offered a few words to acknowledge his presence and excused themselves.

For some reason Thomas wanted to know how often the man came into The Portland Club. Mr. Hodge played a few hands, but didn't sit at the gaming tables for hours like most of the others.

Brian figured it was the elite members that frequented the gambling establishment rather than the games of chance that drew the fellow a couple of times a week. Mostly Mr. Hodge sat quietly in the salon and gave audience to the conversations going on close by.

Old military men reminiscing about their time in India, younger ones bragging of their expertise with women, and a few offering advise on business matters. Hodge nursed his whisky, pretended to read the paper and listened intently.

All that was deadly boring as far as Brian was concerned, but Thomas wanted to know what the man was up to so he would do his best to find out.

Not an especially challenging assignment, nothing remotely exciting like jumping from rooftop to rooftop chasing an adversary, or the reverse, making a wild dash from an enemy across the same gables.

There was also the exertion of hiding in rafters of a portico in order to fall upon unsuspecting prey. That exercise called for strength, stealth and lots of practice, he found people never look up for some reason.

The young man smoothed his mustache and glanced at the ornate clock on the mantle above the fireplace. A little after eleven, Mr. Hodge would be leaving soon, the man seldom stayed much later than midnight.

Brian made his way out of the club and hailed a cab. He could easily walk but decided he was too tired after practicing with Alec and Danny earlier in the day.

One had to keep on top of things . . . prepare for the next catastrophe that lurked around the corner.

Thomas was ever the skeptic when Brian spoke of such things, but it never hurt to be prepared for any event no matter how unlikely. That's why he carried a sgian-dubh. The dirk nestled in a leather scabbard tooled with Celtic knot work.

Alec and Simon preferred a modified Khanjar. A traditional Afghanistan dagger was about ten inches from curved tip to hilt. Those two decided a smaller blade, about seven inches, could be concealed better.

Brian liked the feel of the weapon that rested in his boot, the handle was beautifully worked in silver filigree, the steel blade honed razor sharp . . . better a villain's throat cut than his.

Thomas also carried a knife and a pistol, even if he didn't believe in something apocalyptic happening in the near future, he never doubted the wicked ways of human kind.

Brian closed his eyes and thought about Scotland. The town of Falkirk and Dunmore Park, the ancestral home of the Earls of Dunmore triggered memories of running wild and playing on the remains of the Antonine Wall.

The old Roman wall was constructed about 140 A.D. to try and contain the Celtic tribes living in Scotland. The original wall was thirty-nine miles long, ten feet high and sixteen feet wide, build of turf and stone foundation. Brian imagined finding hordes of gold coins buried and left behind by the Roman Army when vacating the wall.

Alas, nothing like that was ever located in the remnants he clambered upon, so much for childish wishes . . . nonetheless it had been fun.

Norton Engle consumed the rest of his drink. He always enjoyed Ruben's Glenmorangie, single malt, whisky. The spicy, malty taste went down smoothly. At least something was smooth; he was still upset at having parted with four pounds and little to show for such expenditure.

"I have no idea what you are wittering about," Ruben said without much enthusiasm.

Norton poured another drink from the carafe. "I paid a deal of money and received little in return, I hoped for much more."

"What did you anticipate?"

"More than a few lines of religious clap-trap from a long dead monk secluded away in a cess-pit abbey in Northumbria."

"So you paid someone to gather this information and whatever it was didn't meet expectation?"

"Exactly, the idiot clerk from that bookstore on Henrietta Street, you know the block of businesses you want to get ahold of."

Ruben set his glass down with a loud thump. "The bookshop, the one that belongs to that old git Archer Varrus?"

Norton took another swallow before answering. "That's right, he and his sodding niece."

Ruben sat a little straighter in his chair. "Tell me more."

After his friend told the story of the stones, Ruben stared into the fire. Norton was resting his head on the back of the easy chair mumbling about missing persons.

The more he thought about Archer and Olivia Varrus the more he decided he should learn what they were up to. His agent, Mr. Clegg, didn't have much to do with them, not like the other owners, why was that?

In the morning he would find the reason, call Clegg into his office now that the room had been scoured and painted. The new furniture, rug, and bookcases had been delivered; he still must find more books to fill the shelves. The expenses were piling up, especially the cost of having the building patrolled by guards after business hours.

His jumbled thoughts turned to Roanne being away from home two nights in a row. She was spending the evenings with that insipid Bunty, rather, Beatrix Atherton, what the two had to discuss was beyond him. Evidently they were planning a tea to celebrate an engagement, some old maid cousin of Bunty's had finally snagged a poor sod.

Roanne would be asking for funds to help finance something expensive, like party favors for all the guests, one must have party favors, the more costly, the better.

As usual Mr. Fiske ignored George Clegg for the first few moments after the agent asked to see Mr. Hodge. Eventually and with great effort the secretary moved toward his boss's door, knocked then opened it to announce the estate agents presence.

Clegg was amazed at the new look of the place. The old look wasn't really that old, but who was he to try and figure out why Mr. Hodge did anything.

"Clegg, what is going on with that bookshop on Henrietta Street?"

The agent swallowed several times and twisted his hat nervously. "I don't understand sir."

"I gather you have made little progress since nothing is mentioned in any of your reports."

"It's like this . . . I can't get past the niece, she is very protective of her uncle and won't let me speak with him ... "

Ruben leaned forward with elbows on the desk, steepled his fingers, and glared. "His niece won't let you speak to him, may I ask how she does that, threatens you with a weapon of some kind, knitting needles or a hat pin?" he said softly.

"No, no nothing like that, it's just how she talks and, and looks at me, and, and there is a man . . ."

"A man!" Ruben hissed. "What man, not that young, ineffectual, milksop clerk?"

"No, not him, this person might be a friend, perhaps more than a friend, I've seen him coming and going several times . . . a most unpleasant gentleman."

"I suggest you find out who this "unpleasant gentleman" might be. Surely there is someone on that block who knows who he is."

Clegg took a few steps backward. "Yes Mr. Hodge, I think I know just the person to ask."

"What are you waiting for, I don't pay you to stand around looking like a simpleton, get out before I become angry."

Mr. Clegg was only too happy to comply with the order. He knew whom he might seek out to answer the question posed by Mr. Hodge. The tailor who rented the space near the end of the block was somewhat friendly. Probably because he didn't own and was resigned to moving when the proprietors decided to sell.

Chapter Twenty-One

George Clegg stepped inside the small shop. The tailor, Roger Hargrove, looked up from his task, stopped sewing and inserted the needle into the material. He moved the garment aside then heaved his portly body out of the chair and came to the counter.

"Mr. Clegg what brings you here, I doubt you wish to help with the packing, the owner has given me notice, he plans to sell the building."

"Sorry to interrupt but need to ask a few questions."

"Questions about what?"

Clegg moistened his lips. "One of your neighbors, Miss Varrus at the bookshop . . ."

"I'm afraid she has been spoken for, got herself married

she did."

"Married!"

"Didn't go to the celebration, but heard it was quite a do, it was."

"Her husband, know anything about him?"

Hargrove's eyes narrowed. "Why you asking?"

"No reason . . . ah, just surprised to learn the lady was married."

"Mr. Brandyce is a right nice fellow, it's him that makes sure no one sully's up the stores, has people watching at night he does. He and Mr. Varrus tries to help them that needs it. Been to the meetings I have, reckon that's why folks is not selling out."

Clegg thanked the tailor, left the shop, and walked slowly toward Cavendish Square to think. He liked the little park; it was quiet, shady, and enjoyed the sound of water splashing over the statue with the umbrella.

George knew Mr. Hodge was expecting him to disclose his findings, but perhaps he didn't have to tell everything, just that the Varrus girl had gotten married.

The agent sat on a bench near the trickling water. He wasn't a brave man, in fact he was rather faint–of–heart, but hated being a part of what Hodge was doing to these people. They had to be frightened; yet determined to hold out against the violence calculated to make them sell their property.

He would report his findings . . . Miss Varrus was married . . . period.

～

I leaned against the fireplace surround and watched my husband apply finishing touches to his disguise. "Is that really necessary?"

241

"Don't want anyone to make a connection with Thomas Brandyce, Privatus or you. I keep my personal life separate from any business activities. I prefer to stay in the background if at all possible."

"I know you are up to something, just what, I can't discern but Brian Murray is such an open book. *'like a book of sport thou'lt read me o'er.'*

He pressed on the sideburns to make sure they were secure. "Shakespeare, the man developed wonderful and devious plots."

I moved behind the chair and wrapped my arms around his neck and looked at his face reflected in the mirror. "You are a canny animal, devious and hard to pin down my darling, please be careful"

His blue eyes locked with mine. I'll take the circuitous route to entice . . . promise."

"And I will be unable to sleep until you return, I've gotten use to you hogging the covers and puffing like a steam train all night."

"You can't be serious, I prefer no covers to being bundled up like a mummy, and a train doesn't puff it's more of a hiss."

"Hiss, puff, chuff . . . whatever, strange sounds in the night don't bother much, I expect you to come home safely with all body parts in working order."

He chuckled. "No need to worry I'm not doing anything dangerous just have to remember the story Brain and I concocted and hope we have an audience."

Thomas and Brian arrived at the Portland Club and drifted in and out of various rooms looking for Ruben Hodge, eventually found him playing cards. They watched the game for a few moments then moved on to the upper gallery, which featured the billiard room, library, dining area and drawing room.

"We can't just wander around all night might look suspicious." Thomas muttered.

"Fancy a game of billiards, I noticed a table open when we passed." Brian indicated with a nod of his head.

"Might as well, we should be able to see Hodge if he decides to make himself comfortable across the way."

The men played two rather pathetic games of cue sports before Ruben Hodge passed by and went into the drawing room. They waited in the alcove near the small bar for space by the fireplace and across from Hodge to become available.

After making themselves comfortable in the tufted leather chairs, began their conversation. At first they discussed the excellent brandy the club served, then went on about the task of acquiring another horse for a young relative. At last the subject of politics was raised.

Brian drained his glass and called the steward over to order another drink. "I have to concur with Lord Wakefield about the rat-bastards in Parliament. Can't trust the lot of them."

Thomas nodded his head in agreement. "Probably why he lives most of the year in Spain."

"Thinks he lives there for the warm weather according to Nigel."

Thomas stretched his legs toward the fire. "How is the Marquess of Atholl, haven't seen him in donkey's years."

The steward returned and Brian took the drink off the tray. "Fine, trying to keep the estate running smoothly. Speaking of Lord Wakefield, according to my cousin, he wants to sell the property on Storey's Gate but is keeping it quiet."

"How does he plan to sell something and not publicize it?"

Brian leaned closer to Thomas. "Seems he doesn't want the government to find out."

Thomas frowned. "Don't follow old man, what does the government care?"

"Nigel says he doesn't want the powers-that-be to have the place because they are simply drooling to get their greedy hands on it."

"Still not following . . . sell the property to the highest bidder and be done with it."

Brian sighed and downed more brandy. "Something about a long-standing grudge, and knowing how much the government wants it for expansion. That parcel is right in the middle of Whitehall and all the civil service offices. But you have it correct about going to highest bidder. Wakefield has sent out invitations to a few people that might be interested and of course have the wherewithal to afford such a property."

Thomas took a nonchalance peek at Ruben Hodge; the man was avidly listening to their conversation. "I gather Nigel is one of the few to receive such an invitation."

"Have no idea, but needs to make up his mind soon, the bidding closes in three days, according to the gossip."

"Doesn't seem like his lordship has given much time, I mean three days is rather soon."

Brian managed to look puzzled. "Oh, guess I forgot to mention that all this started some weeks ago, it ends three days from now."

Ruben Hodge had given up pretending to read the

newspaper; instead sat with eyes half closed apparently enjoying the warmth of the fire.

Thomas continued. "Well, the warm weather during the day should be agreeable to the old boy."

"Probably doesn't matter one way or another. His lawyer is handling everything, the old curmudgeon, Reginald Thorpe, has a document giving him authority to act in Wakefield's behalf."

Thomas rubbed the back of his neck. "Don't think I'd give that kind of authority to anyone."

"Don't know and really don't care one way or another." Brian looked at the clock on the mantel. "Come along Rathbone, we should at least make an appearance at Warren's party, his social gatherings are dull, but the food is excellent."

The men made their way out of the Portland Club, hailed a cab, and discussed what had taken place. Hopefully Mr. Hodge swallowed their story, it was now a waiting game to see if the man made inquiries. Greed might drive him to enter the bidding.

Ruben's brain was spinning; he's heard about that property on Storey's Gate, the original mansion burned years ago. Many people clamored to buy the large plot of land right in the middle of Whitehall, especially the government. Now it was for sale, if he could get his hands on such a prize . . . due diligence was required.

He called the steward over and asked about the gentlemen who just left. The helpful attendent had no trouble in identifying the Honorable Brian Murray, son of the Earl of Dunmore, and his guest, a mister Rathbone.

Ruben had names, Wakefield, Atholl, and the lawyer

Reginald Thorpe. Time was of the essence if he wanted to be in the game. He'd get Engle to help; he should know something about this fellow Thorpe.

All the other names, if real, should be found in Debrett's, a guide to the nobility of the United Kingdom. He would look into the matter; there was a copy of the book in his library, always useful to know the titles of those breathing rarefied air.

Next and most important, was how to get a hold of the capital on short notice, not an easy task. Couldn't ask his investors, they were clamoring for results on the Henrietta Street properties. He might be able to secure a loan, use his residence and other properties for collateral if necessary. What he did know . . . that plot of land wouldn't be cheap.

He had contacts in Parliament, shouldn't be difficult to learn how much the government would be willing to pay for that large patch of dirt. Could be a tremendous spot of luck or a horrible calamity if all went pear shaped.

So many things to do and so little time to get it done.

Ruben hoped Roanne would be home from her visit with Bunty, this stupid party must be the event of the century with all the planning and expense. To quote his wife "I can't let Bunty pay for everything, after all, dear Daphne is my friend too." 'Dear Daphne' could go to hell and take Bunty right along with her as far as he was concerned.

He didn't like his wife going out in the evenings alone, but the thought of spending long hours in the company of a twit like Howard Atherton made his head ache.

As soon as he got home he would write everything down, bring some order to his thought processes. In the morning get ahold of Engle to locate this Thorpe person, shouldn't be too difficult, there must be a reference guide about solicitors and barristers somewhere.

Jingo Rush gazed into the window of the bakery. He couldn't believe the place looked good as new, maybe better, the boards were gone, and windows glistened in the morning sun. Only thing different was a folding metal grate like the one at the bookshop. The milliner's place had one too.

The aroma of fresh bread baking drew him inside, and the overpowering smell of cinnamon and vanilla made his mouth water. He had a few coins left from the last job he and Burt did for Lida Devore.

"What will you have?" The young woman at the counter asked.

"Looks like everythin' is all fixed, passed by when the window's was busted, real sad that was."

Lucy Sullender bubbled with enthusiasm. "Yes, it's wonderful to have glass instead of boards. Thanks to the gift, there was enough to make all the repairs and pay for the new screen outside too. It was Mr. Varrus who helped us . . . so what can I get for you, the apple turnovers are just out of the oven."

Jingo tapped on the new glass case. "Them apple dainties will do me fine . . . jist fine missy."

Rush had come to Henrietta Street to see what was going on since he and Ellicot had been occupied elsewhere. They needed to get back in the good graces of Mr. Hodge and make some money.

Finn, the barkeep, at the Hanged Man read the notes left for them but they had decided to stay away. Their last effort hadn't gone well, they'd been real lucky not to get nabbed by them blokes wot chased them.

They planned to make up a good story to tell Mr.

Hodge, spending time in the nick for being drunk and fighting was always a good reason to be out of touch. If Hodge couldn't be bothered, they might have to steal clothes off the washing lines. One could fetch a few coins from the ragman for cotton and linen sheets.

Rush dipped his hands into the water at the fountain to wash away the sticky remains of the apple turnovers. He had a lot to tell Ellicot . . . things he had learned from the girl at the bakery.

As much as he hated to lick old Hodge's boots there was a chance to make some money by telling him the information and maybe given some work. He and Burt would visit the bastard this afternoon, worse that could happen was to be insulted with nasty remarks, called a few names and ordered to leave.

That little squint, Fiske, wasn't a threat, in fact Jingo would enjoy pounding his head against the wall a few times.

I couldn't hear Jennie sneaking behind me this time. We had been practicing stalking each other for a while. According to Simon, being able to creep up on people was essential if one was to have the advantage.

The old scarf had been knotted in the middle; this was done to crush the larynx of the victim. Garroting was a gruesome method to do away with an enemy, but necessary when silencing a person keeping watch, again, according to Simon.

I had failed miserably in obtaining much information from my husband about any of his military exploits. Probably thought I was too delicate or whatever to be exposed to such talk.

If Thomas only knew how many times I eavesdropped

on private conversations when his friends were around he'd be livid. How else was a girl to find out what was going on?

I did manage to glean information from the fellows who spent time in the shop. When the place wasn't busy I chatted. Their cases, when not with me, were mostly run of the mill. The evasion and downright lying transpired when I asked about activities in regards to Henrietta Street, which left me wildly curious.

Of course I was constantly reading mystery and adventure stories, forget the overly sugar-sweet romance drivel that many women sighed over. I wanted to fire the gun or arrow, wield a knife with extraordinary skill and escape from precarious situations without coming to any harm.

One could not help being enamored with the likes of Robin Hood, Edmond Dantes, Ivanhoe, Sandokan, "The Tiger of Malaysia "and Quentin Durwood.

But all that was the stuff of fiction and wild imagination that never in a million years happened in the real world. Thinking back on the crazy man I knocked down the stairs wasn't exciting at all, I was terrified.

So I guess play-acting with Jennie was as close as I would get to an exciting adventure . . . pirates. I do enjoy the thought of swashing and buckling and swinging upon a yardarm or whatever one was supposed to swing upon.

However, meeting a real pirate might result in something very unpleasant, not in the least romantic.

"Tell me again how the garrote works?"

"Simon says the Afghans adapted this scarf idea from India. Use a length of material, scarves do nicely, and knot it in the center. Place a hand on each end of the scarf, which should be taut, bring over the head . . . like so . . . against the throat. Now cross your hands and apply pressure both ways, pull down and backwards while applying pressure to the villain's back with a knee."

The attempt to strangle me resulted in the two of us falling on the bed in hysterical laughter. "That was pathetic!" I giggled.

"I think we need more practice, Simon is very good, as are the rest of his friends."

"I assume my husband is to be counted in this group."

Jennie nodded. "Shall we continue, remember, practice will make clear what one doesn't do well."

I couldn't help but smile. "Since when have you become such a philosopher?"

"I have watched and learned many things living with you and Mr. Archer, and for that, I'm truly grateful."

"After those kind words, by all means let us continue with the lesson, it will come in handy when the house is overrun with brigands."

If Norton Engle was surprised by the question, he didn't show it. "There are ways of finding solicitors and barristers. There is a certificate book of admissions found in court records, and the Law Society has annals of lawyers. Such information gives addresses and dates of confirmation to the Central Court."

Ruben tapped his fingers on the desk. "I need to know about a Reginald Thorpe, someone you know perhaps?"

Engle shook his head. "Haven't heard the name, but there are hundreds of lawyers in London."

Hodge was in no mood to continue the conversation. "It's imperative to find this Thorpe fellow as soon as possible, how long will it take?"

"Have to determine if the person is still practicing law, might be retired, might have moved to another city or changed address since being admitted."

Ruben pounded his fist on the desk. "I'm paying good money for your services, so get the hell out of here and start looking for the bloody man. I expect something by this afternoon or more readily later in the morning . . . can't be that difficult even for . . ."

Engle stifled a rude remark; he didn't need to be insulted by the arrogant prat. He had his own dilemma to work out, namely, how to deal with Archer Varrus and his niece. He was certain they had to know something more than that stupid clerk had provided, and he was determined to find out what it was.

Chapter Twenty-Two

Roanne Hodge was ready to leave; it had taken several days to get everything sorted. She had rented a nice room across the river from where she lived and shopped. The first place her husband would look was at her brothers and close friend's so this was the best temporary solution.

She had confided in no one of her intentions. It was fortunate Ruben had become occupied in whatever business that consumed his time. He had been gone most of the past two days and into the evenings.

After his departure this morning she had one of the large trunks brought into her room and oversaw the packing. Of course her maid was curious, but Roanne remained silent.

Ruben's valet had the afternoon off. Roanne told the other servants, including her maid to do the same. She didn't want anyone to know where she was going. A wagon would be calling for her in an hour and there should be no witnesses to the departure.

After everyone had gone, she ventured into Ruben's bedroom and proceeded to cut every pair of trousers at about knee level into sections and strew them about. Then took the scissors and shortened the sleeves of each coat for good measure.

All cufflinks, stickpins and rings of value were pilfered. Finally, placed the letter she had received telling of his betrayal on the bed with the added words . . . ROT IN HELL . . . as a postscript.

From the "secret" compartment of the case where the jewelry had been kept she removed a key. In the study proceeded to open the locked drawer of his desk. The beautiful carved wooden box contained money Ruben kept on hand for household expenses, it would be added to her considerable cache.

The wagon should be here in a few minutes. Once away, she would decide her next move in the safety of the small room across the Thames in Lambeth.

She sat on top of the trunk in the foyer, surrounded by a carryall and her substantial purse, took a calming breath and waited.

<hr />

"Where are we going, or shouldn't I ask?" Brian inquired.

"To look over the office of one Reginald Thorpe." Thomas replied.

"So old Reggie is a real person?"

"Of course he's a real person, can't just invent someone. Ruben Hodge will be making inquiries, if in fact he is making inquiries."

"So Thorpe will be helping us convince Mr. Hodge to submit a bid for the Storey's Gate property?"

"Ah . . . not really, lets just say his office will be helping."

"Brandyce, tell me this is not what I think it is!"

Thomas grinned. "All right I won't."

"Is there a chance we shall be arrested? My father won't be pleased; of course he's in Scotland and probably won't find out. Unless we need bail money, then he'll find out, how much will it cost for impersonating a lawyer?"

"Swafford will be impersonating, has a real talent for such things, should have gone on the stage."

"Ben Swafford . . . thought he was dead, should be dead . . . why isn't he dead?"

"He looks somewhat dead, which is why he's perfect for the part of an old curmudgeon lawyer."

Brian nodded his head as if he understood, but the look on his face told a different story. "So Swafford will be Thorpe, fine . . . you still haven't explained about the office."

"Lets just say I was asking around for a semi- retired lawyer who still maintains an office. Heard about Reggie, who only does a few wills and contracts, so for the most part, the office is closed."

Brian rubbed his temple. "So what happens if Reggie decides to visit?"

"Let's hope he doesn't, at least for the next two days."

"Right . . . sounds like a full proof plan, where is the office?"

"Essex Street, first floor, number One Hundred."

After providing the information for Ruben Hodge about the lawyer and receiving little thanks for his efforts, Engle decided to return to the bookshop. Surely he could convince Archer Varrus to reveal something further about that Bible, there had to be more than the trifling bit the clerk provided.

He was good at persuading people, it was what he did best, cajole and entice, he'd make a greater effort this time and hope the cow of a niece wasn't around.

Engle studied the display in the window for a few moments, then strode through the door.

⁂

I turned from shelving a book to find the odious Mr. Engle standing near the bargain table. Our eyes met and I knew he wasn't thrilled to see me.

"Mr. Engle, what may I do for you?"

"Ahh . . . Miss Varrus, you look especially nice today."

I nodded slightly at the patronizing flattery. "Thank you."

"I was wondering if I might converse with your uncle?"

I looked to where Danny St. Jules was perched on the sofa. He instantly stood, edged closer and feigned interest in a book on the shelf close by.

"My uncle is not here, but I'll tell him you came by."

Mr. Engle wasn't pleased with my retort. There was a brief flash of anger before he smiled and pressed his hands together, probably to prevent himself from smacking me in vexation.

After several moments of staring at each other he dropped his gaze. "It's quite important that we speak."

"If it's about what was written on the stones, the matter is closed, as previously stated, the inscription was damaged in many places making it impossible to decipher. If you are not interested in finding reading material, then there is nothing more to discuss."

"Perhaps your uncle should speak for himself, the matter my be closed in your opinion, but not necessarily in his. After all he is the expert is he not?"

Obviously, Mr. Engle was not easily discouraged. "He is indeed, but since we have examined the issue many times, decided there was no reason to look any further."

"Then perhaps your uncle would consider selling the stones to me, I could satisfy my curiosity and not bother you anymore."

I could sense Danny getting ready to assail this persistent fellow, but I wanted to handle the situation.

"Mr. Engle, listen carefully, the stones are not for sale. The information written on them will not create a stir in academia or those interested in early Saxon religious institutions. So please stop hounding us with your request for material that doesn't exist."

My protector had now moved behind me. From the way the lawyer looked at me then at Danny, I knew the man wasn't going to accept anything I had to say. This individual was more dangerous then expected, but preferred to seem unaffected by my diatribe.

"There is nothing wrong with my hearing, I will not trouble you again Miss Varrus."

Danny and I watched the lawyer march out of the shop. His statement was nonsense; he absolutely would trouble me again.

⁓

Ruben sat on his bed in complete bewilderment and confusion. He read the letter once more before slowly tearing it into tiny shreds. The room was littered with his clothes, rather, the pieces of his trousers and coats.

His wife was gone; most of her gowns and jewelry were missing, as were his valuables. The letter was a complete lie; he would find Roanne. She probably wasn't far, most likely at her brother or friends.

The shock was turning to rage; his wife hadn't given him the opportunity to deny the accusations, instead, became a vindictive bitch. He had lavished her with everything she desired, put up with her pouting and moody temperament.

After everything he'd done for her brother to preserve the family estate she should have had the decency to let him rebut the lies and accusations mentioned in that poison pen letter.

When she was found, and he would track her down, he'd make sure the ungrateful bitch realized who was in control. Any objection would be handled swiftly and severely, leaving little doubt who was master and who was nothing more than a trifling ornament.

The servants had been questioned; the stupid creatures explained how the mistress had surprised them with the afternoon off. When they returned Mrs. Hodge couldn't be located. No one, even his wife's maid, knew where she might be.

Ruben ran his fingers over a mutilated remains of a coat then threw it across the room. There was nothing to wear; he would have to replace everything, which would cost a small fortune.

The thought of finding a ready-made suit, even if temporary, made his stomach churn. He might get away with the one he was wearing for another day, and change into a different shirt, at least Roanne hadn't damaged any of those.

He would seek out his tailor and insist that at least two suits be made-up as quickly as possible, of course he would pay an exorbitant amount for such quick service.

He had to look presentable when delivering his bid for Lord Wakefield's property. It had cost him dearly to secure two loans on such short notice, but if his offer was accepted he was sure to at least double his money by selling it to the government.

His ministry contact divulged a ridiculous sum had been extended and refused in the past by his lordship. Ruben estimated half that amount would be an acceptable figure to submit. He was good at estimating what things were worth, vigilant attention paid to the rise and fall of the real estate market.

The ache in his head was becoming worse, he would take something; maybe a tonic after the mayhem in his room was cleared away. Right now he required whisky and to think about who might have written such a letter.

If he was a superstitious man, one might conclude all the horrible things that had happened were due to the curse the mad caretaker raved about.

There wouldn't be a damned curse if Roanne hadn't insisted on a country house! He was letting his anger get in the way of rational thoughts, first have a drink or two, take the headache powders and tonic then rest. Of course there was no damn curse!

<hr>

"Thomas, its time we had a chat. I know you and your cronies are up to something, probably diabolical, hopefully not life threatening."

He pursed his lips pensively, his eyes narrowed. "Not especially diabolical, more like a connivance to capitalize on greed."

"Optimistically, whatever you have in mind is concluded before Brian ruins another tablecloth, wine stains are difficult to remove. He was in the shop and almost knocked over an entire bookcase, said he was looking for something on the top shelf. And candles shouldn't be allowed anywhere in his vicinity."

"Dumpty is a disaster, except in a conflict, then he seems to know what is going to happen even before the opposition does. Can't explain it, but wouldn't want to be without his skills."

"I can feel a certain energy, please tell me what is going on."

"I guess one might say we are in a waiting game, see if our man does what we want him to do."

"This man wouldn't be Ruben Hodge?"

Thomas grinned. "Excellent guess, old greedy Ruben just might make the transaction of a lifetime."

I smiled sweetly and unfastened the ribbon on the nightgown. "I promise to take you to my bed and engage in mad passionate love if you will divulge the plot?"

He looked around the bedroom and smoothed the sheet draped over his body. "Such a thought would never have occurred to me, I'm surprised at the suggestion, why I'm shocked, absolutely shocked you think I could be bribed with your indelicate behavior."

I ran my finger down his neck and inched closer. 'I promise not to hurt you."

"Oh . . . it has come to making threats has it? You give me no choice but to reveal the truth. It's complicated, so I'll try and simplify.

Our friend is enticed to pay an exorbitant amount for something he thinks will make him a deal of money. The whole thing is a farce, there is no property for sale, no bidding war, and no trace of anyone involved. Rather like an

allusion, what seems true is the opposite. That is, if everything falls into place."

"Why are you going to such lengths?"

"I want Ruben Hodge to experience fear . . . of being
unable to control what is happening to his world. I'm sure
this is how most of his victims felt when losing homes and
businesses, often facing ruin."

"Mr. Hodge will be enraged."

"More like crazed, if the plan works."

"You're sure he won't be able to find out who is behind
all of this?"

"Can't find people who don't exist or beyond re-
proach."

"What about any money collected, what happens to
that?"

"It will all go to worthwhile causes."

I put my head on his chest. "You really are a catch, glad
you were persistent and incredibly lovely . . . much nicer
than I."

"I do believe you have admonished me about not harm-
ing others, I've tried to remember that, for the most part. I
think the exact quote is, 'Thomas, you can't just go around
hurting people!'

"I may have been a bit hasty about Ruben Hodge, he is
someone I wouldn't mind seeing the back of, same goes for
an annoying lawyer."

Thomas wound a strand of my hair around his finger.
"Danny said Mr. Engle was making a nuisance of himself."

261

"He went away, but will be hovering around, I'm sure we haven't see the last of him."

·⁓·

The tailor would have two suits ready tomorrow, at double the usual fee . . . extra charge for an extra long work day. Ruben was in no position to argue, but was boiling inside.

He took several calming breaths before knocking on the office door of Reginald Thorpe.

There was no answer, so he tried again a little louder. Finally a voice said to enter. Sitting behind a large desk was a gaunt individual with a deeply lined face and white grizzled hair. He was busily writing in a journal of some kind.

Ruben waited, then cleared his throat to remind the fellow of his presence.

"Well, what do you want?"

"I wish to submit an offer on the Storey's Gate property."

The man didn't look up from his writing. "Storey's Gate! Storey's Gate?"

Ruben controlled his temper. "The property belonging to Lord Wakefield."

The gentleman slowly set his pen aside and peered at the man standing in front of the desk. 'Oh, yes, that Storey's Gate nonsense."

"When will the results be known . . . the person who submitted the most significant offer advised?" Ruben asked eagerly.

The lawyer took out his watch and examined it closely. "The office closes at six o'clock, all proposals will be scrutinized after that."

"I would expect the winner will be notified tomorrow?" Ruben said impatiently.

"Tomorrow, or the next day perhaps." The lawyer picked up his pen dipped it in the inkwell and returned to his writing. "Storey's Gate nonsense," he muttered.

Ruben removed an envelope from his coat pocket. "Where shall I put my proposal?"

The gentleman tapped a wire basket sitting on top of the desk then continued his task.

Eager to be away before he did something rash to the insufferable prat, Ruben hurried out of the office and strode down the street. To take his mind off the bidding war, he'd hunt for Roanne, the first place to look would be at his brother-in-laws.

It had only been one night and part of a day in the room that overlooked the garden. Roanne paced in front of the window, she hadn't made up her mind

about where to go and how to get there.

Ruben would have been to see Charles by now, probably accusing her brother of hiding her away somewhere in the house. That was reason not to involve any family or friends even though they would be worried. Eventually she would send a note, but right now had to remain hidden.

Her husband would hire people to look for her, she was sure of it. The room had been rented under an assumed name but what if he advertised in the papers, gave a description, offered a reward for information.

She would cross that bridge when it became necessary, but should be prepared and purchase the most popular daily publications to look for anything untoward.

Chapter Twenty-Three

Ellicot and Rush lingered near the door and waited for Mr. Hodge to speak.

"You have important information?"

Jingo Rush took several steps forward. 'Ya see it were like this, had a hankerin' fer somethin' sweet so got me some dainties."

Ruben impatiently tapped his fingers on the desk. "I really don't care about your sweet tooth … why are you here after all this time?" He barked.

"We got nicked Mr. Hodge, all them blue-bottles fault, can't have a pint or two anymore…"

"Lies and excuses, get out before I…"

"But Mr. Hodge it's about them places on Henrietta Street," Jingo exclaimed.

The angry man paused from his outburst. "What about Henrietta Street?"

"Wot Jingo was tryin' to say is someone is givin' lots a dosh for fixin' up the damage. Everythin' is good as new and some gots them fancy metal screens fer the windows and such. Seems that gent wot owns the bookshop is holdin' meetin's and even gots guards watchin' out."

Ruben Hodge slowly came to his feet and stared at the two men across from him.

"How do you know all this?"

Rush took several steps closer. "Like I said, were in the bakery and the girl wot sold me the eats told about the money and the meetin's and how someone is watchin' all night."

"You mentioned the bookstore owner?"

"Yes sir said it was Mr. Varrus wot gave 'em money," Rush said eagerly.

Hodge moved toward the windows and looked out for several moments, then turned to face the two men.

"I want you to find out if people are on guard at night. Don't do anything more than take a look, report back when you have something worthwhile and not just some conversation with a girl."

Jingo and Bert almost stood at attention. "Yes sir, Mr. Hodge, be glad ta find out fer you. Ahh . . . Mr. Hodge, it's like this, we're a little short after bein' away . . . and could use something ta tide us by . . . jist a few coins." Ellicot solicited.

"Come back with the information and you will be compensated. If I give you something now you'll probably drink it all away and forget what I want you to do. Now get out!"

The men hurried from the building and wandered down the sidewalk. "Wot is compencent," Jingo asked.

"Don't know, probably means he wasn't goin' ta give us nothin' till later."

"Guess we'll hang around a few pubs and watch fer drunks stumblin' home, might have some luck."

Ruben put the paper inside a folder on his desk. It was the second report from the firm hired to find his wife. There had been no sightings at the different train stations in London. There was an ongoing investigation of hauling companies that resulted in nothing thus far; obviously, someone had helped Roanne with the trunk the maid said she had taken.

Charles Bartlett, Roanne's brother, didn't have any idea where his sister might have gone; he'd even allowed Ruben to search the house and outbuildings. Charles wasn't especially happy being accused of hiding Roanne, but Ruben didn't care if the sod was offended.

He'd had to tread lightly when it came to Bunty, but she seemed genuinely surprised to learn that Roanne had disappeared. The woman said she would contact mutual friends and let him know if anyone had any ideas where Roanne might be.

Everything seemed to be spiraling out of control, a dead body, robbery, rats, fires, a missing wife and the anxiety of waiting to learn about the Wakefield property. Probably the reason his headaches were more frequent and the medicine didn't seem to help.

It was the second day after he had submitted his offer and still no word from that pathetic excuse of a lawyer.

Ruben stalked out of the office and into the alcove where his assistant resided. "Has the post arrived?"

Mr. Fiske nervously adjusted his tie. "No sir, nothing from a Mr. Thorpe this morning. The next delivery will be around mid-day I'll check everything that arrives myself."

"Make sure you do, it's a matter of vital importance."

"Yes, Mr. Hodge, don't worry, I'm sure the correspondence will be here soon."

Ruben rubbed his temple. "I do nothing but worry Mr. Fiske, it seems I'm in a constant state of worry. Going for a walk, will return before noon."

"Yes sir a walk always clears the head."

Ruben wanted to see for himself what was happening on Henrietta Street. One must admit he hadn't been paying much attention the last few days, too many distractions. If the information was correct, someone was preventing the business owners from becoming discouraged enough to sell out.

He would have to do something about that. After the two idiots reported back, he'd consider making sure the properties were beyond a little repair, not much could be done for a burnt out pile of rubble.

Roanne scoured the papers for a second day. So far

nothing regarding a missing woman resembling her.

The "personal" section was often amusing with columns hoping to generate romance and friendship. *Wealthy bachelor looking for a well-borne lady,* or *Searching for the girl who attended a masquerade ball dressed as Marie Antoinette.* This next one was probably from someone in the military. *Patriotic woman of intelligence and good sense, willing to travel to warm climates.*

There were several "searching for missing wives, husbands or children" but nothing that could be attributed to her.

One of the most interesting items was called "Privatus" which offered to help with problems, assistance for those in need. Roanne had given the small advertisement some thought; right now she was fine, bored, but fine. She hadn't fully worked out where she might go, but couldn't hide forever, and there wasn't any help other than her own competence and resourcefulness. But sometimes one required a little guidance, she'd reflect on it, save the address just in case.

◦◦◦

Ben Swofford gulped down the remains of his second pint of ale. Thomas thought his frizzy white hair was wilder than ever, but his friend didn't seem to mind all that much. "Just wanted to thank you for your performance, I'm sure Mr. Hodge was impressed."

"Don't know if he was or not, but nice making the fellow squirm after what you confided about his dealings, awfully eager to find out if he was the high bidder."

"I mailed the congratulatory letter late yesterday, he

should receive it this afternoon. I'm sure the real Mr. Thorpe won't miss a single piece of paper with its inscribed letterhead. The scoundrel really wants that property, the offer was quite liberal."

"Heard tell the mansion that burned all those years ago was thought to be worth fifty or sixty thousand pounds, so his bid of thirty-five thousand was generous."

Thomas nodded his head in agreement. "Just make sure you are nowhere near Essex Street when the bastard comes looking for Mr. Thorpe."

"Not much chance of him finding me at The Black Sheep, this pub isn't a place the likes of him spends any time."

"My father liked it well enough, thought it had character. I'm partial to the old beamed ceiling, great roaring fireplace and excellent tankards of ale myself."

"One shouldn't forget the witch marks on the stones in the entrance to protect us from evil. Of course, I would never have been able to buy this place if your father hadn't loaned the money."

Thomas clasped Ben's shoulder. "That was over twenty years ago, and you paid him back with interest."

"So, what happens next to the Hodge bastard?"

"In all likelihood he goes to the bank and deposits the funds in an account I've opened and quickly close as soon as the money is credited. Ruben Hodge will not have a happy experience.

"Where on earth did you see witch-marks?" I asked.

"At an old pub that belongs to a friend of my fathers. I

270

just wondered if you know about such things."

I turned around in the chair after setting the pen aside. "I believe during the middle ages people painted or carved designs on doors, stones, even furniture to ward off evil spirits."

"Is there a mark of just the opposite? I mean something that would identify a witch from a . . . a . . . non witch?"

I strolled over to my husband who was taking his turn as guardian of the shop. "We don't carry books on the occult, but one might find reference to such things in medieval times." I walked to the history section and selected a tome and searched for something on witchcraft.

"This might give us information, a reference to a Richard Baxter, *The World of Spirits, Apparitions and Witchcraft,* might give you some idea how folks in the 1600's felt about witches.

Thomas took the book and headed for the sofa and I returned to my desk. One couldn't help but wonder what my devious husband was considering now. Witch-marks and witchcraft, hopefully he wasn't on the hunt for a witch or warlock in this day and age.

I continued working but glanced at Thomas from time to time as he read. When he smiled and closed the book I knew he was up to something. "That didn't take long, did you find what you were looking for?"

"I wanted a little clarification. A witch-mark is sometimes called a daisy wheel, a six lobed flower pattern contained within a circle, which offers protection. A pentacle is a five-pointed star important in the evocation of evil spirits."

"And this is useful because . . ."

"Because, our old friend, who will remain nameless, seems to be superstitious."

"How do you know that?"

"He had an overabundance of good luck charms. Many people have some item they consider lucky, but not many have an array of such things.

Even though I was wildly curious, knew better to inquire how he came by this information. Thomas Brandyce was a master at subterfuge; he had an ability to look . . . blank, the best description of his face . . . totally vacant.

"You've used the word "had" in reference to his lucky items."

Thomas grinned wickedly. "He doesn't have them anymore."

I narrowed my eyes and tried to look stern. "Well, that certainly explains everything. We should take a stroll in the park before it rains, it's starting to cloud up."

⁂

Ruben was almost giddy after reading the letter. His offer had been accepted and now must follow the unusual instructions. The funds were to be deposited at the Bank of England into the account of The White Tower Collective. When it was determined the funds had been credited he would be notified to come into the office of Reginald Thorpe and sign the necessary papers to transfer ownership.

He was also advised to keep all matters pertaining to this business transaction confidential at least until things were settled. Lord Wakefield did not want anyone to know

of the sale, especially the government, at least until all documents had been signed and recorded.

Ruben thought the contrary old man was making too
much of all this secrecy nonsense, probably because he was
half mad, ill or both. Whatever the reason he just wanted it
finished.

❧

The lights had been out for over an hour. The three figures silently made their way into the garden, waited for several moments before edging toward the flagstone terrace.

There was no sign of any guards patrolling the premises
as there were at Hodge's office building. Thomas thought
Ruben might have added another layer of security at his
house, but nothing was different from the last time they were
here.

That was reasonable since nothing untoward had happened at his residence, no robbery, rats or things set on fire.
Tonight was different; a valuable collection of jade figurines
would disappear as if by magic.

In their place a large red pentacle would be painted on
the wall in the room that housed his collections. Before entering the garden they had painted another five-pointed star
on the front door. People were still afraid of such a talisman
that proclaimed a witch might be using magical powers for
evil doings.

The French doors on the side were opened in seconds.
This was a small reception area, which led to an oval foyer.
They scuttled over the marble floor and into the room that
contained the locked cabinets of colorful jade. Shades of

green, lavender, red and blue stones were crafted into jewelry, sculpted objects, small vases, cups and intricately carved incense burners.

Thomas, Danny and Rob worked quickly unlocking cabinets and filling their kits with the beautiful objects d'art. The small container of red paint that had been set aside was opened and Thomas did a rather nice job of reproducing a large pentacle on the wall.

Danny listened at the door, then opened it a crack to make sure no one was wandering around. Rob and Thomas stepped behind him and waited for the all-clear hand signal.

Once away from the house they walked swiftly through the quiet neighborhood keeping in the shadows to a waiting carriage. Simon drove out of the area and headed for Mayfair.

"Wonder what the reaction will be when Ruben discovers his treasures gone and the decretive pentacle in place of," Danny mused and settled back on the seat of the transport.

Thomas chuckled. "Amused wouldn't be a first guess."

Rob removed the black scarf from around his neck. "Think this will be reported to the police?"

Thomas nodded. "Probably, an out and out robbery isn't like rats, yes, the authorities will be notified. I'm sure the pentacle will make the newspapers, something like that will fire the imagination of the public. People love to be frightened as long as it's not happening to them."

Thomas walked softly into the bedroom after removing his black garments and placing them into the bottom drawer of the cabinet in the dressing room.

"Your lady-friend must be disappointed you left so early." I said sweetly.

"Oh she was, well the first one was not happy at all, the second one was resigned to it."

"Two! My, that is ambitious."

"It is, I should slow down and not spread myself so thin from now on."

I plumped up the pillow and leaned against the headboard. "They must be lovely creatures."

Thomas crawled in beside me. "They are completely opposite from my wife. Short, plump, blond, and never question where I have been and what I'm doing."

"That is nice, we should invite them for dinner sometime."

"Excellent idea."

"All kidding aside, my love, I do worry when you leave our bed in the early hours of the morning. I know when you and the others are prowling about, doing whatever it is you get up to, but perhaps you might confide in me before something awful happens to your little band of warriors."

Thomas gathered me close, his fingers brushed through my hair. "I don't have anymore adventures planned for Mr. Hodge at the moment."

"Do you think he will leave us alone now? I'm sick of it all, so is everyone else. I'm sure your friends are also tired of hanging about the shop."

"They haven't complained, the task is easy compared to many others we have encountered. This will end soon, one way or another."

The little voice inside my head wasn't whispering anymore it was getting louder with each passing day. 'One way or another' wasn't comforting.

⁂

Ruben Hodge had thrown a tantrum of epic proportions after the housekeeper scurried into his bedroom that morning.

He smashed the three empty display cases with the fireplace poker, then flailed at the wall where the pentacle was painted. All the while screaming and cursing like a madman.

The servants cowered in the foyer then hurried to the kitchen not knowing what to do. Mr. Hodge's valet tried to calm his employer and was eventually successful, then sent to notify the police.

The scullery maid and Mrs. Hodge's ladies maid announced to the housekeeper they were leaving and asked for a reference. They were frightened of the crazed man and the graffiti painted on the wall and front door, who knew what would happen next.

Mrs. Hodge had disappeared, maybe the same thing would happen to them, witches could do those kinds of things, make people vanish . . . it was time to leave while they could.

Chapter Twenty-Four

Ruben had followed instructions to the letter. Waited for two days after making the deposit and was now knocking on the lawyer's office door. He paused and knocked again then tried the door, which was locked.

He checked his watch made an angry grunt and thumped on the solid oak portal and rattled the handle. Ten o'clock was the time for the meeting. It was now a quarter past and no indication anyone was inside.

He'd give it some more time, return in a half hour; perhaps the old fool was caught up in some legal matter.

There was a small cafe down the street where he could wait. Strong coffee was what he needed, calm his nerves. He tried not to think about his missing jade it was too painful.

The police were a sorry lot, asking stupid questions, milling about the place looking for god knows what! No windows or doors had been damaged, but the thief had gotten inside . . . obviously!

An inspector "somebody" said they would investigate pawnbrokers and moneylenders, might come across a few suspects. Ruben doubted such inquiries would be successful . . . his beautiful treasures were gone.

As much as he wanted to believe there was no such thing as a curse, how could one explain all the horrible things that had happened? The awful red pentacle made him think of blood dripping down the wall.

He wasn't the only one effected, one of the constables, upon entering the room stared at the defacement and crossed himself, probably to dispel any demons lingering about.

Ruben barely touched the coffee set before him, instead looked out the window then pulled the gold watch from his vest pocket. He left some coins on the table and hurried back to Thorpe's office.

The door was still locked; perhaps he could inquire at one of the other places down the hall, someone might know if the man had been around this morning.

His inquiries reveled Mr. Thorpe retired a few years ago and rarely came into his office. No one had seen him for several weeks. That was concerning, but Ruben shouldn't be alarmed, so the old man was retired, it wasn't all that unusual to retire and work part time.

The sod could have forgotten he had an appointment this morning, that's probably what had happened, old people forget things, he would come back in a few hours.

After a fitful night, Ruben was eager to return to the lawyer's office. He had left his house early without breakfast after inspecting the display room. All the glass and broken cabinets had been cleared away.

The pentacle was gone along with the Japanese motif wallpaper leaving an unsightly round space with ragged, torn edges.

Once again the lawyer's office remained closed even after Ruben violently assaulted the door. Employees from other workplaces came into the hallway and stared, one announced the authorities would be notified if he didn't leave immediately. After one last angry kick at the door the enraged man hurried away.

Ruben was furious, he tried to remember details from the moment he'd learned about the property being for sale. The conversation at the Portland Club, the two men, that Murray fellow and his friend, he'd make inquiries.

The head steward knew Mr. Murray slightly; the fellow hadn't been around the club recently and seemed to remember something about being off to Scotland. Couldn't recall his guest at all.

Thoughts niggled inside Ruben's head, a feeling of unease. He had to locate Thorpe, which meant enlisting Norton Engle to find a home address of the old halfwit and get this business settled.

Engle hunted through another stack of papers for the information he'd found on attorney Thorpe; his search wasn't helped by the angry glare and cursing from Ruben. "Why don't you sit down, I know it's here somewhere."

"I want the address of that bloody fool, his home address, not the office where the sod seldom makes an appearance."

Finally, after much shuffling of documents a folded sheet of paper was discovered. Norton had copied the date of admission to the Central Court of Reginald Thorpe, and his address from the Admission Book.

The residence listed was Carlyle Square in Chelsea. "This is a rather posh area, one doesn't just barge in and order people about," Engle exclaimed.

Ruben finally stopped pacing and sat on a chair near the window. "I don't give a damn about propriety. I want my business taken care of whether at his office or home, makes no difference to me."

"Better be on your best behavior when asking to see Mr. Thorpe, else you will be chucked out on your arse."

Ruben rubbed at his temple. "We both shall go, you seem to be able to charm the snobs."

Norton fiddled with a pencil, then took a deep breath. "Why not, we can only be turned away at the door, then what?

"I don't plan on being turned away, but if it happens I'll go to the authorities and file charges. I have a letter to substantiate my claim."

The white stone residence was indeed in a fashionable area, the two men paused outside the black wrought iron gate, then climbed the three steps to the door and knocked. The door opened and after a brief discussion they were ushered inside.

Mr. Reginald Thorpe received them in the study . . . and obviously not the Reginald Thorpe, Ruben had met a few days ago. This person did not represent Lord Wakefield, only knew the name and that the gentleman lived abroad most of the time. He was perturbed and concerned someone had impersonated him and used the office.

Norton could tell Ruben was shaken by the news and escorted him away before the man did or said something rash.

"This can't be happening!" Ruben muttered through clenched teeth. "I know people in banking they will be able to tell me about this White Tower Collective, I deposited thousands of dollars in that account. I want to know what is going on."

Engle had a good idea of what was going on, Ruben Hodge had been swindled, but he'd let him figure it out on his own. Going to the bank would be futile; officials of financial institutions were very reluctant to reveal anything about their customers.

Engle had to trot in order to keep up with Hodge. "What do you intend?"

"I intend to see an acquaintance in financial affairs, there are ways to get information on accounts, especially assets and liabilities of businesses."

"What business?" Engle panted.

"The White Tower Collective, there will be a record of the owner and who opened the account."

Norton was sure nothing favorable would be found. Ruben had to know; even if he was unwilling to admit it . . . he had been duped. Engle hid a smirk, the great Ruben Hodge had been taken down a peg or two.

Ruben's world was coming apart, the White Tower Collective account had been open for several days and closed immediately after his money had been deposited. The collective owners were listed as William Fox, Peter Easton, Edward Low and Lionel Wafer.

If it took forever he would track every one of those bastards down and make sure they suffered and begged for death.

There was some encouraging news, Roanne might have gone across the river to Lambeth, a hauling company delivered a woman and her belongings to a rooming house. An employee of the agency he had hired was watching the place.

The bitch would pay dearly for the humiliation she had caused. It hadn't taken Bunty long to inform anyone who would listen that Roanne had run away. Oh yes, his wife would grovel and plead to be taken back . . . perhaps a few months in an asylum would do her good. Make her more reasonable . . . a dutiful and grateful wife.

⁕

Roanne peered out the window through a tiny gap in the curtain. The man was still there, no question of being followed yesterday. She was concerned and frightened.

That was why she sent a note to the Privatus person, or group, or whatever they might be. She needed help; if Ruben had tracked her down she didn't want to think of the consequences.

Roanne glanced at the gold and enamel brooch watch pinned to her blouse. In a moment she would go downstairs to the parlor and wait for a Mr. Brandyce. Roanne smoothed her hair, took a deep breath and left the room.

The sitting room was small but comfortable with a sofa and two wingback chairs near the fireplace. Roanne perched on one of the chairs and looked at the clock on the mantle . . . a few minutes before three.

The sliding doors opened and her landlady, Mrs. Roberts, announced a visitor and escorted a tall, interesting looking man into the room, then rolled the doors shut.

"Mrs. Jefferies, I'm Thomas Brandyce."

"Thank you for coming so quickly Mr. Brandyce, I read your advertisement and require some assistance."

Thomas recognized Roanne Hodge immediately; he had seen her several times while observing her husband and at Claridge's Hotel with Olivia. This encounter should be extremely interesting. "How may I be of service Mrs. Jefferies?"

The lady shifted in the chair and folded her hands in her lap. "Since haste is required, I shall be direct, little time for the niceties. I have taken leave of my husband and wish to travel out of London or England as soon as possible. I know I have been followed and a man seems to be lurking outside."

Thomas went to the window and looked through the lace curtain from the side. After a few moments of studying the street, returned to his new client. "I think you are correct madam, there is a person on the other side of the street, rather obvious, in my opinion."

The woman played with a ring on her finger. "Any suggestions?"

"I assume you are not using your real name in case of inquiries?"

"That is a correct assumption, Jefferies was my mother's maiden name."

"Names associated with family or friends should be avoided, we shall choose another, something simple, common, and easy for others to forget. But we'll attend to that later. The first thing to do is leave out the back way, hopefully it is not being watched."

Roanne rose from her chair and took a deep breath. "What about my belongings?"

"Take only what you can carry, money and valuables, until I can send for whatever baggage you brought."

The lady nodded her head. "I shall be ready in a few minutes."

Thomas was surprised at her willingness to follow his instructions; she didn't dither over leaving her things behind. He was sure she would have taken all or most of her jewelry and whatever available money, so wasn't destitute.

He was also feeling a tad guilty for writing the letter about her cheating husband. He wanted to cause Ruben problems but hadn't stopped to think what Mrs. Hodge might do or feel. He was duty bound to help her in anyway possible.

It only took minutes for the lady to return to the parlor with a small bag and a coat and hat. "Shall we go Mr.

Brandyce?"

They went through the garden; Thomas carefully opened the back gate and looked down the alley. It was empty other than a few large rubbish bins.

The alley was long and narrow and eventually opened onto another street where they hurried along to the shopping area and found a cab.

It was quiet inside the vehicle, both occupants lost in thought. Thomas broke the silence. "Have you decided where you might like to travel?"

"I thought about France, it's close, but perhaps too close, and an obvious place to look if one is so inclined."

"Do you speak French?"

"Yes, also a smattering of Italian, but I think I should like a place where one can communicate in English."

"I have to agree, there is Scotland, Ireland and Wales."

Roanne closed her eyes and leaned back on the seat. "Again much too close, no, I want to get lost far away from the man who thought he owned me. I have dreamed of leaving but wasn't brave enough to do it . . . fear is a great deterrent Mr. Brandyce."

Well, so his letter wasn't wholly responsible for her leaving. He felt much better. "What about Australia, it's definitely far away, a new country for a new life." Roanne chuckled softly. "Perhaps not that far."

"There is always Canada or the United States, one can travel there in a week or so. I have relatives in New York, been there several times, you might like it."

She looked thoughtful. "New York . . . interesting."

"Right now you need a place to stay, there is a quaint, suitable hotel where you'll be safe until we decide what to do next."

"What about the rest of my things?"

"I'll take care of it, I'm sure your landlady will be more than happy to pack whatever is left in your room for a nice compensation."

❧

I stopped organizing the books for the display window. "Where would I buy what?"

"A black dress and . . . stuff for a woman in mourning," Thomas replied.

"Most of the larger stores carry ready-made items for the bereaved . . . and you need these clothes . . . why?"

"I have a new client who requires such things. I know it's an unusual request, but could you pick out something appropriate and make sure there is a veil, the darker the better."

This was the first time my husband had included me in a case so I tried to act as if this request was perfectly normal. "Do you know what size I should look for?"

Thomas frowned in thought. "Ahh, kind of medium I guess."

"Medium . . . tall, medium wide . . . just medium!"

"Yeah, about so high and so on, like a regular person."

"Well, finding something like that shouldn't be too difficult, when does this "regular person" require the medium outfit?"

"As soon as possible, is tomorrow morning too soon?"

286

"I'll do my best, never shopped for something like that before, an adventure to be sure."

"One must be prepared for new experiences, it broadens the mind and relieves boredom, tedium and monotony."

'You will tell me more about this mission sometime soon?"

"Absolutely, one might say . . . this task is poetic justice in a way."

"An emotional impact or deserved retribution?"

"Both! I believe it's almost closing time, Rob looks much too comfortable with so little to do. That's why he'll be delighted to hire a horse and wagon and haul a trunk to the warehouse."

Rob yawned and rose from the sofa. "Probably take Alec along for the ride he likes lifting heavy objects and his turn to buy dinner."

"Must have a word before you and Olivia leave," Rob announced.

Thomas wandered across the room. "Something important?"

"Could be, Simon was on duty last night, said there were some men loitering about, seemed harmless enough and didn't do anything threatening. They didn't notice Danny in one of the dark alcoves or Simon hidden across the street."

"Pass this information on to the rest of the fellows, keep a sharp eye, could be nothing more than a passer-by, or something more ominous."

Rob nodded. "You and Dumpty have the watch tonight,

be careful. So tell me more about this trunk I'm supposed to pick up."

Thomas gave him a paper with an address in Lambeth. He briefly described the situation . . . probably a watcher across the street, deliver the note from their client to the landlady and pay her handsomely for packing the belongings. Leave the wagon and Alec around the corner, deal with the landlady, then drive around to the alley and haul the trunk out the back.

Rob said he would invite Danny to come along too, someone had to mind the horse and cart while he and Alec heaved the heavy stuff.

I went upstairs to get Jennie; Nyles checked the back door making sure the bar was in place. We always left the store together to make sure everyone was safe, the carriage would arrive soon and take us home, Thomas, Jennie and I to Mayfair, Nyles and Rob to their quarters across town.

How ridiculous to live this way, it had to stop soon, our lives being dictated by one evil man. I probably should have let Thomas do what he wanted to the rat-bastard. But one doesn't hurt others who get in their way; it makes a person just like the evildoer doesn't it?

If one reflected on the subject, civilization might be nothing more than a thin veneer, easily cast aside by those with no respect, a mind without compassion, savage and unaccountable.

Perhaps the only way to stop such a person is to use the same tactics the aggressor is using . . . I should think on it.

Chapter Twenty-Five

Roanne had to admit she never would have come up with such a novel idea herself. Her new name was Sarah Martin, a recent widow, and would be on her way to New York in two days.

Mr. Brandyce advised to stay sequestered in her room, have meals delivered, and if she did go out, wear the black dress and cover her face with the veil. Once on the ship do the same, one could never tell who might be traveling and recognize her.

According to Mr. Brandyce a new trunk should be purchased since the other was distinctive. The steamer trunk had a deal of brass fittings on the camel back top; the honey toned oak and dark leather chest displayed initials tooled above the massive brass lock. The new one was to be plain and easy to overlook.

Roanne studied the second-class ticket that would be the start of a new life, in a new land far away from Ruben Hodge. She would miss her brother but would write as soon as she was settled.

Her guardian counseled that any communication should be sent to his post office address and he would forward them on to her brother in an unremarkable envelope. That way an over inquisitive servant wouldn't be able to reveal anything to anyone offering a few coins for information.

Those suggestions and other recommendations were much appreciated. They had discussed a fee; Roanne was surprised and grateful for such a reasonable amount, far less than expected.

Two days, just two more days, and Roanne Hodge would be gone forever and Sarah Martin would make her debut and never look back.

∞

Ruben hardly felt the fiery sensation as the whisky made its way down his throat. Everything was gone, his money, the beautiful collection of costly jade, the stupid country house and his wife . . . the bitch.

It had been reported that the woman resembling Roanne no longer resided at the boarding house in Lambeth. The landlady said Mrs. Jefferies left quite suddenly without a word to anyone. The agency would continue to monitor the trains; they also had her brother under surveillance.

The debts were substantial, more than he could pay, but something might be done to stem the tide of financial ruin . . . Henrietta Street. Reports from Rush and Ellicot found no guards wandering around to prevent any "accidents" to the properties.

He'd buy what was left after a devastating fire and reap the benefits of the tragic situation and perhaps keep his head above water.

Tomorrow he would send for the two louts. They knew where to hire men willing to engage in the required activities. Ruben especially wanted that bookstore owner to pay for his meddling.

He would send Mr. Clegg to speak to the owners one last time. He had been a very patient man, yes, one might say quite tolerant of those foolish people . . . but no more.

<hr>

I turned as that Clegg person entered the shop and looked cautiously around. He approached in haste. "Please listen to what I have to say Mrs. Brandyce, its important."

I huffed a little in exasperation. "All right Mr. Clegg, what is it?"

"I have been instructed to inquire if you and your uncle are interested in selling this property?"

The fellow seemed genuinely unsettled so I refrained from making a caustic remark. "No, we do not want to sell, not now, not in the near future."

His eyes darted around the shop then lowered his voice. "Please take care, be vigilant. Good bye Mrs Brandyce."

The man was frightened; a better word might be terrified. Yet he had issued a warning, something bad was going to happen very soon. I looked for Simon; he could get word to Thomas.

The hair on the back of my neck prickled. I knew for certain that Ruben Hodge had made a decision, and it wasn't going to be pleasant.

Danny was back after accompanying Roanne Hodge (Mrs. Jefferies, Sarah Martin) to Southhampton, and aboard the ship sailing to New York. Thomas smiled as he thought of her reaction at finding a quantity of jade and small bag of gold coins tucked inside her trunk. All courtesy of her husband, Thomas had to admit the woman wasn't as snobbish or entitled as expected and wished her luck and happiness.

After listening to Olivia and her concern over the brief conversation with George Clegg, Thomas called his companions together. This wasn't the first discussion about what might happen when West End Brokers became really nasty. He had hoped Hodge would be in such a state that he'd forget about the block of properties, apparently that wasn't the case.

Their little band had to be prepared for an assault of some kind. Probably an encounter with ruffians brought in to inflict as much damage as possible, more than breaking a few windows. Ruben Hodge wasn't above setting places on fire when other methods of intimidation failed.

Tonight they would seek out every nook and cranny on both sides of Henrietta Street. Areas of concealment, shadowed alcoves, balconies, alleyways, staircases, places to hide before engaging the enemy. Just like Afghanistan, same tactics applied, only difference was the urban setting.

I listened to the light banter at dinner. On the surface everything seemed normal, but there was an undercurrent of excitement, or anticipation. It didn't take a genius to know they were planning something and looking forward to whatever it was with exuberance.

Uncle Arch and I left them to their business after engaging in polite conversation in the sitting room. The coffee was served, questions asked about recent books and what my uncle was researching, all very trivial and civilized.

Thomas came into the bedroom around eleven. "Will you and the fellows be going out?"

He tossed has coat on the chair. "You weren't fooled in the least, should have known better to even try. Yes, we shall be on our way in a couple of hours."

I threw back the covers and perched on the side of the bed. "One could say I'm being horribly dramatic but choose your actions carefully."

Thomas sat next to me. "That is why we have to be prepared for what is coming."

"You seem certain a battle is brewing." He nodded, then took my hand. "Tomorrow . . .

I inhaled a deep breath. "You know this because Ruben Hodge posted an invitation, just to be sociable?"

"I know because Lida Devore sent me a note."

My eyes narrowed a little. "Who is Lida Devore, an old girl friend?"

"An old client who needed help, and never forgets a favor. The rumor is a rather nasty group has been engaged to cause trouble."

"So this Devore person magically knows who will be in trouble?"

"I put the word out with a few people to let me know when two rotten apples suddenly have funds to hire a number of exceptionally bad people to do a "job"."

I felt a shiver run down my back. "And the "job" will be tomorrow. My friends must be warned, I won't see them harmed, a shop can be replaced, people can't."

"First thing in the morning everyone will be advised about the situation. Your uncle can visit and try to soothe an already frightened group. I might add, for your ears only, if properties are damaged, funds are available to make repairs."

I started to laugh. "Your devious plot to lighten the pockets of Mr. Hodge must have succeeded."

"Beyond my wildest dreams," he said gleefully.

"Are you positive that nothing can be traced back to you and your accomplices?"

"Very doubtful . . . Dumpty hasn't visited the Portland Club lately and there is gossip the Honorable Brian Murray is in Scotland. The Reginald Thorpe, with whom Hodge rubbed eyeballs isn't around either, and the names on the White Tower account at the bank were infamous pirates from the 17th century."

"I'm sure your brigand friends are pleased their names were used in vain," I mused.

Thomas drew me close. "Enough talk of doom and

gloom, there are more pleasant ways to occupy our time."

"But Thomas . . ."

"Hush, be quiet and listen to the night.

Ellicot had hired Beddie and his followers before, when Mr. Hodge wanted something more than paint sloshed and windows broken. The eight men were like wild animals with Beddie the most out of control. His name described the person.

Beddie, was short for Bedlem, the notorious asylum for the crazy sods chained to walls. One might say the punter had a byname for a nickname.

Beddie was a hulking brute with strange eyes, one was brown the other an olive green. He had streaks of white running through greasy brown hair that hung to his shoulders.

Rush was leery of him and kept his distance, said he had "bad eyes", whatever that meant. Ellicot didn't care if the bloke's eyes were bad, evil or hideous as long as he earned the pay.

The job wasn't complicated, burn the block. Torches would be provided to toss into windows not protected by the metal screens. On the places with grates, try and lob torches soaked in pitch into the upper floor windows or anything that could easily catch fire.

The cart would contain clubs, hammers, torches, rags and a barrel of pitch. Once fires began to burn it wouldn't be long before the whole block was raging.

The constable who patrolled the area would be removed before an alarm could be raised. Easy enough to smash him a few times and leave bound in an alley. Any bystanders would be handled the same way bash 'em up and send 'em packing.

All and all a quick night's work for a pouch full of dosh, he and Jingo could pay the rent, eat more than one meal a day and stay drunk for a week . . . pure heaven.

❧

There was no possibility I could stay home waiting for news. I had to convince Thomas to listen.

"I will be perfectly safe watching from your office across the street," I rationalized.

He was wrapping a scarf around his head to complete the unusual outfit. Loose fitting slipover shirt that extended to the knees, over baggy pants tied with a draw
string. Everything was black from head to toe. He looked the proper villain.

"Why is the scarf so wide and long?"

"This is much shorter than the ones worn in Afghanistan. It has many uses, wrapping up against the cold at night, tie a horse, and hide one's face, even a weapon if necessary. And you can't come and watch."

"Why not, give me one good reason."

"It's too dangerous."

"I would be across the street, locked away on a second story, out of sight."

"No, I don't want to be worried about you, and besides Warren Downing will be using it."

"Why is Warren going to be there, not very ambulatory with his cane an all."

"Just because he doesn't romp around like a dervish doesn't mean he isn't useful in a fight."

I was puzzled. "How so?"

"Warren is a fine marksman, can shoot the eye out of a snake. He will even the odds considerably."

"Thomas try and put yourself in my situation, a place you love is in danger, possibly destroyed, wouldn't you want to know what is happening rather than notified later that it's gone. Not to mention my husband will be in danger too, I don't want to learn any bad news after the fact. So second best is for Uncle Arch, Jennie and I to wander around in the park, to see for myself."

Thomas tied another scarf around his waist; it secured a wicked looking knife. He moved to my side and gazed into my eyes. "You have a valid point . . . so against my better judgment, you can stay in the office with Warren. The thought of you rambling around Cavendish Square at night makes my headache.

What I said about war, isn't romantic, harmless or fun, it's ghastly, lethal and devastating."

I took a deep breath. "Nevertheless, I want to be there."

He sighed and nodded his head. "All right, but follow any instructions Warren gives you without question."

"I understand, you won't be sorry."

"I might not be sorry, but perhaps you will," he cautioned.

I sat in the corner out of the way. The men went about their business quietly, conversation at a minimum, Thomas glanced my direction several times but didn't say anything.

Their uniform, I guess one might call the outfit's uniforms, were all the same, turbans, slipover shirts and baggy trousers in basic black.

One item was intriguing, a short, round, wooden tube with notches carved down one side and a hole in the middle. Rob caught me looking and held the device up and rubbed a strip of wood over the notches creating a chirp like a cricket.

He chuckled. "Just another night sound, nothing to cause alarm."

One had to agree; no one would give such a noise any notice. Ingenious!

Warren hobbled over to the window that had been opened to allow his rifle to protrude. "Nice and dark especially with the lamps extinguished."

"No trouble at all to turn off the gas jets, just need a small ladder and a flick of the knob to douse the sickly glow, darkness is our friend tonight," said Danny.

I wasn't sure how much the night would help but kept my mouth shut. A few minutes later they were gone and the room was quiet and black until my eyes adjusted.

I maneuvered to the window and looked upon the street below. Couldn't see anyone moving, which was a good thing since the men were supposed to be hidden away somewhere.

"You should settle back, it might be hours before anything happens," Warren stated.

I searched the street for several more minutes then moved to the sofa. "Aren't you nervous with all this waiting?"

"A little, but we became good at biding our time and

being patient . . . lots of practice." He adjusted the rifle on the windowsill.

I had noticed the weapon had something attached to the end of the barrel. "Warren what is that round thing on the rifle?"

He chuckled. "Oh, you mean Silent Night?"

I came over to take a closer look. "You've named the weapon?"

"During the war we were often concealed and wanted to stay that way. In the desert, when it's quiet and dark, sound travels and light can be seen for miles. There is a flash when a weapon is fired, which can give away the position.

It was often discussed how one could eliminate the flash, so the gunsmith was tasked with trying to solve the problem. Eventually, after almost a year, the talented craftsman created a tube with holes and a baffle stack that could be inserted inside the barrel.

This device can significantly reduce the flash and has an added bonus of muffling noise. Almost silent other than a whooshing sound and the glare is more like a wink."

Impressive, I had heard the awful noise of guns being discharged and it could be deafening. This cylinder thing was awe-inspiring, a new concept to be sure. "Whoever came up with the idea is a mastermind, hopefully it helped when your band of rebels needed it."

"Worked like a charm, made us safer that's for sure."

I must have dozed and awoke with a start when Warren gained my attention. "Listen to the crickets," he whispered.

I went to the window in order to hear and started to

count . . . five chirps from different directions. A few moments later came ten more trills, then everything was silent.

"The first sounds identified where each man was positioned, the second set was how many thugs are coming. Not bad odds, only out numbered by five."

My mouth was so dry I couldn't respond and I gripped the windowsill tightly until my hands hurt.

I heard a faint rumble, then some shadowy figures appeared hauling a cart. Thankfully the horse, if there had been one, was safely out of the way. Didn't much care what happened to the human rats as long as innocent animals were not involved.

The cart stopped by the curb in front of the milliner's shop, which was located in the middle of the block. I couldn't see what the men were doing, but they were gathered around the cart.

Warren was watching intently his attention on what was happening below. He calmly adjusted the weapon and waited.

I waited too and made myself breathe and silently count . . . one, two, three!

Chapter Twenty-Six

A sudden brightness shattered the darkness as a man held up a torch and waved it around. I could see men split away from the group, two ran left, a couple trotted off to the right, all had hammers or clubs. Those who remained at the cart dipped their cloth wrapped sticks into the barrel of what was probably pitch.

I could hear glass breaking at each end of the block. Then the fellow with the firebrand screamed, clutched his shoulder, and stumbled into the cart. The torch fell next to the barrel of pitch and everything was instantly engulfed in flames including a fellow who must have had something flammable splashed on his clothes.

Warren muttered. "Two down." A soft whoosh came from his rifle and a third man grabbed his knee and fell to the ground. By this time there was shouting, cussing and confusion as the human torch twirled in circles and staggered into the street.

I watched in horrified fascination as silhouettes appeared from nowhere. One could detect the dark shapes from the second-floor advantage as they scrambled toward their unsuspecting prey.

The flames were smothered when something was thrown over the poor sod that lay screaming and rolling on the ground. A dark figure knelt down by the injured man then quickly moved away.

Out of the shadows further down the block darted more black-clad figures, crouched close to the ground almost cat-like. At the end of the block came a scream then silence, more yelling could be heard in the other direction.

Dark shapes ran toward two confused men who stared at the burned creature on the ground. These bewildered sods were slashed on the back of their legs, their attackers quickly raced away.

A large brute was flailing his arms and bellowing like a crazed bull after being sliced on both legs, he then staggered and fell on the walkway.

"Warren what is happening?"

"Cutting the back of the ankle just above the heel severely impairs the ability to walk. The foot will dangle loose at the end of the leg and bleed like hell, the pain is excruciating. Most likely those bastards won't be hurting anyone again."

Warren was probably right, severing the Achilles tendon was a sure way to incapacitate. The words Thomas had uttered came flooding back, war is a horror and I had caught only a brief glimpse. Often necessary to stop a bully, but doubted Ruben Hodge was one of those screaming in pain.

People were starting to gather in the street, I could hear whistles, an indication of police making their way to the scene.

"The boys will be on their way back to Mayfair, we shall wait for things to calm down before leaving. The fire brigade should be here soon to put out the burning cart or douse the remains," Warren remarked as he locked the rifle away in the cabinet.

I sat on the sofa and tried to stop my hands from trembling. "It wasn't what I expected . . . I really don't know what I thought would take place . . . at least it was over quickly.

"Hit hard and get out fast, no rules, create as much havoc as possible and disappear."

"What about the man who started this war, Ruben Hodge gets away again?"

"There will be arrests and when that happens tongues will wag. The police can be persuasive when seeking information. Especially when influential people become involved and Thomas has contacts that will be of help."

"My husband, the man of mystery, strikes again," I said softly.

Two hours or so later Warren and I left the office and went to where a carriage waited to drive us back to Mayfair. Simon drove and Thomas sat inside the closed vehicle.

Thomas grasped my hand. "Are you alright?"

"I have been better, not something I'd like to experience again. As you said, war is unpleasant . . . terribly relieved you are safe." I searched his face for any indication he had been hurt, and found nothing untoward. "The others, what about them?"

"Everyone is fine, Alec received a nasty clout to the ear, and Rob has a gash on his arm, which has been cleaned and tended. As planned, hit fast and hard, don't hang around afterward."

"The burned man, something was used to smother the flames."

Thomas grunted. "My turban can be replaced, no one should experience what that poor fool was going through, a horrible way to die."

I could feel tears prickling. "True . . . even though that person didn't care if he was the cause of innocent people being trapped inside a burning building."

Thomas sighed and squeezed my hand. "Man's inhumanity to man makes countless thousand's mourn."

I closed my eyes and thought Robert Burns, the Scottish poet, was most accurate.

The papers had articles about the fight and fire on Henrietta Street, not one mentioned the real culprit. I said as much to Thomas in not the politest of terms. Uncle Arch smoothed things over in his usual way.

My husband had little to say other than he was working on it, then continued to spoon more jam over his toast.

The following morning, I opened the shop as usual, before I could remove my hat and jacket Mrs. Sullender dashed in accompanied by the Portman brothers. They were positively bursting with news and spread the paper across the counter.

On the front page was a story about West End Brokers, and how Ruben Hodge had paid thugs to burn out the block of businesses on Henrietta Street.

There was outrage from property owners on Oxford Street directly behind the intended fire. The entire shopping district could have gone up in flames, not to mention, people might have died when trapped on the upper floors of their apartments.

Unfortunately, Mr. Hodge had not been located at his place of business or residence. There was also a rumor about his wife who had gone missing, what might have happened to her was a concern to the woman's brother and friends.

The police issued a warrant for Mr. Hodge's arrest and sought help from anyone who might have seen or heard from this man. A concerned citizen offered a sizable reward for information.

"I can hardly believe the nightmare is over," gushed Mrs. Sullender.

Paul Portman shook my hand. "Thank you Olivia, it was Archer, Mr. Brandyce and you that kept us from giving up. Andrew and I were on the brink of selling, isn't that right brother?"

Andrew grinned and nodded vigorously. "True words Olivia, true words indeed."

"There is more cleaning up after the attack, Uncle Arch will see that windows are replaced, he has money left from our generous benefactor."

Mrs. Sullender nodded her head vigorously. "Most of the rubbish from the fire has been removed but the black muck will take some time to fade out."

"We were hoping to thank Mr. Brandyce, is he here?" inquired Paul.

"He was off early, business matters that required his attention."

Andrew began to clear the newspapers from the counter. "I'm sure he will be around, please give him our regards."

"I will let him know how much he is appreciated."

I ushered them out and placed the OPEN sign on the door. I would definitely let him know how much he was appreciated after I smacked him up side the head for not telling me what he was doing.

Not for one minute did I think all this detailed information in the papers came from the police or a nosey reporter. The fine hand of Thomas Brandyce was behind it all.

It was amusing about the reward, most likely part of the money Thomas had bilked from Hodge. Same went for the repairs to the three stores that had windows broken during the attack.

I smiled as I wandered back to the counter to arrange the newly arrived bookmarks. My clever husband wasn't the only one who could keep a secret; I had one of my own thanks to Simon.

After much pleading, Mr. McQuade agreed to teach Jennie and me how to shoot; the hard part was sneaking away to the shooting school. There were several such places in London, mostly for gentlemen interested in hunting birds and other unfortunate creatures.

I was interested in protection for my loved-ones and me, so it seemed perfectly natural to be as self sufficient as possible. I also remembered how terrified I had been when that crazy man chased Jennie up the stairs and knew for certain he was bent on killing whoever got in his way.

Therefore, I became the owner of a delightful Webley, five-shot revolver, which could be concealed in a pocket.

Nice to have, but now that the troubles were over, it would be like the truncheon under the counter. The painted club the sodding copper left behind after I confounded his pathetic mind . . . like the baton, untouched, but available.

For three days the guest had been hiding in his house, Engle found the company boring and dreary. Thankfully his housekeeper wasn't especially curious about "Mr. West" she wouldn't have any reason to make the connection to Ruben Hodge, he'd never been to the house before.

The man was a liability after the newspapers revealed a litany of bad behavior; the only bright spot was a substantial reward.

Perhaps if he waited a few more days the purse would increase then he'd notify the authorities. Norton could invent a story how the crazed man barged into the house and threated his life. It wasn't until the villain passed out from drinking himself into a stupor that Norton escaped.

It wasn't far from the truth; the arse had locked himself in the bedroom with several bottles of cheap whiskey and only came out to sit in the study and whinge. Moaning about the theft of his money, one-of-a- kind trinkets, something about the bitch of a wife, and a ridiculous curse.

Ruben was almost apoplectic after reading the papers and the account of what had taken place on Henrietta Street.

Difficult to believe that "devils" materialized out of nowhere and struck down a menacing group of thugs then disappeared into thin air.

The man who was burned wasn't expected to live; the others might never walk again or be crippled even after the severed tendons were repaired. Recovery would be long and painful.

One of the business owners, Mr. Archer Varrus, mentioned intimidating letters, constant harassment, and destruction of property the entire street of shops had endured.

The proprietor of the Ink on Paper bookshop hoped things could return to normal now that Ruben Hodge, the owner of West End Brokers, had been identified as the person behind the reign of terror.

Norton continued on the subject of the bookshop, and his difficulty with the same individual, obviously a coincidence. That conversation rapidly deteriorated into accusations of how Varrus prevented the sale of the much-coveted properties. It was the bastard's fault that he, Ruben Hodge, was in such a desperate situation . . . the troublemaker should be shot.

Before the irate man passed out he assured Engle there would be hell to pay, Archer Varrus would regret his actions and words . . . everything would be put to rights again, all would be just as before.

❧

It had taken only a day to glean information needed to find the whereabouts of Mrs. Lydstrom's daughter, Julia. Once Thomas knew where she and her husband, Liam Moore, settled twenty some years ago it was relatively simple to locate the family. Thomas sent Rob to investigate after Cecily Lydstrom became their client.

Lawyer Engle had somehow been correct in locating the town, but evidently didn't care about searching for anyone. He could have made the hunt last for days or weeks and charge a handsome fee for all the hard work.

Julia and Liam had gone to Keswick, in the Lake District. The area was known for beautiful lakes, fields and woodlands. Painters, poets and tourists flocked to the area.

Liam Moore had been successful on a small scale, his paintings were poplar with tourists and eventually a shop was opened near the town square. Julia and Liam were the parents of five children and seemed content with their life in the colorful little place.

Mrs. Lydstrom had written a letter to her daughter, to be given if and when she was located. Rob handed it over after explaining his mission; any further contact was up to Julia Lydstrom Moore.

Archer Varrus and Mrs. Lydstrom had become friends while he was trying to organize the mass of historical papers, leaves of ancient writing, and parts of old books. The job was time consuming, like solving a puzzle with many of the pieces missing; nonetheless he had enjoyed the task, and the company of a bright woman like Cecily.

Their friendship flourished after cataloging everything and making sure measures were taken to preserve the ancient literary works. He had discussed the Hartlepool mystery and they spent hours speculating where members of the monastery and nunnery might have gone.

The book about Saxon churches, barrowed from her library, had been a great help in locating those still in existence. It was only a guess, but they narrowed it down to three possible places. Darlington, Durham, and Escombe.

Thomas closed his eyes and wiggled his toes in front of the fire. I marked my place in the book with one of the pretty new tags. "Do you think Mrs. Lydstrom's daughter will make contact with her mother after all this time?"

Thomas inhaled deeply. "Don't have any idea, not any of our business, what happens is up the them."

"It would be wonderful if there was a reunion."

"Twenty some years is a long time, and the past is not easily forgotten or forgiven."

"I don't think one really forgets but to forgive isn't wrong, carrying a grudge can weigh heavily."

Thomas laughed. "Where did you come up with that philosophical statement?"

"Can't recall, I think it's all mine, but could be a mish-mash of several different thoughts."

"Might be true in many cases, but there are some things one can't forgive."

"I suppose you're correct . . . . I'll have to think on it."

"Has your uncle mentioned going to Northumberland?" Thomas inquired as he rolled his shoulders back and forth several times and stretched his arms.

"He has indicated it might be interesting to have a look at some Saxon churches. Go on a quest for lack of a better word." I grinned and reached over with my foot to tap my husband's leg. "He's invited us to go along . . . might be fun."

He grunted. "Just like King Arthur, looking for the Holy Grail . . . wonderful."

"King Arthur didn't look for the Grail, it was Galahad, the purest of the pure."

"Truly . . . awe inspiring."

Wilfred Fiske hadn't wasted any time after reading the scathing articles about his employer. The bank account for reserve funds was emptied except for a hundred pounds or so.

No one would question his removal of money, because that was part of his duties as Mr. Hodge's assistant. That account often had large sums added and removed fairly often, mostly by him, as Mr. Hodge requested.

Mr. Fiske would be leaving immediately for parts unknown after writing letters of reference for the three clerks in the office and household employees. It was the least he could do under the circumstances.

He would also provide a nice severance allowance. Fiske could afford to be generous, what were a few pounds when he had acquired thousands. Duplicating the scrawled signature of his former employer wasn't difficult.

All ledgers and accounts were stored in the large desk; Mr. Hodge had given him access to everything, but locked them away at the close of business. Wilfred kept the records and balanced the books as part of his job; he prepared the cheques except for the signature.

It had been effortless, the lock on the desk popped open after a few jabs with the letter opener, and the cheques removed from the account books.

The following morning he notified the workers that the office was to be closed, handed them an envelope with reference letters and twenty pounds. After the clerks left, he locked the doors, went to the Hodge residence and did the same thing for the household staff.

By that afternoon Wilfred Fiske and his substantial carryall was on a train headed for Scotland. He would catch a ship out of Edinburgh bound for somewhere warm, the West Indies perhaps, Barbados might be just the place.

❧

Ruben lay on the bed, his head ached and his throat raw. He had no idea what day it was, didn't even care. It might be daylight from the sounds coming from outside the windows.

He looked around the unfamiliar room. A moment later remembered where he was and tried not to let the anxiety seep into his mind. His life was in shambles, according to the papers, the police were looking for him as well.

Engle had reported that constables lurked about the office building and his home, waiting to arrest him for every crime committed in London over the past year. What was he going to do and where was he to go? Ruben needed money desperately but going to the bank was risky someone was bound to be waiting for him.

Perhaps he could send a telegram to Fiske, his loyal assistant could access the reserve accounts. He would do that just as soon as he dealt with that Archer Varrus creature.

He knew Engle kept a weapon in his desk, the fellow had bragged about it often enough. Yes, he would contact Mr. Fiske to get his funds and meet him at the King Charles Pub after he took care of the bookstore bastard.

Everything would quiet down after awhile, the newspapers would stop spreading lies and the authorities would tire of hunting him. He could start again in some other place with a new identity, but right now he would go back to sleep; perhaps his headache would be gone after resting a few more hours.

Chapter Twenty-Seven

The shop had been busy most of the morning. As usual, I looked around for my guardians before remembering they were gone, no longer needed to make sure the store and those inside were protected.

I had always felt guilty about taking them away from their real jobs. At least no one person worked more than a few hours a day, but still, it must have been tremendously dull to be unobtrusive as possible yet alert when customers entered the store.

Hopefully Thomas's business hadn't suffered, he would never admit to any problems when I asked. He said they managed to juggle things around . . . vague as usual.

New clients were mentioned, the Lydstrom-Moore inquiry, a tiny village with a trouble causing bully making life a misery, and a delicate matter of stolen jewelry possibly a member of the family.

When asked what was being done about the troublemaker in the small hamlet, Thomas smiled and said, Mr. Shaw, a friend in the shipping business had taken care of the problem. I didn't inquire further, couldn't imagine what ships had to do with anything.

Uncle Arch sat at the desk studying his notes on the Escombe Saxon Church. "Olivia, come see this drawing of the church, it's quite detailed."

I ambled over to see what he was talking about. "How lovely, but small as churches go."

"The stones were taken from a nearby Roman fort, the markings on the purloined materials mention the Sixth Legion. There is also a 7th Century sundial and a relief of an animal head on the south wall.

The building is typical Saxon, narrow and tall with small high windows and room enough for about sixty people. A cemetery surrounds the place on three sides. Imagine the dates and inscriptions on the tomb stones, if time and weather haven't obliterated them."

I picked up the drawing. "Material from an old Roman fort was used to build this church?"

"Many of the bricks had Legio VI stamped on them. Nothing unusual about such practices, it was convenient and cost nothing to repurpose the items."

315

"I know that . . . I'm referring to the legion. The 6th was famous, commanded by Julius Caesar in Gaul, and later by Mark Antony. Often known as the Ironclad Legion. Wonder how they happened to be in Northumbria?"

Uncle Arch huffed a bit and looked at me like I was the village idiot. "Legions were moved around and went where needed and hopefully you can't think these soldiers were the same ones that served under Caesar. Nevertheless, good to learn you paid attention to your history lessons.

I chuckled. "Who knows, they might have been remarkably fit for being three or four hundred years old. And I love history, its math that eludes me.

"Daft as a donkey!" He mumbled.

"I heard that! But what I was thinking, my darling uncle, is that something could be hidden in the crumbling remains of an old Roman fort close to a Saxon stone church. The Vikings were rambling about the country-side, so the church would have been an easy target, old ruins might be a convenient place to stash valuables."

Uncle Arch looked over the rim of his glasses and blinked several times, then smiled. "Never thought of that . . . old Roman fort . . . interesting."

I stood in the doorway and looked at the dark clouds forming, rain was on its way, the pleasant weather would soon be gone. The changing seasons brought new colors to the trees, but not to the sky, which seemed limited to shades of brown and gray often accompanied by a dull mist of autumn.

The nights were getting colder and the days light shorter. We would need the fireplaces to be lit in the morning to take off the chill. I enjoyed the cozy atmosphere the fire created in the store; our customers seemed to like it too.

I should start looking for interesting books to display in the windows. Robert Lewis Stevenson came to mind. *Treasure Island, Prince Otto, New Arabian Nights, The Body Snatcher,* stories to read while sitting by the fire.

The throb in Ruben's head wasn't any better after sleeping all morning. Engle sent his housekeeper to the apothecary for medicine to alleviate the thrum; a quantity of opium usually calmed the pounding into a dull ache.

The newspapers were still full of the happenings on Henrietta Street, seems the reading public couldn't get enough of "invisible creatures" who left their victims maimed in the street.

To make matters worse people were coming forth to complain about the acquisition of property due to underhanded and violent practices. How thugs caused bodily harm or intimidated them to sell to the West End Brokers at pathetically low prices.

Ruben ripped the paper apart and ground the pieces on the floor. Where was that bloody woman with his bloody medicine? Shouldn't take this long for a bottle of elixir to be prepared, the apothecary shop was only a few blocks away according to Engle.

While everyone was out he should remove the gun from the desk drawer. When he felt better, maybe tomorrow, he would settle with that medaling bookseller, get his money from Fiske and leave the city. Yes, tomorrow would be a great day.

Thomas idly wondered where Ruben Hodge might be hiding, the fellow's office was closed and a constable patrolled outside. Same at his home, it was under observation as well.

Doubtful the brother-in-law would have taken him in, Roanne Hodge said there wasn't much love and affection between the two. The business arrangement was the only thing that brought them together other than rare family gatherings. Not that she ever mentioned her husband's name in conversation; she was always vague about her past.

There was a possibility that Norton Engle might give him shelter, but Thomas didn't really care that much to find out. He had achieved what he had set out to do, take everything away just as Ruben had done to others.

From what he could glean from acquaintances in banking and finance, Hodge had barrowed against his office building, personal residence, and other properties.

The country house and land was expensive, same with the jewelry for his wife, the lot for sale in Westminster created a gaping hole that couldn't be fixed.

Too many loans and not enough money to pay them back.

Thomas's thoughts turned to a quote by Edmund Burke. *The only thing necessary for evil to triumph is for good men to do nothing.* Not that he was particularly "good" he had done plenty of rotten things in his life. One can always justify his actions in many ways, but sometimes there was a need for swift justice to help those who couldn't do it for themselves.

So much for all this philosophy, he had work to do and Brian Murray to manage. The Earl of Dunmore was seeking his help to find a suitable girl for his son . . . how the hell was he to do that!

He envisioned Dumpty's awkward conversation with a "suitable" female limited to a stammered *"Delightful . . . ah, ah . . . care for a pickled eel?* or *"Which do you prefer a Bradoon or curb bit when riding?"*

Thomas couldn't think of any worthy young ladies that would consider the disheveled, red haired, bear of a man as a "catch". Even if some misguided female took on the challenge, she would have to keep him away from open flames, formal dinners, and dainty teacups.

He would talk to Olivia about this situation perhaps some of her more posh customers fell into that category. A chance meeting in a bookstore was respectable, if Brian didn't knock over the bargain bookshelf or drop a large dictionary on the young lady's foot.

Uncle Arch had received a note from Mrs. Lydstrom who mentioned she was in contact with her daughter. Mother and child had agreed to meet in Keswick at a comfortable Inn on the lake. I thought it was a good idea, if things didn't go well; neither would be obligated to prolong the visit.

Mrs. Lydstrom and Julia could acknowledge each other and say their hellos and goodbyes and either continue or end the relationship. Might be difficult, but at least Mrs. Lydstrom knew what had happened to her child, which was better than the alternative.

"Now that things are back to normal I should make a decision," Uncle

Arch announced at dinner.

"What decision is that?"

"Where I should live. You and Thomas have often stated that I'm welcome to stay on in this lovely house if I wish. Quarters over the shop are a little more cramped, but they are cozy. I'm in a dilemma at the moment."

I clasped my hands together and rested them on the table. "The choice is yours, of course, but I would miss the pleasure of your company and our conversations at meal time."

"Thank you my dear girl, as I said, must mull it over."

"It doesn't have to be right now, plenty of time for

"mulling".

Nyles had tended to the fires; the day was dark and showers threatened, the rain couldn't make up its mind. At least the shop was warm and one was tempted to grab a book and sit close to the flames that gamboled.

Not much in the way of customers this morning, perhaps it would pick up in the afternoon. My thoughts rambled about the conversations with Thomas, what to do with Brian Murray and the request from his father to find a match.

I was trying to remember any customers that might qualify. Miss Allenby was too silly, Annabelle Grove was too stuffy, and poor Prudence Udlock was ruled by a cantankerous mother who probably made her life miserable. I would have to think on it a little more.

⟡

Ruben added more coal to the fire, for some reason he couldn't get warm. The house was quiet, Engle was out and the housekeeper, Mrs. What's-Her-Name, was doing what servants do to keep out of sight.

At least he had his medicine, but needed more, the bottle was almost empty. He could take care of that later after his visit to the bookstore. He knew all his problems would disappear when that dozy old sod was gone.

He reckoned a few minutes before the shop closed was a perfect time to make an appearance, finish his chore and meet Fiske at the pub. Ruben would leave for the telegraph office in the next hour, the one near Oxford Street was convenient to his destination.

I sent Nyles home a little early. The gloomy weather had conspired to keep customers away, every once in a while thunder rumbled overhead. Only a few people entered the shop after lunch and I doubted there would be a stampede in the last hour before closing.

Uncle Arch was dozing by the fire while I put things in order for the next morning.

The other display window should be changed, perhaps something on seasons, poets were always good at describing colors and feelings at the end of summer and coming of fall. I'd figure it out later.

I turned as the door opened and a man entered. I couldn't see his face because of the coat collar and scarf.

"Good afternoon, may I help . . ."

"You can help me find your uncle, I know he is here somewhere in this miserable place," snarled Ruben Hodge, as he kicked the door shut.

My voice faltered and my mouth was probably hanging open in shock. "M . . . Mr. Hodge . . . ah . . . wha . . ."

"Shut-up you stupid cow, where is he!"

The fellow's eyes darted around the room as he rushed toward me and grabbed my arm. The other hand was at his side and half concealed a weapon, which he swiftly brought up and pointed at my head.

He was frenetic, the emotions crazed, confused, everything from being over the moon to a black despair in a matter of seconds. His face was gaunt and gray, a far cry from the polished gentleman I remembered.

"Mr. Hodge you seem ill . . . you're in need of a doctor." I knew the ache inside his head was bad; a pulse visibly throbbed in his temple. If I kept talking softly he might actually listen, it was a chance.

For moment he paid attention to my words, but started to blink rapidly as if to clear away the fog. "I should have crushed you insignificant maggots and this pitiful excuse for a business a long time ago . . . I'll put a bullet through your brain if you don't take me to that bastard . . . now!"

"No need for that Mr. Hodge," Uncle Arch stated and came around the corner of a bookcase. "Let my niece go!"

Hodge shoved me away and leveled his weapon at my uncle. "Meddling old fool, savior of these grubbing worms eking out a pathetic existe . . ."

I didn't feel like listening anymore so shot at him. The first bullet went into the wall, the second hit his arm, which he grabbed with his other hand, hunched over and crumpled to the floor. The weapon skittered away.

So much for my schooling with fire- arms . . . I had to make sure Ruben Hodge couldn't destroy anyone ever again. I fixated on the ache in his head, which was causing the man a tremendous amount of pain, far beyond the wound in his arm.

I felt there was some mass slowly spreading in his

brain and had been doing so for some time. The man was dying a slow painful death; it would be a mercy to end his agony.

Concentrate, breathe deeply, expand the mind. There are moments in ones life that calls for something beyond the pale, I watched his eyes narrow slightly, then glaze over. He moaned and muttered one word . . . "bitch"!

Uncle Arch's moon face had lost all color, little beads of sweat formed on his forehead. "My god, Olivia what have you done . . . I, I think you killed . . . you actually shot him!"

This was no time to give into fear that crawled around the pit of my stomach. "He gave me no choice, the man would have killed us both."

My uncle stared at the body a little longer then moved to my side and put his arms around me. "My dear child, why don't we sit down, remove ourselves from this tragedy for a moment."

The door banged opened accompanied by a loud clap of thunder. Thomas and Simon struggled with the door for a moment then turned around. "The wind is picking up, we might be in for a real down pou . . . " He didn't finish the sentence.

Thomas took in the figure on the floor, the two of us, and finally the weapon in my hand. He told Simon to lock the door, then examined the body and picked up the gun.

One had to admire the efficient manner he took

control of the situation, not giving into the temptation of demanding an explanation. "Where are Nyles and Jennie?"

"Jennie went home after lunch and Nyles left early." I replied.

I could see Simon was relieved that Jennie was gone and out of danger.

The only reason I knew Thomas was unsettled was by the set of his jaw "Good, glad to know they are safely out of the way. Archer?"

"I'm not hurt, mostly frightened and concerned."

"Olivia?"

"He was about to shoot Uncle Arch, couldn't let that happen."

"Seems Mr. Hodge wasn't expecting a sweet young lady to get the upper hand. An innocent with a Webley must have been quite a shock," he said in a rather patronizing tone.

Simon examined the body. "Looks like he was shot in the arm probably shouldn't have killed him, so why is he dead? Perhaps the shooter forgot to aim at center mass in all the excitement," he stated, and glared at me in exasperation.

I set my pistol on the counter. "Probably had a bad heart. "I'll find something to cover the poor sod," and walked toward the stairs before Thomas could ask any more questions.

After covering the body with an old quilt, we escorted Uncle Arch to a sofa in front of the fire. Simon left to find Danny and Rob. I knew the dead man and any trace of what happened would be removed, no police notified, and the elusive Ruben Hodge would quietly fade into obscurity.

Uncle Arch was a pragmatic soul, who took things in stride, knowing life had its ups and downs, the sun would come up in the morning and apple pie is best served warm from the oven.

When questioned by a still upset husband later that evening about my shooting ability and procurement of a weapon, I simply smiled. I could be just as vague as he; one must never reveal their sources or contacts.

Considering the events and misadventures occurring on a regular basis it was prudent to be resourceful, one couldn't rely on others to protect them forever, I muttered. Nothing was said about the real reason Ruben died, certainly not from a wound to the arm.

He went on about how fortunate I was that Hodge hadn't overpowered me and taken the pistol away. My reply was truthful, there was no possibility the fellow would have done that because he'd never believe a woman capable of thwarting his evil intentions. I thought it sounded plausible . . . maybe.

I was capable of whatever I set my mind to achieving; did a man always have to be involved to save the day? I let him sputter and fume knowing he was frightened and he'd calm down after assuring himself I was fine.

I guess I was coming to terms with what I had

done, admonishing Thomas not to engage in such behavior, and guilty of the same thing. After a tremendous
amount of thought . . . I was glad not to have tried a
headshot, aiming for center mass had been a dismal
failure. I'd stick to controlling a physical condition by
using my mind. After all, Ruben Hodge did have a really, really, bad heart.

Chapter Twenty-Eight

A cold drizzle replaced the pleasant warm days. Autumn had arrived in all its glory, overnight frost on the ground, dead leaves clinging to the trees, and a chill to remind of the cold yet to come.

Yet there was a festive feeling on Henrietta Street, people were still celebrating our good fortune. The relief of not being afraid drew us closer as neighbors, concern for the welfare of others not just oneself.

Uncle Arch decided to stay with us at the Mayfair house, which created another dilemma. What to do with the living quarters over the shop? We weren't keen on the idea of renting it to complete strangers, who knew what kind of people might inhabit the place.

Jennie solved the problem. Evidently, Mrs. Patton, Nyles mother, was looking for new quarters, their old residence was being sold and the family had to move. Why Nyles hadn't mentioned anything to me was a mystery.

Probably because he is a boy person and for some reason the male of the species don't think about such things. Mothers, or women in general, provide a warm bed, clean clothes and tasty meals no matter what.

Nyles was ecstatic when I asked if he and the family might like to live above the shop. Of course he would have to ask his mother what she thought of the idea, but sure "mum" would be pleased.

Mrs. Patton sent a note with her son the next morning thanking me, inquiring about the rent and practical things like furniture and cooking facilities. More likely than not, many properties had no running water, let alone cooking facilities.

Fortunately my young assistant did know the amount charged at the previous place since he contributed over half. Couldn't see any reason to change what they had been paying so left the rent the same.

I instructed Nyles to tell his mother there was hot and cold running water, inside comfort facilities and full kitchen.

A week later Mrs. Patton, Gemma and Nyles were installed upstairs and thrilled to call the place home. Most of the furniture remained except for items in my uncle's study that he couldn't live without.

The arrangement was good for me as well. I didn't have to hurry away to open the shop every morning, as Nyles was on hand to light fires and make the place ready for business.

There was an added bonus of young Gemma shyly asking if she might do something to earn a few pennies . . . thus the dreaded task of dusting went to the eager girl.

The study at the Mayfair house was given to Uncle Arch. The large space had room enough for his "needful things" and after much debate all items were situated in their "perfect" places.

Thomas didn't mind shuffling a few things to the library where he preferred to be anyway. Most of the Privatus matters were kept at the office across the street from the bookstore, and Warren Downing handled the silk business accounts.

There was another source of revenue, property acquisition, which Thomas maintained the files. This enterprise was slowly growing, with three warehouses by the waterfront, and several buildings featuring four to six apartments in posh neighborhoods, all brought in decent revenue.

Danny and Rob had flats at one place, Simon and Alec in another, Warren and his wife, Catherine, lived in a third. Brian Murray made do with the substantial family home Lord Dunmore kept in London for the rare times he ventured away from Scotland.

"How was dinner at Cecily Lydstrom's, Uncle?"

"Very nice, a pleasure to see Cecily so happy and to meet her daughter and grandchildren."

I sipped more coffee. "I gather its turned out to be a joyful ending after all these years?"

"I would imagine from having no one to finding a

daughter and five grandchildren might be overwhelming at first. But only the two oldest came with their mother, Andrea is twenty and Brandon, eighteen, both well mannered and not in the least intimated by their formidable grandmother."

Thomas returned to the table with his plate of bacon and eggs. "Mrs. Lydstrom is rather intimidating, I can vouch for that."

"Once you get to know her she is down to earth, intelligent and has an inquiring mind. We have spent pleasant hours speculating about Hartlepool and Saxon churches, even discussed a trip to Northumberland to have a look around."

"Hopefully not this time of year, it will soon be bone-chilling cold and the farther north one travels the colder it gets. I'm sure Thomas can tell you all about Edinburgh in the winter."

My husband grunted. "Fog, rain, wind. Not uncommon to experience all four seasons in one day. Gloomy with rain and fog in the morning, by afternoon the sun comes out and it's almost warm, then moments later clouds over and rains again. But I have to admit Edinburgh is a wonderful place."

I reached for his hand. "Perhaps we shall visit one day, you can show me where you went to University. Uncle, you may be surprised to know my very talented and learned husband achieved a L.L.B."

Uncle Arch looked over his glasses at Thomas. " I had no idea, a Bachelor of Laws is quite the accomplishment, you never practiced?"

Thomas shook his head. "There were other matters to

attend, couldn't find the time and maybe no inclination to be truthful."

"It's where you met Brian?" I quarried.

Thomas laughed. "We did have some memorable adventures, can't imagine him as a lawyer, but one never knows what the future will bring."

I was relieved that Thomas had come to terms with past events. He blamed himself for not hunting down Ruben Hodge. I reasoned how anyone could know the man would come to the shop looking for my uncle as if he was the cause of all the ill fortune. I don't think he ever set eyes on Archer Varrus.

There was no accounting for the actions of others, and why they thought as they did. The fellow was in pain; something to do with the headaches I had sensed, which might have caused his unpredictable behavior. Ruben Hodge created his own problems; he was a foolish and greedy man who made dreadful decisions.

There was no use blaming anyone but Ruben Hodge for his lot. Couldn't change the past; it was the future we might be able to do something about, I'd have to think on it.

A few days later Uncle appeared in the small sitting room where I was happily reading by the fire. He sat across from me and fiddled with his glasses, a sure sign he had something on his mind.

"Olivia . . . ah . . . would you mind hosting a small gathering for Mrs. Lydstrom and family?" Uncle Arch finally asked.

I sat aside the book. "Is there a celebration of some

kind?"

"I want Cecily to meet you and for you to get to know the family. I'm sure you'll like them and it would be nice for Julia to have someone young to be her friend. As you know our class-conscious society can be unforgiving and the girl created quite the scandal when she disappeared."

"After all this time why would anyone care?"

"You'd be surprised, people love to look down their noses at those who disturb the status quo, makes them feel superior in some way."

"Now that you have mentioned social class we aren't in the same league as Lady Cecily Lydstrom, widow of Baron Whatever."

Uncle Arch sighed, removed his glasses again and began to clean them with his handkerchief. "You're probably right, just thought it would be a nice gesture."

I should have kept my opinions to myself, Uncle Arch looked crestfallen. "No reason why we can't have a gathering for the family, what did you have in mind?"

His face brightened considerably. "I was hoping you might have an idea . . . nothing elaborate."

"Perhaps a simple buffet luncheon . . . serve cold ham and beef, cheeses. I'll speak with Mrs. Reed about the rest, I'm sure we can come up with something fitting."

His eyes glistened. "Mustn't forget the apple pie . . . remember nothing formal, just a few friends."

"When would you like to have this friendly celebration?"

"Soon, perhaps Saturday next, I'll speak to Cecily tomorrow."

After Uncle Arch wandered to his study I thought about whom to invite. The little band of friends, Catherine Downing, Warren's wife, Alec's fiancé, Leah Owens and Jennie. Her duties had changed to that of personal maid, housekeeper in charge and companion since my marriage. Mrs. Reed's daughters were full time now and kept the house sparking.

I had an idea that Jennie's status would be changing again in the coming months. She and Simon were together whenever possible, a lovely couple.

Oh dear . . . Brian Murray. Since it wasn't formal and people would serve themselves and sit at various places around the room he might be able to make it from the buffet table without mishap . . . or not.

I'm sure the dear man had been truant the day they taught social graces at school, unfortunately he could be counted on to do something disquieting, but it was up to us to handle the situation.

Norton Engle had given up looking for Ruben Hodge. The fellow simply disappeared much to the lawyer's disgust. No chance of claiming the reward, even the newspapers had relegated the story to a few articles off the front page.

Engle was also agitated at losing a potential customer like Mrs. Lydstrom. A reply to his last offer of help to find her "grandchild" was short and to the point. Basically it stated that she wasn't interested in any further communication . . . in other words, go away and stop bothering her.

Stupid cow . . . but there were other potential customers

he could concentrate his talents. He would miss old Ruben, not the man, his money and the profitable deals he brokered.

He did wonder if Roanne was dead, wouldn't be surprised if Ruben had done away with her as the papers speculated. Too bad, she was a beauty.

There was still a possibility of finding that old Bible in Northumbria, he would keep an eye on the bookseller and his condescending niece. Do some more looking into the archives about Vulgate Bibles, and northern monasteries. That old goat, Varrus, wasn't the only one who could solve a mystery.

Come to think about it why not make use of that clerk. He could easily intimidate him with threats to reveal his theft of important papers. The fellow was sure to know if his employer had found information on the location of a Bible.

Shouldn't be difficult to watch the young man's comings and goings and find an opportune moment to have a conversation. He was still perturbed about the four pounds paid out with nothing much to show for it. Norton congratulated himself on this potentially profitable idea.

❦

I wandered around the room one last time to make sure all was in order for the party. Round tables had been set up in various places and each one featured a different color tablecloth. Red, orange, brown, deep plum, and yellow cloths topped with glass bowls of white and purple heather, red cyclamen, and sunny-yellow mahonia, an acknowledgement of the season.

A long buffet table covered with crisp white linen was

pushed against the wall and would soon groan with cold meats, breads, cheeses, nuts, pickled beets, carrots, roast potatoes and onions and a selection of sweets, including apple pie.

Thomas leaned against the doorframe and let out a soft whistle. "I thought you said this was a little informal luncheon."

"It is informal, no long dining table with five different place settings and untold amount of silverware and glasses. One plate, knife, fork and spoon, casual dining, hopefully no confusion."

He came toward me and encircled my waist with his arms. "Everything is beautiful including you. Your frock is fetching, I like the colors."

I offered a haughty expression. "This old gown was just hanging in the wardrobe begging to be worn before the moths got to it."

"Funny, don't remember seeing it before, must have been hidden behind something."

"Easily overlooked, the maroon velvet and peach lace sleeves blend with everything."

"That must be it, the gown mingles so well. Speaking of mingling, the fellows promised to be on their best behavior. Rob and Danny will guard Brian, one on each side."

I couldn't help but laugh. "Oh, for goodness sake, let Brian do what he likes, everything can be easily replaced . . . and not a candle in sight."

"You are an incredibly decent lady, remind me to ask for your hand in marriage."

"I'm afraid I've been spoken for, but if you come to my room later tonight we can discuss the situation over a rare vintage brandy," I whispered.

His blue eyes sparkled. "Who could resist such an offer?"

Uncle Arch introduced Thomas and me to the Lydstrom-More family. Cecily was small, her silver hair held in place by combs garnished with deep blue stones that matched her dress. She used a cane to maneuver about the room and seemed to appreciate the flowers and colorful tablecloths.

Julia Moore, was much taller and on the plump side, a pretty woman with a charming smile and laughing gray eyes.

One might consider Andrea Moore a sprite. The young lady was a small bundle of exuberance, with bright blue eyes, and an interesting mixture of dark blond and light brown hair.

She flitted from table to table admiring the winter flowers, the view of the garden from the tall windows and picked up the ceramic cat from the mantle and suggested the name must be Bartholomew. She was a captivating young woman.

Her brother, Brandon, was quiet, he watched his sister with an amused look, resigned to such effervescence.

Other guests were shown into the room and introduced, the place began to buzz with conversation and guests were offered liquid refreshment. The aperitif was uncomplicated; a choice of dry sherry, light white wine or sweet cider.

Andrea Moore engaged in conversation with first one small group then another until she had spoken to everyone. I watched the pixie beguile her audience, heard the tinkling laugh and thought she was totally delightful.

The true test of her mettle was when Brian Murray spilled wine down the front of his waistcoat. Out came her handkerchief and she calmly dabbed away at the stain.

Brian turned beet red and began to stammer. Andrea guided him to a table, sat next to him and began a story of how she once dropped a jar of pickles on the vicar's foot. The poor man smelled of vinegar for several days.

The rest of the afternoon went smoothly. By the end of the party, a small group made plans to visit the National Gallery . . . Brian included. Andrea Moore had Brian chatting about the family in Scotland, horses and hounds.

Thomas sidled up to me and said softly. "Me thinks Miss Moore could be considered a suitable match for the Honorable Brian Murray. After all she is the granddaughter of a Baron."

"Me thinks you're a bit touched to be making marriage plans."

"He is going to view all the pretty paintings tomorrow, probably a first for him."

"A stroll through the National Gallery doth not a marriage make."

"We shall see, one can only hope."

Cecily Lydstrom and Uncle Arch had their heads together as we approached the table and sat down. "It's been decided, we are going to Hartlepool in the spring," my uncle announced.

"Who are "we" may I ask?"

"The four of us, do a little investigating, some sight-seeing, Cecily want's to explore the area, look at the Saxon churches and whatnot."

Mrs. Lydstrom chuckled. "Your uncle has revived an interest in history, with a hint of mystery thrown into the mix."

"A journey to Northumberland is tempting, but don't count on discovering anything more than shipbuilding, glassmaking, coal mining and portions of Hadrian's Wall."

Uncle Arch tapped his fingers together. "Never know what might be waiting in some long lost nook or cranny."

Nyles looked distraught as he approached. "Miss Olivia, I need your help."

I stopped sorting books and looked at his pale face. "My goodness, what has happened, are you ill?"

"No, no nothing like that . . . it's that man, Mr. Engle he, he's . . . well, he wants me to, to spy on your uncle."

"Spy! What could you possibly uncover about Uncle Arch?"

⁂

Nyles nervously ran his fingers over a basket of potpourri on the counter. "It's the same old thing, the Bible, says he will inform about the theft of papers if I don't give him information."

I laughed. "What nonsense, can't disclose something that has already been disclosed. The man is pathetic."

"But he says he will be watching. Said my sister is a charming child."

"Nyles, the fellow is bluffing, making idle threats, although mentioning Gemma is disturbing. "I will speak to my husband I'm sure he'll have an idea of what to do. Please stop worrying."

That evening I mentioned what Nyles had disclosed. Thomas didn't appear concerned, said much the same thing I had explained to my young assistant. Can't blackmail someone who has nothing to hide. Norton Engle was a nuisance and a scoundrel, ignore him and the pest would go away.

Which was exactly what he did a few days later, according to the newspaper. The lawyer had been drinking to excess in his local pub and decided to walk along the Victoria Embankment beside the Thames River. Several people saw him balancing precariously on top of the wall and evidently fell into the water. Very few survive the treacherous river.

Not a subject I planned to become distressed about, after all, no one actually saw anything untoward. No accounting for fools.

Now that the troubles were over, Thomas and I wanted to travel to St. Ives and enjoy being together. The weather should still be nice in the south, and even if it rained every day we wouldn't care. So much to talk about, "shoes and ships and sealing wax, cabbages and kings", possibly secrets to discover. Time together and time to care, next week couldn't come soon enough.

◦○◦

Thomas wandered into the shop. He waited until I finished with a customer then drew me to the sofa by the fire. "I received a letter this afternoon, a gentleman wants to find a brother that might or might not exist."

I wrinkled my nose and sighed. "As Uncle Arch would say . . . daft as a donkey."

"The gentlemen's name is Lord Brand, wants to know once and for all if the rumors are true that he has a half brother."

I was at a loss for words, then started to laugh. " It seems you are being hired to find yourself."

Thomas shook his head, and grunted. "What do you think I should do? If I make an excuse and refuse the job, he will probably find someone else to investigate, wouldn't be terribly difficult if one is bent on tracking this elusive brother."

I rested my head on his shoulder. "Six of one and half-a-dozen of another my darling . . . I'll have to think on it."

Jeninne Taylor

About the Author

A college professor and administrator, Jeninne Taylor made the San Joaquin Valley in Southern California her home for many years. After she retired, she moved to the Big Island of Hawaii, outside of Hilo. Here, she says, she can enjoy the vivid colors of green, fresh air, rain, and the many visitors who make her laugh as well as broadening her horizons.

What makes Taylor's books special? "My female characters are very independent," she said. "Plus they're talented in something unusual. As a writer, applying ideas such as martial arts, facility as a sniper, and or the ability to profile in Victorian terms can be a challenge. And I also love to add a touch of the mystical just for fun."

Taylor has two rescue dogs who keep her company.

"They're both kind of special ed," she said, something she's familiar with having been a special education specialist for many years.

As for the rest: "I have travelled the world, love England and try not to get thrown out of foreign countries. I collect yard art flamingos, the more tasteless the better. Even though I'm not brave enough to display them in the front of my house, my friends can't wait to see what godawful *objet d'art* I might find next!"
"As I have mentioned before, I have three goals in life: move to Hawaii, write something other than school curriculum, and marry Johnny Depp. Two out of three ain't bad!"

Jeninne Taylor's books can be found on Amazon.
Search by title or author.

More Book by Jeninne Taylor

Never Star Crossed

After the untimely death of her father, Juliette finds herself shouldering the responsibility of a vast business enterprise stretching from England to the Americas. She soon discovers that she must fight for her survival, for there are greedy men intent upon taking advantage of her youth and inexperience. In this fascinating tale spanning the globe from Barbados to London, Juliette finds more then she expected; not only does she manage to salvage her father's empire, but she finds the one man who can see her for herself.

Watch for Me

The widowed Arabaya, Viscountess Westbrook, has no intention of sitting idly watching the world pass her by. Outwardly conforming to the role required of her by Victorian Society, Arabaya adopts the persona of Madam Paradis, a reader of Nordic Runes, and finds herself involved in also the quest to solve a mystery, a puzzle that has eluded treasure hunters for more than two hundred years. Here is a fascinating tale of romance, espionage, and murder.

Looking Through Time

Jordis Azgard has the ability to see into the past whenever she touches an antique. When her client is sold a fake instead of the real piece, however, Jordis has to find out who made this million-dollar switch and make it right before the reputation of her family's business is ruined. Here is an adventure and romance spanning two continents.

Listen to The Wind

Life for a female orphan child in Victorian England can be dismal beyond belief. And so, when Alyse is dropped at the home of her distant relatives, she is more than happy to agree with a proposal that she marry her cousin James. While her husband travels in America, hoping to replenish the family coffers, she comes to know her reserved grandfather-in-law, as well as other inhabitants of the ancestral home including the down to earth housekeeper and her talented, street wise, husband who teaches Alyse the art of pickpocketing. The years pass and eventually Alyse must make a decision: does she accept an exciting, yet forbidden romance, or continue to honor the family name and the bargain she struck when little more than a desperate child?

Step into The Light

In mid-century Victorian England, Shaleen Brandon is finding it difficult to secure employment, until she is hired as a secretary for an Inquiry Agency. Soon, however, she is caught up in the more active aspect of the work, and pleasantly surprised at how much she enjoys it. That is until they take on a horrific case A mad man is murdering young women and leaving their bodies in the squalid and shabby areas of London. He also leaves cryptic notes attached to each victim. Solving the bizarre messages takes time and intuition, and even more danger when the search eventually leads to a member of the upper echelons of society.

Circle of Fire

Mary-Corinne Aldridge experiences a sudden tragedy when her father and brother are brutally murdered. The killers are known, members of a ruthless mob that is the scourge of East End, London. When she begs the authorities for help, however, they're not interested. Mary-Corinne discovers that she is going to have to find a resolution herself. This leads her down a very unusual path.

Trained by her best friend's uncle, Mary- Corrine eventually becomes a master of an ancient Asian philosophy and martial art. At last sure of herself and no longer defenseless, she becomes the hunter … only to run into the one official from the Home Office who decided to look into the situation himself. Now working with Andrew Preston, Mary-Corinne discover that this investigation is taking them far beyond an East End mob.

Right Side of The Moon

Joanna Mallory has a knack for finding ancient relics, and uses this talent to uncover items long hidden, a profession that is surprisingly lucrative. During her travels, she meets Ethan, a young archeologist excavating the ruins of a Roman fort. While she is not the typical Victorian lady, Ethan is yet delighted by the unusual, surprising, and occasionally nonsensical lady. But Joanna is being stalked by a vicious malefactor. Soon this mix of unconventional characters find themselves wrapped up in a mystery, contributing to a clever tale of discovery, danger, and of course, romance.

Slightly Different

A perfect Victorian lady, Mrs. Colfax's time is spent serving tea with impeccable style. That is when she isn't pursuing bad guys, saving the kingdom from terrorists, or loving a secret agent. Yes, the widow Colfax appears to be the perfect picture of a well-bred Victorian lady, but her unique family and unusual friends have no idea that she's leading a double life, the recipe for either disaster or for some hilarious situations. How does she balance such disparate facets of her complicated personality? Carefully. Very carefully!

The Trouble with Legends

Like every other teacher in the country, Maris Connelly is looking forward to the end of school and the long summer vacation. But she didn't plan on becoming the target of an obsessed stalker. Or being haunted by the spirit of a long dead bandit. And, to make life more interesting, a new neighbor moves next door - Jim Hayden - immature, irresponsible . . . not her type at all. Although he is incredibly good-looking . . . but still not her type!